TRIPLE DIVIDE

J. E. Tobin

Pale Horse Books

ISBN: 978-1-939917-20-1

Cover Design: Sally Stiles

www.PaleHorseBooks.com

Also by J. E. Tobin: *WHEN WE WERE WOLVES*

available from:
- Amazon
- Barnes & Noble
- PaleHorseBooks.com

PRAISE FOR *TRIPLE DIVIDE*

Triple Divide is a fast-paced novel exploring the long-term consequences of the hard decisions made in war on those who fight. Tobin vividly describes both people and the landscapes they move through, giving particular care to the deep, oft-unspoken bonds between men. I couldn't put down this gripping book!

— **Kayla Williams**, author of the memoir, ***Love My Rifle More than You***

Triple Divide is a terrific novel. J.E. Tobin expertly crafts a propulsive and thought-provoking narrative that is as literary as it is entertaining. He writes expertly about the ugly realities of modern warfare as well as the trauma that so often follows soldiers home. Pick this one up and read it. You won't regret it!

— **Chad Dundas**, author of the acclaimed novels ***The Blaze*** and ***Champion of the World***

J. E. Tobin writes with a readable style that opens his characters, and his audience, to the often hidden, and always fascinating, inner world of men. *Triple Divide*, loosely based on *The Odyssey*, is indeed epic in its journey, and in its intimate details of relationship, landscape, challenge, and emotional release. I highly recommend this novel not just to men, whose lives it reflects, but to women who are interested in bridging gaps between the inner worlds of women and men. While this novel is first and foremost an adventure and a thriller, *Triple Divide* is also an inspiring take on the human condition, able to open human hearts to self-awareness and, I think, a deeper peace.

— **Michael Gurian, New York Times bestselling author of *Saving Our Sons* and *The Stone Boys***

J. E. Tobin has taken what he learned from returning soldiers in a New Jersey VA hospital and woven a masterful novel as finely observed as if he had lived it himself. The story takes me back to my many days with soldiers and Marines (and their interpreters) in the mountains and deserts of Afghanistan, and the encounters I've had with those who suffered upon returning. It breaks your heart and rings all too true.

— **Martin Smith**, Emmy and Peabody award-winning documenarian, most recently writer, producer, and correspondent for **FRONTLINE** series, *America and the Taliban*

Infused with pain and regret, *Triple Divide* is a compelling story of three soldiers on leave in the States after a harrowing incident in Afghanistan, each battling his own demons and sense of responsibility. Many books have been written about the horrors of war; this one explores what happens afterwards, when soldiers come home haunted by the ghosts of dead comrades and weighed down by all they've seen and done.

— **Bill Glose**, author of *All the Ruined Men* and winner of the F. Scott Fitzgerald Short Story Award

In the impenetrable darkness of war there is one consoling ray of light—the unbreakable bond of love and loyalty forged between warriors. They fight and die for each other; then, if fortunate enough to survive, they bring each other home. *Triple Divide*, a deeply human, radiant homecoming story, focuses on that light, while never denying or diminishing the darkness that surrounds and threatens it. For the countless others who never went to war, *Triple Divide* brings the gift of understanding.

— **Robert Emmet Meagher**, author of *Killing from the Inside Out* and *Albert Camus and the Human Crisis*.

For my son, Matthew

Tho' much is taken, much abides; and tho'
We are not now that strength which in old days
Moved earth and heaven, that which we are, we are;
One equal temper of heroic hearts,
Made weak by time and fate, but strong in will
To strive, to seek, to find, and not to yield.

~ From "Ulysses" by Alfred Lord Tennyson

CHAPTER ONE
September 12, 2021

A period. Call it a full stop. At the end of a sentence or a chapter or a book. That's what Brian wanted today to be. A period. An ending. Then he could move on.

The Amtrak Acela train from New York City pulled into Washington's Union Station at eleven in the morning, just four minutes late, a good sign. Brian stood and stretched so his six feet of bone and muscle could unwind after three hours in the quiet car. He had chosen this car because he wanted to read and think and didn't want cell phones and the chatter of children to distract him. He left a dog-eared copy of *Catch-22* on his seat and hustled down the aisle toward the exit door. As he ascended the escalator to the terminal, he extracted his iPhone from his khaki-colored technical vest.

When Kate answered, her voice surprised him. "Hi. You're home? I thought you'd be at church."

"No church this Sunday. I figured you'd call when you arrived in D.C., and I wanted to be here for you rather than having you talk to my voice mail."

"Her voice is kind of sexy."

Kate laughed. "Good. The next time you reach over for me in bed, I'll turn on my phone."

She didn't wait for his response. "Are you going to be all right?"

"I'm fine. This is something I need to do. I promised Hector."

More than promised, he thought as he followed passengers through the concourse into the Main Hall. Kate continued to ask him questions, and he answered each one, but his mind had drifted to a land several thousand miles away. The war in Afghanistan had officially ended thirteen days ago, on August 30th. He watched on TV as the last man, a major general dressed in fatigues and a battle helmet, carrying a rifle, boarded a C-17 in the dark of night. How many times had he done the same thing? Flown into and out of battle at night. How many times did he feel the chill of the air in the Hindu Kush mountains? Even now, he felt it as he glanced up at the massive vaulted ceiling above him. Almost twenty years after the war had begun, its end had triggered all kinds of emotions in him. It had also triggered the promise.

"What's that, Kate? I'm sorry. I didn't hear. Lots of people in here."

He knew she didn't buy it.

"Your father called. He wanted to know where you were."

"Did you tell him?"

"You asked me not to."

"That's good. It's better this way. Listen, Kate, I need to go. I'll be back tomorrow evening. Love you."

Brian pocketed his phone and scanned the entrance hall. People weaved around him and each other like dancers in a musical. All of them were rushing somewhere, maybe to a hotel, a museum, or the National Mall; some returning home after visiting somewhere else. Sounds of traffic outside blasted through several open doors and merged with the last calls for passengers to board. Behind him, light poured in from large Diocletian windows high above and sparkled on the Vermont-marble floor at his feet. On either side, statues of Roman legionnaires stared down at him, holding their shields as if they were on guard. The train station was a neoclassical masterpiece. If he had more time, he'd explore every inch of it. But he had somewhere he needed to go.

After Brian exited the station, he got his bearings under the central bay of the triumphal arch gracing the entrance. In front of him, the sight of about three dozen tents of different sizes and colors radiating out from a large fountain surprised him. At first, he thought the tents were part of a festival or craft show, then quickly realized that the men, women, and children milling about were homeless. He heard the strumming of a guitar; smelled roasted pork wafting from a small grill. Above the people's heads, in the distance, he spied the rotunda of the U. S. Capitol piercing a sky of cloudless blue.

My America, he thought.

A young man in blonde dreadlocks stepped in front of him.

"You want a taxi?"

Brian turned to his left and spotted double lines of red taxis waiting for passengers.

"I think I can find one myself."

"But you don't know the best driver. I do. For a dollar, I'll lead the way."

Brian looked at the smiling man. He was in his late twenties, high on something, and so emaciated he looked like he'd collapse at any moment. "I'll give you ten bucks if you buy food with it."

He seemed taken aback. "Food? Yeah, I guess. Does ramen count?"

Brian removed his wallet from his forest-green cargo pants and gave him a ten-dollar bill. "What's your name?"

"Lenny."

"OK, let's go, Lenny."

The fidgety vagrant led Brian to the first taxi on the left and opened the rear door. "Take good care of this gentleman, Anna," he yelled to the masked driver. "He's a friend of mine."

Brian slipped into the back seat, and Lenny closed the door with a theatrical flourish. "Glad to be of service."

"Arlington National Cemetery," Brian instructed the driver.

She turned to him. "You must wear a mask. Mayor's orders. Covid, you know."

He reached into his vest. "Oh, sorry. I forgot." Putting on the white N-95, he noticed the taxi driver's license hanging off the rearview mirror. "Your name's not Anna, is it? And the skinny guy who just left is not Lenny."

She laughed. "Right on both counts. Every day he picks a new name. Yesterday, it was Elvis."

He grinned. He liked her face — as much of it as he could see above the pink mask decorated with strawberries. The colors went well with her pink hair rising above her head in a natural afro bob. "Reinvention, I like it. Anyway, he said you were the best driver. Can you take me to the cemetery?"

"Do you want to go the scenic way or the fast way?"

"What's the difference?"

"The scenic way goes down Constitution Avenue past the museums, the White House, and the Lincoln Memorial. The fast way uses the I-395 expressway. It's cheaper and saves you about five minutes."

"Five minutes, that's all? Let's take the scenic route."

As the taxi pulled out of the line and entered traffic on Louisiana Avenue, Brian sat back and stared out his window. The war is over, Brian thought, but the burials continue. Just four days before the final withdrawal, a suicide bomber had detonated a twenty-pound explosive at the Kabul airport, killing almost two hundred Afghans and thirteen U.S. service members. This morning, he might need to walk past open gravesites awaiting those thirteen soldiers. The thought made him squirm in his seat.

To get his mind off the dead, he studied the photo identification of his driver. The image showed a young woman in her early twenties. She had black hair and an oval face with high cheekbones and a smile that curled upwards on the right. The same spiral silver earrings dangled from her earlobes. The name on the ID was Ayana Johnson.

Brian leaned forward. "Excuse me, Ayana. May I call you Ayana?"

Without turning around, Ayana answered with amusement. "Sure, just don't call me Anna."

He chuckled. "When we get to the Mall, can you point out the museums and the monuments as we pass by? It's been a while since I've been in Washington."

"Sure. Are you a soldier?"

"Not anymore," he said, then added: "How did you know?"

She laughed. "You look like the poster boy for the Marines: tall, fit, erect posture. My brother is in the Corps, so I recognize the template. And besides, your first stop in DC is at Arlington National Cemetery. Who does that but a soldier or a member of the family?"

"Well, I'm not a Marine, but otherwise, your assessment is spot-on."

"So, what's your name, soldier?"

"Brian McEnroe."

Ayana raised her right hand as if making a tribute. "Well, Brian, let's begin our special tour of Constitution Avenue, shall we?"

As the taxi turned onto the thoroughfare, Ayana began her improvised tour, mixing history and little-known facts with news of current museum exhibits. Brian listened attentively, soothed by Ayana's voice and the notion that each of these institutions was free to the public. It made him feel good that the nation had set aside these buildings, and the great swath of green behind them, for the common good. Today, more than any other day, he needed to know there was something about America that still inspired him. The scenes on January 6th and the Taliban's takeover of Afghanistan had tested his faith in the ideals for which he had risked his life and the lives of the men he led.

He swiveled in his seat as the taxi entered the circle around the Lincoln Memorial, then exited onto the ramp for the Arlington Memorial Bridge. On the other side of the expanse, Robert E. Lee's former home, Arlington House, perched on a grassy knoll gleaming in the morning sun. Just below it, the cemetery's entrance appeared straight ahead. Brian patted the pocket of his vest to make sure his leather pouch remained in place. Two years ago, he had carried the small pouch and its contents home from Triple Divide Peak and stored it, waiting for this day. He didn't want to lose it now.

He patted his pocket again. Still there, he thought.

Just thinking about Triple Divide reminded him of the mountains of The Hindu Kush. The Kush remained with him like a piece of shrapnel embedded in an inoperable part of his body. Yes, the war had ended. On paper, at least.

"I'll leave you off at the Welcome Center, all right?" Ayana asked.

"That's fine," Brian said. "Do I need the mask?"

"You do while you're inside, but not outside. For security reasons, visitors also must show a government-issued photo identification and go through screening."

"Thanks for the heads-up, but I'm good."

The cab stopped at the entrance and Brian paid the charge plus a forty-dollar tip. "Elvis was right. You are the best driver. And the tour was terrific."

"Take care, soldier."

Brian nodded, and, after Ayana drove away, he turned to face a row of granite stairs ascending to the doors of the Welcome Center.

He had made a promise, and he was this close to fulfilling it. All he needed to do was walk up these stairs, pass through inspection, walk on the hallowed ground until he found the grave marker, and do what he came to do. Yet he could not take the first step. He thought he was ready for this, but suddenly he wanted to call another taxi and return to Union Station. A thousand cuts, the terrorists had warned. That's what he and his brothers-in-arms had to face. He had no rifle pointed at him from a balcony; no IED waiting to explode under his feet. But the fear was genuine. His enemy lurked inside him like a sniper, waiting.

He wiped the sweat from his brow and pulled out his phone. He dialed Kate's number. She could talk him down when he got like this. In the last year, the times she had to do so had gradually decreased. Everything about his future seemed to be right on track. Maybe even perfect. Then came the images on the TV, Facebook, and Instagram. The media showed people storming the airport; a baby passed over a fence; families crushed behind a gate, and a young man grasping the wheels of a jet taking off.

Eight years of his life for this?

Kate's phone rang.

It would be good to hear her voice.

To talk with her.

A voice answered.

"Hello, this is Kate . . ."

The voice mail asked him to leave a message.

CHAPTER TWO

Two Years Earlier

Bagram Air Base, Afghanistan, time 0200 hours.

A moonless sky hung over the base like a black shroud. A chill froze the air into stillness. Four men strode, two by two, toward a one-story building dwarfed by a cyclopean hangar.

The night before, Taliban militants had launched a mortar attack that gouged several holes in the concrete building. The explosions aroused the men from a deep sleep and propelled them from their barracks to defend against the assault. But a follow-up attack never materialized, and the enemy had little to show for another night of endless war. But neither did the men, who hoped tonight might be different.

The lieutenant colonel captured the gist of the night's plan in the briefing room. "I don't want heroes, just professionals. Do the job and get the hell out."

Special operations team Lance-1 knew its mission: Fly at night through the Hindu Kush Mountains. Land on a small plateau and climb to a remote village under enemy control. Capture two high-level ISIS-K leaders. Minimize casualties and collateral damage.

The last part of the orders rankled Jenner Chapman. How do you minimize casualties and collateral damage? Too tricky a balancing act, he thought. When the shooting starts, you choose one or the other.

But Jenner and the rest of the team were ready. They wore multi-patterned camouflage uniforms, black Kevlar helmets, and dark vests with ceramic disc protection. Their garments bore a host of clips and pockets to hold grenades, ammunition, knives, GPS devices, explosive charges, fuses, a medical kit, quick-tie tourniquets, batteries, and other tools designed for each man's combat specialty. Jenner's forte was weapons. Brian McEnroe's was communications. Alex Vilanova's was engineering. And Hector Flores' was medical. Brian served as the team leader with the rank of First Sergeant, but the squad operated as one unit like the arms and legs of a single body. That way, they stayed alive.

After the team pushed its way through the building's steel double doors, Brian directed his men — all in their early thirties and superbly conditioned — to settle in a cluster of folding chairs beneath a large photo of the President of the United States. The interior space reflected government-funded human engineering. Dull-yellow paint covered the walls. White fiber ceiling tiles hovered above them. A grey concrete floor felt hard underfoot. The message was obvious. "Don't linger. Ready yourself for battle."

"What are we waiting for?" Jenner asked, his hulking frame poised for takeoff at the edge of his chair.

Brian glanced at his watch. "We're waiting for Aarmaan."

Jenner shook his head in disgust, his shaggy red hair and beard adding emphasis. His green eyes glared at Brian. "The terp is coming? I thought interpreters don't deploy on snatch missions. Didn't you say the risk for them was too high?"

Alex took a sudden interest in the conversation and leaned in.

Brian noticed Alex's movement but said nothing. He knew how his brothers-in-arms felt about Afghan interpreters, especially this one. Jenner showed little trust for anyone outside the team; more so when the team expected enemy fire. But he took a particular dislike to Aarmann, whose quiet demeanor proved impervious to his verbal sorties. On the other hand, Alex found most Afghans honorable people, and his forty-nine-year-old interpreter as good a friend as he ever had.

Brian's blue eyes held his men's gaze for a few seconds before answering. "The brass wanted him. A last-minute decision. They said his language skills were essential. His supervisor says he's on his way."

Brian didn't question orders. He believed in the chain of command. His superiors wanted the interpreter along, and his job was to follow orders and bring everyone back alive. To Brian, the soft-spoken Aarmaan was a proven asset. Born in the United States to an Afghan diplomat and an American schoolteacher, he moved with his family to Afghanistan when he was a boy. In Kabul, he attended school, graduated from college, and married the daughter of a Kandahar physician. Fluent in English, French, Arabic, Dari, and Pashto, he often defused tense situations with the locals or gleaned information from a tribal leader's convoluted story.

And the man has courage, Brian mused. When the Taliban came to power in 1996, Aarmaan was a young instructor of modern languages at Kabul University. Though it meant death to do so, he continued to instruct his female students in secret. After Operation Enduring Freedom began in 2001, he volunteered as an interpreter, although the Taliban targeted interpreters and their families for horrific reprisals. Those who "betrayed Allah" and helped the infidels faced beheadings and bombings. Thousands died. More fled to the United States on special visas. Some quit their jobs and hid in fear. But Aarmaan stayed on the job and refused to cover his face to mask his identity. When warned, he would simply say, *"Insha'Allah."*

If God wills it.

Brian admired that kind of intestinal fortitude. It gave

Aarmaan a certain grace during tense situations. Once, he faced down an angry crowd wanting to stone a boy falsely accused of planting a bomb for the Taliban. Another time, he accidentally broke a tripwire stretched across his path, and when the explosive device failed to detonate, declared *"Insha'Allah"* and continued walking.

Yes, the terp would be useful.

Brian checked his watch.

Hector yawned as he spoke. "Are you sure he's coming?"

"He'll be here," Alex said.

Jenner stood up and paced. "I don't enjoy waiting. We're supposed to be in the hangar now. I say, 'Fuck him.'"

"We wait for Aarmaan," Brian said, enunciating each word for emphasis. "Orders."

Jenner opened his mouth to argue but stopped himself. No use, he thought. His team leader had a hard-on for following the chain of command. But Jenner distrusted the generals, especially those who flew into Bagram to burnish their resumes and earn an additional star. Sure, a few proved honorable and competent, but even they sank into the quicksand of ancient religious and ethnic rivalries with no end in sight. One day, orders would get him killed or maimed. His only allegiance was to the men with whom he served.

"OK, Falcon, orders." He sighed and sat down. "But don't forget the eagle we saw."

During a training exercise with Afghan special forces three days before, a golden eagle hovered over their heads while clutching a small bird in its talons. The Afghan soldiers grew agitated — falling over themselves, making mistakes, talking among themselves — and Jenner knew why. "The eagle grasping the dove. It's an ancient omen of imminent death and destruction," he told his teammates. "Look at their faces. They know. They're terrified."

Jenner believed in omens. He studied classical tales of war and knew how omens foretold the future. Of all the sagas, he loved most *The Odyssey* and its story of a warrior king and his ten-year-journey home after years of battle. Fighting in distant lands, being a pawn to powerful forces, driven by honor and duty, Jenner saw in Odysseus's struggles a template for his own. To remind him, he had the head of the warrior tattooed on his left arm.

He turned to Alex and Hector. "You guys want to know about the meaning of the eagle in *The Odyssey*?"

Hector moaned. "Read another book for a change, Icarus. Please. Something with jokes maybe."

"Yeah," Alex said. "Something less than three thousand years old."

Jenner laughed. "You fucktards know you love it, no matter how many times I tell it. Where are you going to get warriors and gods and giants and sorcerers all in one tale?"

Hector cackled. "What about Harry Potter?"

"That's for kids."

"Don't tell our team leader."

They all turned to Brian, who scoffed and glanced at the outside door.

At that moment, the door opened with a resounding crash. A tall, gaunt, and greying man in an ill-fitting camouflage uniform and an oversized helmet stumbled toward them. His right hand pressed against his heart in greeting. "*Salam Alaikum,*" he said, his words sputtering with exhaustion.

"*Wa Alaikum as-salam,*" the men answered, except for Jenner.

Aarmaan bent over to catch his breath.

Brian placed his hand on the interpreter's shoulder. "Sorry about the late call. At the last minute, Command added you."

Aarmaan rose, shaking his head, his piercing brown eyes scanning Brian's square-jawed face. "You're abducting someone. Is that why you need me?"

Brian looked at his watch. "I'll brief you in the assembly area. Let's go."

The five men hurried down the corridor to the hangar in silence. Their day had just begun, and none of them knew how it would end.

CHAPTER THREE

Hector slipped into the latrine off the corridor, knowing this was his last chance for indoor plumbing for several hours. He chuckled when he saw the words some grunt or flyboy had scribbled on the wall above an arrow pointing down into the urinal.

Home Sweet Home

Except for Army nurses, soldiers spewed the darkest, most ironic humor. Maybe it had to do with the job. It was good to laugh when blood and death filled your days and nights.

Home, he thought. Recently, he calculated it was seventy-two hundred miles from Bagram Air Base to Fort Bragg in North Carolina. From there, it was two miles to his house with its five rooms, garage, and growing family. In the last five years, he'd spent less time there than here in Afghanistan. At this moment, his wife and kids were probably at home eating dinner.

Standing two stalls down from him, a ground crew member interrupted Hector's reverie. "Do you think there's any truth in it?"

Hector turned to the freckled-faced young airman. "Any truth in what?"

"That you get to go back home if you piss here and flush?"

"Let's check it out, shall we?" Hector flushed and looked down at his body as he zipped up. "Still here. It must only work for the Air Force."

The man laughed. "That's cold, man."

Hector grinned and moved to the sink to wash his hands. He glanced at his reflection in the mirror. Somehow, he half-expected to see an unfamiliar face, one altered by eight years of war. So many soldiers wore their battles on their faces and in their eyes, but his dark-brown face was unscathed — no lines, no scars, nothing of note except for his bloodshot eyes and a shaved head glistening in the harsh lavatory lights. He had his mother's features, round cheeks the size of ripe *sapotes* and a small chin stucking out from his face like the knob on a kitchen drawer. His wife, Mariana, said he was handsome, but Hector attributed that perception to the power of love.

He dried his hands and looked at his watch. Fifteen minutes left before he ran out to the tarmac and boarded the chopper that would fly two hundred miles farther east — farther from home — and drop him and his brothers off to invade a village, penetrate someone else's home, abduct their targets, and kill anyone who tried to stop them.

The ground crew member called after him from the sink. "Have a good mission, Sergeant."

Hector nodded and fastened his helmet. "Thanks. Try flushing that urinal again. I heard the second time's the charm."

The man shook his head and smiled.

As he left the latrine, Hector surveyed the long line of soldiers filling the corridor. The men were doing what soldiers do when they have nothing to do: stand, sit, doze, fidget, fart, sweat, scratch, complain, brag, daydream, and pray. Some nodded or smiled as he walked by. Others, so deep into the mind games men play before a battle, didn't notice him, even as they moved out of his way.

As usual, his team was in the front. By the time he hunched down with his comrades-in-arms, their game faces in place, he had twelve minutes left before embarking. He leaned his body against the gray cinder-block wall and relaxed. He didn't enjoy thinking about home before a mission, but sometimes an image or a smell or a word above a urinal wormed itself into his head, and he had a hard time exorcising it. It could only get in his way. There was plenty of time to think about home between missions. The military made it easy, creating an air-conditioned bubble around them stocked with Burger King's French fries, ESPN, the latest video games, magazines, and action movies. In Bagram, they had everything soldiers needed to imagine they were back in the States.

Jenner leaned in. "Nice of you to join us."

Hector grinned. "I had a chance to fly home a few minutes ago, but I knew you rejects would be lost without me."

The men snickered.

"Maybe all of us should go back," Alex said, exaggerating his distinct East Texas twang. "Let's call up the Commander-in-Chief and inform him we're striking for better working conditions."

Brian nodded. "Sergeant Vilanova, that's an excellent idea. When we get back from tonight's excursion, I'll give the President a call."

The men laughed in unison.

Ten minutes to go.

***

Brian said a silent prayer: God, keep me from making a mistake, and if I do, let me alone bear the pain.

In war, prayers were as common as bullets, and the close-cropped, clean-shaven team leader used the same one every day of his deployment. Saying the prayer was just a crazy superstition. His belief in God lay buried with the dead somewhere in these mountains.

"Are you guys ready?" Brian asked.

Alex and Hector gave him thumbs up.

Jenner leaned forward; his eyes fixed on Brian's. "You already know the answer to that."

"You sure?"

"Fifty-five missions, not one casualty. But who's counting?"

"You know why I'm worried."

Jenner's thin-lipped mouth tightened. "You worry too much."

"I have reasons."

"About us being ready?"

"About us coming back with two targets. Alive."

"Them or us?"

"Both. You heard the orders."

Jenner lifted his head and pressed the back of it against the wall. His face reddened, and a throbbing vein slithered snake-like across his forehead.

Brian studied his teammate and waited for him to respond. Unlike him, unlike anyone else he knew, Jenner showed little respect for fear. He raced to the brink of every precipice, seemingly unafraid. Brian loved Jenner, but it troubled him that his friend was turning into an adrenaline junky. On recent missions, Jenner had acted in ways that showed little value for his safety. Brian feared that his lack of caution might someday endanger the team, though Jenner's fearlessness had saved their lives more than once.

"Abduct not kill. Unless absolutely necessary, understood?"

Jenner hesitated. "Understood. Unless there's no choice."

Hector, who was sitting next to Jenner, laughed. "You're like my mother. She wants me to kill every Muslim. She thinks they all want to kill us. All one billion of them. She's bloodthirsty."

Alex chuckled. "Jenner even looks like your Mama."

"No way. Mama is bigger."

Everyone laughed. Jenner was six foot, four inches and weighed 220 pounds. Hector, the son of Honduran immigrants, was five foot, six inches and so small-boned that Jenner said he looked like a Cub Scout.

"When I first came here, my Mama asked me, 'When are you going to kill Osama Ben Lennon?' That's what she called him — Osama Ben Lennon. She thought every soldier spent all their time searching for that skinny bastard. She didn't know I was really on a task force hunting down Osama and other Ali Baba assholes."

Alex looked at Jenner and winked. "So, Hector, what did your Mama say when the Seals killed bin Laden?"

"She said I should come home."

Jenner snickered. "That will be the day."

"I told Mama I wasn't coming home until I did my duty. I said the generals would find something else for us to do."

Jenner pounded his chest. "Kill more of the enemy."

Hector's smile rippled with self-satisfaction. "You see. You're as bloodthirsty as my *madrecita.*"

Hector's smile was a quarter moon framed by the night sky of his dark olive skin, a stub of a nose, and bright black eyes. His looks and small stature prompted many who met him for the first time to underestimate him, but he was a good soldier and tough as they come.

Alex nudged Hector. "And what does Mama say about you reenlisting again?"

"She thinks I'm fucking crazy if I reenlist. She wants me to come home and take over the restaurant. I tell you what, if I do that, I want all of you, wherever you are when this war finally ends, to visit me for a feast of *baleadas, cerviche,* and all the

Salva Vida beer you can drink. It will be my treat."

Jenner chuckled. "A free meal and unlimited booze? I'm in."

Alex grinned. "Me too."

Hector motioned to Brian. "And what about you, team leader? Will you visit me when the war's over?"

Brian hesitated. The war seemed endless. "Yeah, I guess."

"Not guess, *mi hermano,*" Hector said. He was no longer smiling. "Do you promise? As soon as possible after the war ends, our team comes together one more time to celebrate the victory. Promise."

Brian nodded and smiled. "I promise."

"Good. My *madrecita* will be happy."

Alex leaned against Hector and asked, "And what does your Papa think about you reenlisting?"

"He thinks we should just drop some nukes down every cave in the Hindu Kush mountains and come home."

Hector threw his arms around Alex and Jenner's shoulders. "He says that if the Greeks, Persians, Mongols, British, and Russians couldn't defeat the Afghans, then how can white trash from Texas and California ever do it?"

Alex and Jenner both elbowed Hector until Brian said, "Knock it off now. We have only five minutes before we move out. No more talking. Get ready."

The men quieted. The entire corridor sank into anxious silence.

Brian suspected that few people in the States or the allied countries had any idea what it meant to undertake a mission like this. They didn't understand the real odds of success in these mountains. The enemy had lived in the region all their lives. They knew the hidden goat paths like New York cabbies knew the ins and outs of Manhattan. When the Taliban traveled, they traveled light, relying on tribesmen to supply them, while the Task Force had to carry in every bullet, every scrap of food, and every drop of water. What the Afghans lacked in technology, they made up for in their knowledge of how to survive a harsh life in rough terrain. When Delta came in force, the enemy combatants melted into the rubble of rock and ice. But if the operatives let down their guard just once, a sniper's bullet or improvised explosive device made them pay the price. A thousand cuts for the infidels, the enemy promised.

This land was their home.

CHAPTER FOUR

Alex's chest tightened. The tension right before a mission often weighed on him. It reminded him of when he was a kid waiting in his bedroom for his angry father to walk in with a belt in his hand. Alex just wanted to get it over with.

"Recheck your night-vision," Brian ordered. "We move out fast when we land."

Alex checked his goggles and the straps to his vest. He felt confident their MOUT training, short for military operation urban terrain, would automatically kick in when they reached the village. But any mistake might jeopardize the mission and cost lives. Better to review the details a hundred times than lose one man.

He turned his head to say something to Aarmaan but paused when he saw his friend, head bowed, reading his Koran. He thought it ironic that the only book of God carried on the mission was the Muslim Holy Book. But maybe it was fitting. All the men, except for Jenner, admired Aarmaan's devotion to his faith, even if they didn't fully understand it.

Alex noticed rivulets of sweat streaming down Aarmaan's cheeks. "Are you OK, my friend?" he whispered.

Aarmaan looked up and flashed a wan smile.

"Why do you ask?"

"You're sweating . . . a lot."

Slowly, the interpreter touched both sides of his face. "It's hot in here. All these men in such close quarters."

"Brian briefed you?"

"Yes. I know the village. My father and I visited it before the war with the Soviets. It's small. The people raise goats. I don't know why our enemy would go there."

"Just remember, when we enter the village, you stay behind me. Brian will call you if he needs you."

Aarmaan placed his right hand on his holy book. "I'm not afraid."

Alex heard Aarmaan's words and knew his friend had lied. Among all the team members, he was closest to the soft-spoken Afghan. The eighteen-year age difference and their cultural divide meant little to either of them. They often talked when the afternoon sun demanded stillness. Alex shared secrets with the interpreter he told no one else: how he struggled in high school; how the Army rescued him from a ragtag life filled with drunken violence and loneliness. Aarmaan spun stories like fine silk from his youth as a cricket player and a diplomat's son. More recently, he told of his struggles with the Taliban, who whipped him, destroyed his books, and threatened him with beheading for reading newspapers. Though the two men spoke for hours at a time, they more often sat shoulder-to-shoulder and listened to the sound of wind swirling around the nearby mountains, sharing a bond of wordless understanding. That is why, when Alex heard Aarmaan's denial of fear, he knew something was amiss. His friend was terrified.

"You sure you're OK? Did something happen at home?"

"No, nothing," Aarmaan mumbled, and gave Alex an anguished smile.

Alex nodded. What more could he say? The seconds ticked away in his head. Nothing could stop the mission now. Whatever any of them were feeling, the mission locked them into something too big and too powerful to reverse or delay. Nothing that Brian, Jenner, Hector, or anyone else in this cold corridor could abort. All their fates laid like spools of woolen yarn in the Hindu Kush mountains. What became of them would unravel soon.

He touched Aarmaan's arm. *"Insha'Allah,* my friend."

"Insha'Allah, Alex."

Alex leaned over and whispered in Aarmaan's ear. "By the way, I bought a Sims 4 video game for Kohzad and Amin. It's back in my locker."

Aarmaan winced. "You shouldn't have."

"It's just a gift for your boys. No big deal."

"All right, thank you. My sons will love the game."

Brian's voice crackled from across the corridor. "Quit the chatter." His look meant there were no exceptions.

Alex wanted to say more. He wanted to ask more questions but watched in silence as Aarmaan tilted his head in a gesture of submission to Brian's authority and put away his Koran.

As Alex leaned back against the wall, a whistle signaled the teams to move out. Brian jumped up and led his men across the tarmac. They boarded an MH-47 chopper and filled the red pull-down benches closest to the exit ramp. Other Special Operation teams, including a team of Afghan commandos, sat up front ghost-like against the dimly lit gray walls of the cabin. In the cockpit, Night Stalkers — battle-hardened pilots from the 160th Special Operations Aviation Regiment — gunned the engines and lifted the enormous bird off the ground. The noise from the rotors made conversation impossible.

The two choppers flew without lights through an ink-black sky at one hundred eighty miles per hour toward what the men called Indian Country. This section of the Hindu Kush Mountains swarmed with tough fierce fighters who believed that if death came at the hands of the infidel, their souls would go to heaven.

Too pumped up to doze or relax, the operatives prepared themselves to face death one more time. Most stared straight ahead, but some made eye contact with their fellow team members. The tension was visceral. When the choppers touched down, most of the men felt relieved the waiting was over. At last, they could get up and move.

When the ramp opened, Alex followed Aarmaan out of the chopper. He noticed that Aarmaan seemed unsteady. He worried that whatever was afflicting his friend might make it hard for him to keep up. Before they reached the village, they had a steep climb ahead. The squad couldn't afford stragglers. The soldiers needed to complete their mission and board the chopper before the sun rose.

Alex put his hand on the older man's shoulder. "Is something wrong?"

"Keep moving," Jenner said from behind.

"I'm fine," Aarmaan said, then squeezed Alex's forearm.

For the next hour, the men climbed without a word. When they arrived at the outskirts of the village, the teams dispersed to their designated points of entry. Brian pointed to a rock formation twenty yards ahead, and the team followed him. The men gazed at the village, a cluster of twenty mud-brick and stone buildings looking like layers of a wedding cake, one on top of the other, huddled around a common spring. It reminded Alex of an ancient Navaho village he once visited in Arizona. In the middle of the walled compound, the villagers had penned a few donkeys and a dozen Girgentana goats for the night. Alex worried about the goats with their long-pointed ears and twisted horns and shrill cries that warned whenever strangers approached. He couldn't see any sentries posted. But gunmen with AK-47s and grenade launchers could hide in unseen crevices and doorways. He hoped the villagers were asleep, and no one would resist. If they did, some men, and maybe women and children, would die.

Alex stared at the rock outcroppings hovering over them like dark assassins. In his night vision, a green glow bathed the cliffs. Somewhere in the outcroppings, a Seal team of snipers hid, ready to lay down deadly fire and prevent escape. Beyond them were miles and miles of mountains lying on the earth's curving bedrock, oblivious to whatever was about to happen in this village. Armies came and went, but the mountains always remained.

Brian pointed at the village. "I don't see any sentries, but be on the lookout. We'll scale the wall at that point to bypass the goats."

Alex felt relieved. He hated those goats.

Brian brought them into a close circle. "Remember, for a thousand years, warriors have died in the Hindu Kush. Tonight, let's not add any to the list, but if shit happens, make sure it's only the enemy who meets their ancestors. Roger?"

"Roger," the men whispered in unison.

"Hand signals from this point on." Brian motioned the men to take their positions, then led the team to a wall at the north end of the village. Alex extracted a lightweight tactical ladder from a pouch. He unfolded it and inserted its tip into the barrel of his rifle. Carefully, he lifted the rifle and guided the ladder over the lip of the mud wall where its jagged teeth bit down and held. The men scaled the wall and dropped into an alleyway. They ran down the alley and halted at the largest building in the village. Satellite photos had singled it out as the one most likely to shelter the terrorist leaders they were seeking. Other teams would infiltrate different targets, but this one was theirs.

The success of this "house call" depended on a combination of military intelligence, surprise, and luck.

Brian motioned to Aarmaan to stay back. He pressed his back against a wall and pushed against the door, but it didn't open. At Brian's signal, Alex smashed a small steel battering ram into the plank door, tearing it off its hinges. Jenner entered and moved to his right. Alex followed and moved to the left. On Alex's heels, Brian took a position in the center of the room and scanned above him for any overhead space that could harbor a shooter. He saw nothing and signaled to Hector, guarding their rear with his powerful M249 SAW automatic rifle, to enter. As Hector backed into the hut, Brian motioned to Jenner to move into the next room.

Alex followed and glanced at Hector, moving in his direction. Hector gave him the thumbs-up sign. At that moment, a shot rang out, and Hector collapsed as if a giant wave had hit him broadside. Blood spurted from his neck. Instinctively, Alex wheeled around to respond to the shooter, only to see Aarmaan standing in the doorway.

Aarmaan aimed a pistol at him.

Rifles fired, and the interpreter's body crumpled and landed in the dirt. Alex whirled and saw Jenner and Brian in a shooter's position, weapons pointed at Aarmaan lying in the alley.

In shock, Alex stumbled over to Hector and tried to stanch the bleeding. But the blood gushed out of Hector's neck and splattered him.

Jenner pulled him away. "He's dead, man."

Alex's mind grappled with what had happened. It was as if the earth beneath his feet had given way, and he was in free fall. Hector was dead. His best friend had killed him.

Why didn't Aarmaan shoot me? Alex thought. He looked

right at me.

Jenner barked at him. "Hammer, this way."

Alex picked up his rifle and followed Jenner as they searched the rest of the hut. In a large back room, they found two women and six small children huddled together. The smallest children were crying. The women and an older girl tried to keep them quiet. Alex realized none of them could see him in the darkness, but they knew he was there. He could see their eyes sweeping the room, their bodies trembling, eight faces aglow in the sickly hues of his night vision lenses.

He scanned the space. Rugs covered the floors. Three beds made of tree stumps and ropes, plus two large chests, crammed the room. Rough-hewn wooden shelves laden with meager possessions lined the walls. The smell of turmeric and coriander mingled with the acrid odor of gunpowder.

Outside, goats and donkeys screamed the alarm. The sounds filled the house and seemed otherworldly.

Brian's strained voice pulled Alex back to reality. Brian shouted into the microphone on his headset, informing other team leaders of Lance-1's situation. He waited for a response. A gruff voice answered, "Charlie Foxtrot, over. We captured the targets, over."

"Move out," Brian shouted and led the men into the front room, where Brian hoisted Hector onto Jenner's back and shouldered Hector's weapon.

Outside, the sound of small arms fire intensified, and an RPG exploded nearby. Panicking women and children screamed. Men's cries bellowed over the rooftops. Alex heard people scurrying behind the house and wondered if they were frightened civilians or angry men with AK-47s. He didn't want to find out. Time was now the enemy. The element of surprise was no longer on their side.

With caution, Brian exited through the open front door. The alley was empty, but he knew that could change in an instant. He signaled for Alex and Jenner to race toward the gate at the end of the alley while he covered them. Jenner rushed forward, but Alex hesitated and leaned over Aarmaan's corpse.

Brian whirled around. "Leave him."

But Alex didn't obey. Instead, he reached down to pick up the body.

Brian rushed over and grabbed his wrist. "Don't touch him. They might have booby-trapped him."

"But —"

"I said, 'Leave him.'"

"You can't be serious!"

Suddenly, several armed men shot at them from the far end of the alley. The bullets ricocheted off the ground. Brian delivered suppressive fire with Hector's SAW. Two fighters fell. The rest scattered behind a building. Alex rose with his weapon, but Brian screamed at him to run. For a moment, Alex hesitated, then ran toward a gate about twenty-five yards away. Meanwhile, Brian sprayed bullets at men emerging from the back of a house with AK-47s. The fighters ducked for cover, but one returned, holding a grenade. Brian put two rounds through the man's chest, knocking the man off his feet and into a bloody heap. As Brian retreated, Alex covered him. Each man took turns fending off the attackers until they reached the gate and fled down a steep path.

The infiltration teams assembled at the prearranged meeting point. The village behind them seemed eerily quiet to some of the newer operatives, but the old-timers understood the enemy was regrouping. Soon, the enemy fighters would follow. Men from other villages, now alerted, would swarm. The Americans and their two captives had to reach the choppers before the mountains came alive with warriors. The teams moved out as gunfire shattered the calm. Shouts and shots mingled in the din from the village. Fiery tracers from the Seal snipers in the cliffs above the village streaked the sky.

Alex found himself in the rear. To his left, the flash and roar of an explosion came too close. He flinched, then resumed scrambling up the rock-strewn path. The men ahead formed a single, silent line, pulling him forward. He could feel his heart pumping. He stared straight ahead. Two operatives carried Hector's body in a black flex-litter. The sight of Hector's arm flapping lifelessly over the side of the stretcher caused him to shudder. But he kept moving, focused on the path, trying not to think, falling back on instinct. He didn't break stride. He had to get back home. Had to fly like a bird. Get back to where he came from. Away from here.

CHAPTER FIVE

When the chopper landed at Bagram Air Base, the men engaged in none of the usual horseplay marking the end of a mission. The body bag containing Hector's corpse and Aarmaan's empty seat reminded them that the Hindu Kush, or "Killer of Hindus," had won more trophies.

The back ramp opened, and Brian spotted the mortuary service specialists on the tarmac waiting for Hector's body. Brian glanced back at the two hooded and bound prisoners sitting cross-legged on the forward floor. Somehow their capture didn't seem worth Hector's death, but he would leave it to the generals to make that calculation.

"Listen up," he shouted. "Our orders are to proceed to quarters, stow our gear, clean up, and report at 1100 to Room A-108 for action review. Copy?"

"Copy," Jenner and Alex said.

"Any questions?"

Jenner pointed at the two men wearing black hoods. "What about the prisoners?"

"Lance-2 will escort them to headquarters for questioning."

"Who are they?"

"As far as Mako can tell, the taller one is Hazret Ayoub. The other one is Abdul Hamed. Two ISIS-K leaders."

"High value then?"

Brian stared at the black scrim PVC transport pouch that held Hector and said ruefully, "Very high. The mission was a success."

"Like hell," Alex said, and shook his head.

****

The first of two "hot washes," or action reviews, began at 1100 in Camp Vance, the special forces facility located about five-sixths of a mile from the airfield. The first hot wash included the entire troop. Mark Cohen, the senior noncommissioned officer, ordered the sixteen soldiers to sit in a circle. The Major and two lieutenants remained outside the ring and spoke only when necessary. The noncom asked the group three questions: What worked? What went wrong? What would they eliminate or strengthen for the next mission?

When the incident with Hector and Aarmaan came up, Brian did most of the talking. At first, some operatives questioned leaving the interpreter's body behind, but concluded that the level of enemy fire and the possibility of an explosive vest warranted the decision. The troop arrived at a consensus that the interpreter's betrayal was tragic but unforeseeable. The contractor, Military Essential Personnel, did a quality job vetting its CAT III linguists. But no one could see into the heart of another human being.

After the first hot wash, the men split into their respective teams and moved into breakout rooms with no officers. The questions remained the same, but the focus shifted to each team's internal process.

When Brian led the way into their small room, he noticed the blue plastic chairs, milk-colored walls, vinyl flooring, and lack of windows. "Take a seat," he ordered.

Brian turned a chair around and straddled it, and the others followed suit, all facing each other in the center of the room. Brian cleared his throat and spoke. "I know this is hard, but it will be a hell of a lot easier if we follow protocol. So, let's get it done. Question one: What went right about the mission?"

Both Brian and Jenner looked at Alex, who was quietly staring at the floor. For a few moments, the men sat in awkward silence until Jenner rode his chair into the center of the circle. "I'll go first. From my point of view, our team performed according to the plan. We avoided detection from the LZ to the village, gained entry without a hitch, and when we lost the element of surprise, we finished our search ASAP. That's all there is."

Alex looked up at Jenner in astonishment. "That's all there is? How can you say that? Hector and Aarmaan are fucking dead."

Jenner nodded. "Hector did his job. Then a motherfucker took him out. And we took out the motherfucker. I'm as pissed off as you are about Hector, but this is the standard operating procedure in this hell-hole of a country."

Alex shifted in his seat. "And what about me? I fucked up, didn't I? Something was wrong with Aarmaan. I knew he was acting weird. He was sweating like a pig and wouldn't look at me. I should've pursued it. I should have —"

Brian interrupted him. "There was no way you could have guessed what he was about to do."

Alex gasped. "No way? Are you kidding? Something scared him, and I saw it. He never showed fear before. Why didn't I follow my gut and find out the reason?"

Brian answered like a priest, offering absolution. "You did all you could. He was our terp for six months and never gave us any reason to suspect him. He fooled all of us, not just you."

Jenner said, "We're not the first unit this has happened to. The British even coined a term for it: Blue on Green attacks."

Alex leaned against his chair, almost tipping it over. "It

should have been me he shot. Not Hector."

Jenner angrily stood and paced the small room. "That's bullshit. It was the goat-fucker who deserves to be dead, and he is. That's all. I trust none of our Afghan so-called friends, even the Afghan-American ones. They're all a bunch of two-faced rag heads smiling with their hands out for dollars just waiting for a chance to off us. They turn on each other the same way. The Army says we need them, but I'd like to line them all up against a wall and frag them. Hector died, not because of something you did or didn't do. He was just in the line of fire."

When Alex didn't respond, Jenner scoffed. "And what is this crap that the terp should have shot you instead of Hector? Please. We should have dropped the asshole from a chopper six months ago."

Alex shook his head. "You're wrong, Jenner. Aarmaan was a good man . . . a friend."

Jenner's face was livid. "A friend? He was Hector's friend too, wasn't he? Until he shot him."

"That's why it makes little sense. Not any of it. He loved America. Loved it as much as he loved Afghanistan. He told me. God, he still had his American citizenship. He never renounced it. He must have had some reason for what he did."

Brian shot his hand out to get Alex to shut up. "Think hard. This man you call a friend pointed a weapon at you the moment we took him out. One more second, you're in a hurt locker beside Hector."

"I know. I thought I was dead."

Jenner's eyebrows raised. "So, why give two shits about what that son-of-a-bitch's reasons for pulling the trigger?"

"But why didn't he shoot me? He looked like he didn't want to do it."

Jenner pronounced each word as if he were speaking to a foreigner. "That makes no fucking sense. He intended to pull that trigger."

"But he hesitated. Maybe he felt he had no choice."

"He had choices," Brian said in disgust. "We all have choices. He made the wrong one. Now, let's finish this hot wash and get the hell out of here."

Alex placed his hands in his lap, hung his head, and remained quiet for the rest of the meeting. Meanwhile, Jenner and Brian finished the protocol in a lackluster manner, glancing at Alex whenever they answered a question. Finally, Brian checked his watch and rose from his seat. "Is there anything else we need to discuss?"

Alex lifted his head and stared at Brian. "You ordered me to leave Aarmaan's body. You should've let me take him back with us. For his family. We never leave a fallen comrade behind."

Brian's nostrils flared, and he pointed his finger at Alex. "Comrade? Screw that. I'll say this once. Aarmaan betrayed us. He killed Hector and almost killed you. He wasn't one of us. He was one of them."

Brian turned to Jenner. "Take Hammer out of here. Now. Get some chow and shut-eye. The Unit Psychologist set up CISD meetings for us in his office starting at 1600. Alex goes first, then you, and I'll be last."

Jenner groaned. "Why so late?"

"Major Carruthers is in Kandahar and won't be back till later."

"Can't we bailout?"

"You know it's SOP, so suck it up and get through it."

"I don't like it."

"You don't have to like it. Do it."

Jenner looked as if he were going to argue the case, then stood up and hovered over Alex. "Let's go, Hammer."

Alex stood and followed Jenner out the door. But then he returned alone and approached Brian. "Are you coming?"

Brian glared at him. "I'll be there in a minute."

"Listen, Brian, I —"

Brian held up his hand. "Don't say anything. I don't want to hear it. I'd march into hell for you, but don't ever, ever, accuse me of leaving a man behind. Do you understand?"

Alex nodded.

"Now, get out of here, Vilanova. That's an order."

Alex left the building and caught up with Jenner, who was outside leaning against a white delivery van. Neither spoke, and when Brian joined them five minutes later, the three men walked in silence toward their barracks. The road was a beehive of activity. Contractors, soldiers, laborers, military vehicles of all shapes and sizes, and two women in business suits and bright red-and-yellow headscarves in a taxi whizzed by. The smell of diesel fuel penetrated the men's nostrils. Choking dust filled the air. The one comfort came from Jill Scott's voice singing "A Long Walk" from a radio inside an idling Jeep.

When they finally arrived at their quarters, a sand-colored concrete building, Brian told them to get some rest, then climbed the outside steps to the second floor.

Jenner and Alex watched him go. "Home sweet home," Jenner said to Alex. "See you later."

After Jenner left him, Alex strolled to the center of the dusty courtyard that the barracks surrounded on three sides. He reflected on the large KEEP OFF THE GRASS sign that skewered the barren soil. Hector had hammered his homemade sign into this hard ground a week ago. Just like him, Alex thought. He wondered if he should pull the sign out, then decided it should stay. With his head hung, he shuffled to the quarters he had shared with Hector. He unlocked the door and pushed it open. The room was the size of a college dorm. A solitary window framed the outside. A white door led to a bathroom. To the right, a kitchenette held a small stove and fridge. Hooks of varying sizes stuck out of the walls like miniature antlers. On the far wall, a TV hung above an Ikea-type chest of drawers. Near each bed, the men had access to a small desk, a chair, and a tall metal locker.

After taking a mental picture of the space, Alex headed toward Hector's locker, where his roommate had kept his most precious keepsakes. In the front, Hector had affixed mementos his wife, Marianna, regularly mailed to him, along with her sweet *buñuelos* and guava jam. There were also family photos and his kid's drawings, "Humor in Uniform" clippings from *The Reader's Digest*, and most prominently, a funeral card adorned with his little brother's name, a brief prayer, and a picture of Jesus. On the left side of the locker, Hector had taped penciled caricatures he had drawn of celebrities like Penelope Cruz and Lionel Messi. They were quite good for someone self-taught. And on the side closest to his cot, he had taped photos of his time in Afghanistan: The streets and markets. The children playing. And many pictures of his friends enjoying each other's company.

One of these photos was the one Alex was looking for. It was one in which the five men lined up with their arms around each other, dressed in the traditional Afghan knee-length tunic and baggy trousers. Alex smiled with melancholy, remembering how much time it took the five men to stop laughing and find the right pose. Hector, dwarfed by his taller friends, stood in the center of the group like a Wizard-of-Oz munchkin. Jenner and Brian stood on his right, and Alex and Aarmaan on his left.

Before the Army transported Hector's body back to the States, it would send a team to pack his belongings and ship them back home, leaving these quarters stripped for the next occupant. With care, Alex removed the photo of his team from the locker. He wanted this photo for himself.

CHAPTER SIX

After Alex met with the psychologist, he waited for Jenner to finish his debriefing session. He stood under the enormous American flag that covered the entire ceiling of the open entranceway. The cold air chilled him, and he turned up his collar to block the breeze sliding down from the nearby mountains. He could have waited inside but the idea of spending one more minute in the psych unit was anathema to him. The staff was mostly Air Force personnel and as friendly and as competent as professionals anywhere, but their kind eyes and smiles made him feel there was something wrong with him. He knew it was stupid to feel that way, but he couldn't help himself.

While he waited, he paced back and forth in front of the entrance, gazing down each side of the street that paralleled the hospital. Each side was a maze of blast walls and check points that protected the structure from Taliban car bombers. The last time a bomber got through, two people had died.

Jenner emerged from the building with a laugh. "Damn. That was just like the scene in Robin Williams' movie with Matt Damon. You know, the one where Matt toys with his shrink?"

"What did Major Carruthers ask you?"

"She asked me if I hated my mom."

"Stop joking."

Jenner's mouth tightened. "She asked me how I felt about what went down."

"And what did you tell her?"

"Enough for her to believe me; not enough to earn an

administrative discharge."

Jenner punched Alex's arm. When Alex didn't laugh, Jenner frowned and shook his head. "I know this whole thing sucks, but you can't let this pull you down."

Alex turned his head away.

Jenner placed his arm around Alex's shoulders and shook him. "Come on, Hammer. Let's get something to eat and head down to the MWR."

"What about Brian? Should we wait for him?"

"Negative. After he meets with the psychologist, he's got to report to the Detachment Commander. I'm sure they'll talk through the decision to leave the terp behind. Who knows what the brass will do? Leaving behind a potential suicide bomber seems like a no-brainer to me, but what do I know? Anyway, I'm your date for tonight. Kiss, kiss."

"How can you joke after what happened?"

"You really want to know?"

"Yeah, I want to know."

Jenner twisted his head to loosen his neck muscles. "It's simple. It's what I do to survive this war. Compartmentalize. Bagram is here. The Kush is out there. We're alive. Others are dead. Kill or be killed. Friend or enemy. Makes things simple."

"Is it that simple?"

"Damn straight. Now, let's get some food." With his arm, he nudged Alex along.

"I'm not hungry," Alex said.

"So, watch me stuff my face for a half hour, then we'll go play pool."

Alex dug in his heels. "Icarus, listen. You go ahead. I'm going back to quarters. I don't want to hang out."

Jenner threw up his hands. "Chill out, Dude."

"You go ahead."

Jenner grabbed Alex's arm and pulled him along.

Alex ripped his arm away and pushed back.

Jenner's eyes deadened. Alex had seen that hard look before in a Fayetteville parking lot. A drunken Marine called Jenner a pussy while poking him in the chest. Jenner didn't say a word. Instead, he smiled, then blew the grunt a kiss. The enraged drunk unwisely raised his fist, so Jenner head-butted him, splitting his forehead wide open and buckling his knees. A kick to the side of the head then knocked out the man.

"Hammer," Jenner said. "We don't want to go to close quarters with each other, do we?"

"Not unless you push me into it. Maybe we should walk away and start over?"

Jenner thrust his face into Alex's. "What's the matter with you? This is Icarus you're talking to. You don't want to be alone tonight."

"I'm not in the mood for a crowd."

Jenner shrugged. "You want to stand in your own shit, go ahead. But remember this: Hector is dead, and you're alive because I killed the bastard. Me. Think about that."

Jenner shoved Alex hard in the chest and walked away.

As he tramped back to quarters, Alex tried his best to think about something other than the friends he had lost. "Compartmentalize," he said, but his mind betrayed him. "Why them?" he muttered. "Why the guys with wives and kids? And not me? Or Jenner? It's always the friends with the most to lose who the enemy blows away."

He thought of Hector's wife. What was she going to do when she heard the news?

Alex knew that shortly after Casualty Notification Officers

visited Marianna Flores, other Army wives would comfort her. The women would feel both sad and relieved as they banded together for their widows' walk up the front steps with their casseroles and napkins. Fayetteville was a strange town, he thought. It was a military town where women spent their best days loving strong hard men who were always shuffling off to war, then coming back home as different men.

Coming back home? To Alex, the phrase seemed strange. Fayetteville was not home. Never would be. His home was here, with his brothers.

The thought of his fallen brothers triggered tears. "Compartmentalize, Sergeant." Alex flicked his lit cigarette against a trash can a few feet away. Suddenly, he felt a powerful urge to get Hector's SAW and shoot every Afghan man he could find.

CHAPTER SEVEN

Two weeks after the village raid, Brian heard unsettling news. The info came from two friends who were private contractors with the Afghan military. They had just returned from Asadabad, a city less than five miles from the Pakistan border.

Jerry Erskine and Phillip Barstow, former members of Britain's Special Air Service Regiment, welcomed Brian into their tent for Taddy Porters and Nicaraguan cigars. The mingled aroma of cigars and British after-shave greeted Brian as he stepped inside. Light from a jerry-rigged electrical system flooded the interior, and a Van Morrison song played quietly in the background.

The older men clapped Brian on the back and made small talk, then guided him to a corner of the tent covered with Afghan rugs and cushions.

Phil motioned for Brian to sit.

"Glad you could make it, Sport," Jerry said, handing Brian an opened beer and a Prensado cigar. "Here, let me light this for you. Think you'll fancy it."

Brian inhaled the rich oily smoke and savored the scent of chocolate and leather. "How are things in Indian Country?"

"Not good," Phil said. "The commanders we train keep getting shot."

"By the Taliban or their own men?"

"Both, I'm afraid to say. Makes our job harder, as you can imagine. But we didn't invite you here to blamestorm. We brought back some news for you. We figured you might not have heard about this from the official channels, so we thought we'd better tell you."

"Tell me what?" Brian asked, anticipating one of their practical jokes.

Phil cleared his throat. "We were working with these blokes at the camp when an Afghan patrol came in with two boys, about ten and twelve years old. The patrol found the boys wandering in the foothills. The lads looked exhausted and confused and their heads were heavily bandaged."

"At first, they refused to speak," said Jerry. "But finally, the oldest boy, holding the other's hand, asked for water. When the medic removed their bloody bandages, he discovered their ears were missing."

"Jesus," said Brian.

"Nasty business," added Phillip. "Anyway, the youngest boy began to cry, but the twelve-year-old stared at the patrol, dried-eyed and defiant like the finest Gurkha, while he slowly removed his blood-stained shirt. The bastards who kidnapped him had carved into his chest the Pashto words for 'son of a traitor.'"

Brian suddenly knew why Jerry and Phil invited him. "The boys were Aarmaan's sons?"

Jerry nodded.

"Where are they now?"

"They're in the ISAF hospital in Kabul. The Taliban released the boy's mother two days after they let the boys go. She's in worse shape, but alive."

Brian slammed his fist down on the table. "Fuck the Taliban and fuck this war. God damn it. Why did they do that?"

Jerry filled Brian's glass with beer. "Don't you get it, chum?

It was a reward."

Brian shook his head. "A reward? Cutting off their ears and scarring chests? How is that a reward?"

Jerry, who saw the worst of the Troubles in Ireland and the Insurgency in Iraq, gestured to Brian to drink his beer. "The Taliban rewarded the boys with their lives. They would be dead if Aarmaan hadn't killed an American soldier. Killing Hector was the ransom your terp had to pay. It was a bloody transaction, I admit. Cutting off the boys' ears was just a friendly message to other Muslims: Don't help the infidels."

***

As soon as Brian left the tent, he searched for Jenner and Alex to tell them what he had learned. After checking their quarters, he found them eating burgers and fries in a half-empty Burger King. They sat across from each other, chatting until they saw Brian, then greeted him by raising the soft drinks in their hands. Brian settled next to Alex and declined their offers to buy him a meal. He didn't know how to begin so he took his cues from his training in high altitude, low opening parachuting — jump first, then worry about a soft landing. Without a prologue, he relayed word for word Jerry and Phillip's story of Aarmaan's two boys. As he continued, both men put down their drinks and looked at each other. Neither man spoke, but when Brian told them about Pashto words carved on Aarmaan's oldest boy, Alex shoved his food tray into Jenner's, stood up, and stormed off without a word.

Brian called after him, then turned to Jenner who was mopping up the spilled soda on his tray with paper napkins. "What was that about?"

"Beats me."

"He was looking at you the whole time."

"He and I don't see things the same way."

"And what do you think about what I told you?"

Jenner sneered. "Nothing. It changes nothing."

"But, he —"

"He killed Hector! That is all that matters. I don't care what you or Hammer think."

Enraged, Jenner snatched up his tray, dumped the remains of his meal into a trash can, slammed the glass door open, and charged out of the restaurant.

The next day, Brian and Alex asked the captain for permission to visit Aarmaan's family in the hospital, but he denied their request. He said that their team's orders were to return to the United States for two weeks of leave and six weeks of training with a new teammate.

In the afternoon, Alex wrote a letter to Aarmaan's wife and put it in a box with the video game he had bought for the boys. Some fellow soldiers threw in cash, and Alex sealed the package and gave it to a Dutch aid worker to deliver to the hospital. According to scuttlebutt, the embassy was flying the family out of the country as soon as possible.

Brian sat with Alex that night on a bench outside the MWR. Brian offered Alex a chocolate bar, but Alex refused. "Listen, Hammer. What happened with Aarmaan. You were right. I was wrong. I should've let you bring his body back."

"It's too late now."

"I don't know what I would have done if I had to face his dilemma. I'd like to think Aarmaan could have found another way. You know what I mean?"

"Maybe there was another way. Maybe there wasn't. When you're fighting a war, you don't get easy answers."

Alex stood up and looked up at the starlit sky.

Brian stood next to him and placed his hand on his friend's shoulder. "I hope you'll forgive me for leaving Aarmaan behind. He killed Hector, and I thought he might have an IED strapped to him. I don't know . . ."

Alex lowered his gaze until it met Brian's. "There's nothing to forgive. The Hindu Kush makes fools of us all. I'm no better."

He walked off.

Brian's eyes followed Alex until his friend disappeared into a crowd of soldiers leaving the recreation center. Brian sensed something parasitic had wormed itself into his comrade's soul since that awful night. And Jenner had changed as well. While trauma had stalled Alex on the road, Jenner barreled along at two hundred miles per hour with no brakes. A head-on crash between the two was inevitable, and Brian didn't want to pick up the pieces.

He had his own grieving to do.

CHAPTER EIGHT

Just get us home in one piece, Brian thought as the massive C-17 Globemaster descended into driving rain and strong winds. Storms over the Atlantic had buffeted the flight home via Germany, but the weather over the Mid-Atlantic states proved far worse. It felt like the gods had strapped the plane to the rear end of a bucking bronco. The cabin shook, and the metal skin of the jet shrieked. Some soldiers threw up; some gripped their seats until their muscles ached. But true to military tradition, the Air Force captain piloting the C-17 toward Fort Bragg's Pope Field never got on the radio to reassure her passengers.

Don't expect cocktails, headsets, or sympathy on a military transport, Brian joked to himself, as the two-hundred-and-eighty-thousand-pound monster nosed down for a landing.

The Globemaster hit the runway with a pronounced bump. A cacophony of curses, laughs, and whistles followed. The pilot taxied the jet to a terminal, then cut the engines. The soldiers on board rose from their seats and tramped down the aisles. After they entered the terminal, Brian and his men deposited their gear and weapons with the duty officer. Unburdened, the men walked into a reception hall where wives, children, moms and dads welcomed the returning soldiers from the 82nd Airborne.

Brian expected no such reception. He had texted updates on his arrival to family and friends, but didn't expect anyone to greet him or his men. Unlike regular soldiers, their deployments to and from Afghanistan occurred so frequently, and with so little warning, that none of them expected any welcoming signs or crying relatives. That's why a familiar voice calling his name surprised him. When he turned around, he saw Kate walking his way.

"Look who's here, Falcon," said Jenner. "It's the fabulous Miss Porter, you lucky bastard."

What Jenner didn't know was that Kate Porter was the last person Brian expected to meet.

Kate was wide-eyed when she reached them. "I'm so sorry about Hector," she said and hugged the three men. She reached out for Brian's hand and squeezed it. "Your father called me. He said to tell you he wanted to come, but he couldn't arrange a flight on such short notice."

Brian pulled away from her. "So, you came?"

"I wanted to."

"It's a long way from Charleston."

"I wasn't in Charleston when he called. I was on my way to New York City."

Brian sneered. "So, you're moving to New York, for real?"

Kate ignored the implications of his question. "Are you going to visit Marianna?"

Brian looked at his men. "Tomorrow morning, I hope. We're all going together."

"I'm going with you."

Kate's announcement didn't surprise Brian. She loved spending time with Hector and his wife whenever she was in town. Hector always made her laugh, and she viewed Marianna as the sister she never had.

Jenner put his arm around Kate. "Let's take her with us, Falcon. It might help Marianna."

Before Brian could respond he added, "Hammer and I will leave you two lovebirds so you can get reacquainted. Pick us up tomorrow morning at eight at Alex's place."

"Thanks," Brian said as his two friends walked away.

Brian picked up his duffel bag and faced Kate. "Now what?"

"I have my car. I'll drop you off at your place and find a motel."

Brian grabbed her arm. "We need to talk."

She stared at Brian coldly until he released her. "Two months ago, you said all you needed to say over the phone. I'm here only because your father asked me to come. He's worried about you."

"Can I buy you a drink?"

Kate smirked. "I don't think Fayetteville has a rooftop bar."

Brian felt the sting of the remark. They had met three years ago in the rooftop bar of the Vendue Inn near the heart of Charleston, South Carolina. The bar offered a beautiful view of the harbor and historic Fort Sumter, but the young couple only had eyes for each other. Kate had long blonde hair, eyes the color of dark chocolate, and a swimmer's body with broad shoulders and a tiny waist. But she was much more than beautiful. She was smart and so percolating with life that Brian's wariness of beautiful women blew away like leaves off a porch.

Brian shook his head to push aside the memory. "I can't think of a rooftop bar, but we can go to the Mash House for beers and ribs. It may not look like much to you, but compared to where I've been, it's almost heaven."

Kate nodded. "The Mash House is fine. . . . Listen, I'm sorry. I don't want to fight. That's not why I'm here."

They walked to where Kate had parked her Subaru Outback, and Brian noticed that she had jammed the cargo area with cardboard boxes. He slid into the passenger seat and crammed his duffle bag beneath his feet. "So, tell me about this move to

New York City."

Kate turned on the ignition and wipers and pulled out of the spot. "I took a job with *The Raven*, a small literary magazine. I know that going into publishing now is like hiring on as a steward on the Titanic. But the job's part-time, and I can do some freelance as well. Friends are letting me stay with them until I find a place."

Brian clenched his teeth but didn't speak until they passed Fort Bragg's first control access point. For the last three years, he measured his life back home in the miles he drove back and forth to Kate's hometown of Charleston, and the short road trips they took together before his leaves ended with awkward goodbyes.

"So, you're moving on," Brian said. "Where does that leave us?"

Kate sighed. "It was you who called it quits, not me."

"I asked you to marry me, and you turned me down. What was I supposed to do?"

"I like how you put it. You didn't ask me to marry just you."

She gestured to the sprawling military installation engulfing them on both sides of the road. "You were asking me to marry the Army as well. As much as I love you, I won't commit my life to endless deployments and the fear that one day you wouldn't come back. I don't want to be like Marianna."

"But Kate, this is who I am. I'm a soldier."

"And once a soldier, always a soldier."

"That's right. You've known that."

Kate brushed her hair back. "Yes, I have. And that's fine for what we've been to each other. But you want more."

Brian peered through his window at Army men running together in the rain, bellowing their marching song, and wished he could explain what he wanted to Kate. It wasn't marriage per se, though that's what he proposed to her on the phone. How could he explain what he meant? It wasn't about a license or a ring or a church ceremony. Marrying Kate served as his return ticket back into an ordered world after emerging from hell. Somehow, she knew how to defuse his inner rages. Her tenderness, the yielding landscape of her body, and the soft sigh she made when she turned over in bed made him feel almost human again. He wanted to father her children, hold them in his arms, and lose himself in their innocent eyes.

"I missed you," he said.

"Then why did you dump me? We have so much in common. God, you even love to read. And my father likes you, sort of."

"Did you tell him we split up?"

"No, he'll kill you when he finds out."

Brian chuckled. "I know."

"Seriously, we don't need to get married, Brian. We can enjoy our time together until we split for good or grow up."

Brian scoffed. "Grow up?"

"Yes, grow up. Be like normal couples. Talk to each other. Make a life together. Be there when it counts. You know what I mean."

For the next few minutes, they said nothing. Kate drove, and Brian looked out the window. When Kate reached over to turn on the radio, Brian grabbed her hand.

"No, don't," he said. "Listen, the last two months have been hard. You're the love of my life. I don't want to lose you. You make me crazy in all the good ways."

He paused. "Well, most of the time."

Kate laughed.

Brian grinned. "You see, I even make you laugh."

He took her hand and squeezed. "Let's make this work."

Kate steepled her hands and playfully pummeled her forehead. "You are such a jerk. Ugh! I can't believe I'm doing this. OK, let's try one more time. You stay a soldier. I'll stay a civilian. No expectations. For either of us. And let's not go to The Mash House. Let's drive to your apartment and order a pizza."

Brian eyed Kate. He could fight with her or surrender. "Pizza sounds great."

They passed the final checkpoint and headed to Brian's apartment.

***

The next morning, Brian parked his Dodge Ram 1500 in front of Hector's small ranch house in New Hope. Kate and Jenner sat next to him. As he unbuckled his seatbelt, Brian looked past them at the property.

No one had cut the lawn or swept the driveway. The rain gutters overflowed with leaves and pine needles. Streaks of mildew stained the shingle roof. A small, frayed American flag flapped in the breeze from the front porch.

Brian recalled a different flag, a beautiful banner with embroidered stars and stripes waving from a tall cedar pole in the front yard. Hector loved his patriotic display and the house it flew over. Whenever he came home from a tour, he always worked on his home. He'd spend hours patching the driveway, fixing the roof, or fertilizing the lawn. He liked to brag he was the best handyman in the neighborhood.

But Hector's flag was missing. The cedar flagpole was empty.

Jenner pointed at his watch. "We're an hour late."

Hector's wife, Marianna, had asked them to arrive at nine in the morning after her children went to school. She explained, "They've missed too much school already, and Hector wants them to have an excellent education. You will eat something when you come. I have some left-over casseroles I can reheat."

But it was a quarter past ten when Brian parked the car. They were late because Alex had failed to show up at the meeting spot. They had wasted an hour looking for him. How would Brian explain Alex's inexcusable breach of duty to Marianna?

Jenner opened the passenger door. "Are you coming?"

Brian took one last look down the tree-lined street and stepped out. He took Kate's hand, and with Jenner alongside, they walked up the pathway to Hector's front door.

Before they could knock, Marianna opened the door and motioned the three inside with a weary nod of her head. She wore a blue cotton-fleece robe and a pair of red slippers. Her hair was uncombed, and her puffy amber face lacked any signs of makeup. Barely five feet tall, she seemed even smaller, as if grief had deflated her. She hugged each of them and led them to a cream-colored sofa and armchair in the living room.

"We're sorry we're late," Brian said.

Marianna waved her hand. "It's all right, but where's Alex?"

"He's sick," Jenner said. "He sends his condolences."

"I'm sorry," she said. "Sit down, please."

She scooped up the dolls and plastic toys that covered the sofa. With a long sigh, she placed the toys on the floor next to the armchair and sat. "My kids own too many toys."

Brian surveyed the house's interior. Children's clothes and toys littered the floor and most of the furniture. A spoilt-milk odor wafted in the air. The sound of a television talk show echoed from the master bedroom. Someone, probably Marianna, had drawn the blinds.

"A kid can't have too many toys," Brian said, then thought it was a stupid thing to say.

Marianna nodded. "I guess you're right. Hector always said that."

"We're so sorry about Hector, Marianna," Jenner said. "We wanted to be here for the funeral to pay our respects."

"Thank you."

"How was the funeral?" Kate asked.

Marianna wrung her hands. "The Army arranged everything. The ceremony was beautiful. Many of his friends came. His family, his mother, and father, and his brothers. They were all here."

"And your family?" Kate asked.

The edges of Marianna's mouth fell. "They're all in Honduras. No money to fly here."

She paused. "My children still don't understand."

Brian leaned over. "If we can help . . . "

"No. Thank you, but no. They'll come to understand, but they are children. They need to play; go to school."

Jenner placed his hand on Brian's sleeve. "All Brian meant was that we would be happy to come out, take the kids to the park, fix things around the house. You know, give you some time."

"Time?"

"Time to deal with everything."

Marianna's lips curled, baring her teeth. "I don't need time. I need my husband."

It's not going the way I hoped it would, Brian thought, then said, "Marianna, we're so sorry about your loss."

Marianna's eyes hardened. "Everyone's sorry. You. My neighbors. The Army. They send regrets. Give me the flag on his coffin, but they don't give Hector back to me. Can you give my children their father?"

Brian felt his jaw tighten. "No, I can't bring him back."

"No. Hector's not coming back. I thought he would. Even after the funeral. I thought I'd see him walk through the door and tell me it was just a joke."

Brian wanted to say he wished he could have saved him. Instead, he said, "I'm so sorry."

Marianna sobbed. Her small body sunk into itself. Kate rushed over and held her, motioning the men to leave the house.

Ten minutes later, Kate stepped out on the porch and beckoned Brian and Jenner to come closer. When they did, she said, "Marianna wants to thank you for coming and hopes you don't think she's rude for not coming to the door to say goodbye."

Before Brian could respond, Kate added, "She wants you to find Alex. She said Hector always believed Alex had a kind soul."

Brian reached out for Kate's hand, but she shook her head. "I'm going to stay for a while. When I need to leave, I'll call a taxi. We can meet later at your apartment. Now, go."

CHAPTER NINE

Alex felt numb. He sat with his back against the headboard of a bed in a thirty-seven-dollar room in a Motel 6, watching television and drinking tequila from the bottle. A Glock handgun felt heavy on his lap. A series of infomercials flashed across the TV screen. One was for costume jewelry, another for male enhancement, and a third for a training school for health care aides. Who watches this garbage? he thought.

"Just add me to the list," he said. He picked up the prescription bottle on his left side, opened it, and swallowed the last of the pills. Without water, the pills went down hard.

It was three in the morning, and Alex couldn't sleep. The entire day, he had drifted around downtown Fayetteville. He walked past the shops on Hay Street and bought a six-pack of beer at Bob and Sheree's. A cop chased him off a bench at Market Square, then he sat for hours in a pew in the Episcopal Church on Greene Street. When the service started, he moved into the last row and listened. Raised a Catholic, he still found the prayers soothing. At dusk, he left and walked to Cross Creek Park, where he stood in front of the statue of the Marquis de Lafayette, a fellow soldier. He finished the last of his beers and smoked a cigarette. Finally, he found his car parked in a municipal garage and drove to an ABC store, where he purchased a bottle of Jose Cuervo Tequila. When the clerk in the store handed back his change, she asked him if he had someone to drive him home. "My girl's right outside," he told her. "She's sober."

Somehow, he had ended up in this motel watching television. The infomercial ended, and Alex used the remote to flip the channel to the news. A talking head pontificated on the President's failed Afghanistan policy while a second expert kept interrupting him to praise the Commander-in-Chief. Alex thought neither expert made much sense, but what did it matter? They had all lied about the war for years. Made up stories about their progress. Wasted billions of dollars. Shipped coffins home. Left Afghanistan buried in the rubble. For what? No one cared about the war. It was just another reality show with low ratings.

Brian and Jenner were out there somewhere looking for him. He probably pissed them off when he didn't show up for the visit to Marianna. But he couldn't face her or them. Not in this condition. Last night, the nightmares and flashbacks struck again, worse than ever. He feared he'd go mad, then get an "Other than Honorable" discharge or wind up in a locked unit in a VA hospital. Or, in the worst case, sent back to Afghanistan, where he would be a danger to others. In the Hindu Kush, soldiers feared those who slipped over the edge more than the enemy. You couldn't trust them to cover your back or tune out scary voices commanding them to throw a frag grenade into the sleeping quarters.

No, no one, not even Brian and Jenner, could know.

Alex picked up the gun with his right hand and held it against his temple. The metal barrel was hard and cold. He was so numb that the pressure against his head felt almost welcome.

"This is your life. It will end here," Alex murmured, recalling the words he saw written in red marker across his cot on his first day in Afghanistan. At the time, he viewed the scribbling as typical Army humor and a way to cope with the war. But now, coming to his mind at this moment, he wondered if the words meant something else, something more significant. Death doesn't always come from bullets or bombs. It can come crossing the street or sitting on a bed in a cheap motel. It could arrive with your next breath. Why am I alive? What does it mean that I'm alive, and they're dead?

Alex felt the gun in his hand. Just one squeeze of the trigger and it would all be over. No more sleepless nights. No more terrifying memories. Just sleep forever. He had dug himself into this hole and there was no way to climb out. All it would take was a slight squeeze, and his sorry life would end. He had pulled a trigger like this one so many times; it was all muscle memory. Breathe in. Fire. Do it.

"This is your life, and it ends here," Alex said aloud. His hand shook, and his head jerked as if he expected the bullet to pierce his brain, blasting him into oblivion. But he had pulled the gun away from his temple without firing. Tears streaked his face. He took a deep breath to slow his heart, and with two hands, stuck the Glock in his mouth. Do it. Do it. He tasted death. Father, forgive me. Do it. Pull the trigger.

But he couldn't do it. The moment his brain told him to fire, the flickering images from the television caught his attention. The news program gave way to another infomercial. An 800 number flashed on the screen as young actors in swimwear frolicked over a disclaimer in tiny yellow print. The light showed otherworldly.

Carefully, Alex placed the Glock on the night table and forced himself to sit up. He didn't want to die in a cheap motel room, in his boxer shorts, watching TV.

He would not die here. It was his life, after all. He owed it to his fallen comrades not to end it in a place like this. He would go back to his apartment, pack his bags, fly to Montana, see his mother, and then head into the mountains. There, either Fate would take his life or give it back to him.

CHAPTER TEN

Halogen lights painted shadows on the sides of buildings as Brian and Jenner peered from Brian's truck. Most of Fayetteville's residents were home asleep and safe in their beds. The streets and sidewalks were empty. A feathery mist glistened in the arc of the headlamps. Tires hissed as they spun on the black asphalt. A light on the dashboard warned that the gas tank was nearing empty. In the distance, a siren sounded.

Brian and Jenner had searched everywhere for Alex. They had driven to his apartment, then to bars, motels, and all-night eateries. They couldn't find him. The few people they encountered saw no one who fit his description.

Jenner groaned. "Where is he? It's like the town swallowed him whole."

"It's five o'clock," Jenner added a minute later.

"So?" Brian asked.

"Let's try his apartment one more time."

Brian nodded and made a U-turn. "But if he's not there, we go to the police."

Jenner shook his head. "I don't know about —"

"We're going."

Jenner shook his head but voiced no objection.

Twenty-five minutes later, after stopping at a gas station, they walked through the unlocked front door of Alex's apartment complex and up the narrow stairway. They found the apartment door open. When they stepped inside, they saw Alex in his bedroom sorting through a pile of clothes tossed on his bed. He looked tired, and his wrinkled shirt and pants hung on him like he had slept in them.

"What are you doing here?" Alex asked.

"We've been looking all over town for you," Jenner said. "First here, then in every dive bar and taco shop. You left us hanging at Mariana's. The poor woman."

"I'm sorry. My bad."

"She's worried about you."

"There's a lot on my mind. I have a lot of things to do, so you guys need to leave. I booked an early flight to Montana to see my mom."

"Is she OK?" Brian asked.

"Oh, she's fine. . . . I need to finish packing."

"When's your flight?"

"8:30. So please —"

Jenner wrapped his arm around Alex's neck and whispered in his ear. "Jesus, Hammer, you have time. But you smell like road kill. You can't get on a plane like this. C'mon, let's get you spruced up."

Alex half-heartedly tried to pull away, but Jenner pulled him into his tightening embrace and guided him into the bathroom.

Meanwhile, Brian called Kate. "We found him in his apartment. He's OK. Slightly hungover, but breathing. Won't say where he's been. Says he's going to Montana to see his mother. He seems different, not listless like yesterday. Like a different person. Can't figure it out. We're taking him to the airport. Do you want us to pick you up on the way? All right, be downstairs in an hour. Bye. I love you."

Brian fried some eggs and made coffee. A few minutes later, Alex walked out of his bedroom wearing a crisp plaid flannel button-up shirt and olive-green cargo pants, looking more like his old self.

"You look great," Brian said.

Jenner laughed. "He's turned into a poster boy. Line the bro' up in front of the recruiting office."

Alex smiled, lowered his head, then raised it with a proud grin as if the Army had awarded him a medal.

Brian took stock of his friend. Alex appeared two inches taller. His shoulders pulled back as though he had discarded some heavy burden. What happened to the wretch who flew in from Afghanistan? "Here, sit down and eat these eggs before they get cold."

Alex devoured three eggs and four slices of buttered toast while downing two cups of coffee. To Brian, every morsel of food proved that his friend had finally begun the journey back from war.

Jenner returned from the bedroom with Alex's bag. "We've got to go if he's going to catch his plane."

Brian finished cleaning the kitchen while Jenner checked that Alex had his military ID card and boarding pass. When the three men left the apartment, they tumbled into Brian's truck, picked up Kate at his apartment, and sped to the regional airport. The traffic was lighter than usual, and they made good time. They half-ran through the terminal until they halted several yards from the security gate.

Alex hugged each of them. When Alex threw his arms around Brian, he whispered in his ear, "Wish me well on my journey."

"Safe journey, my friend," Brian said. "Anything else?"

Alex grinned. "Can I kiss Kate goodbye?"

They laughed, and Kate kissed Alex as if she were a movie starlet, kicking up her right heel behind her.

"Now, he'll never leave," Jenner said.

Brian chuckled. "She never kissed me like that."

Jenner snickered "That doesn't surprise me."

Alex broke them up and said he was ready to go through security. He shook Brian's hand, then Jenner's. He threw his bag over his shoulder and took a few steps before Jenner stopped him.

"Now, don't forget what we talked about."

"You don't need to worry."

"I hope not," Jenner said, then turned to Kate. "Well, you kissed him. You might as well walk him the rest of the way to the security gate. Better you, than me or your ugly boyfriend."

Kate pulled Alex away, locked her arm through his, and escorted him to the officer checking ID and boarding passes.

Brian wrapped his arm around Jenner's shoulder. "Just you and me now."

Jenner looked at him with mock astonishment. "Don't think so, *Honcho*. Now, it's just you. I'm flying out of here on my bike as soon as I can."

"You're leaving? When did you decide that?"

"Just now. Marianna doesn't want our help, and I have two weeks off. And Fayetteville's too dull for me. You're on your own. Sorry about that."

Brian felt mixed emotions. Until now, he assumed he would spend the next two weeks babysitting Alex and Jenner, making sure they didn't self-destruct or leave carnage in their wake. Now both men were deserting him, and he was responsible only for himself.

"Where are you going this time?"

"West."

"Any place special?"

"Nope. When my ass gets sore, I'll stop and look around."

Kate appeared and snaked her arm around Brian's waist. "What are you two talking about?"

Jenner answered before Brian. "My boy here needs a vacation. Why don't you drag him to New York with you?"

Kate looked up at Brian. "What do you say, soldier?"

Brian pointed his thumb at Jenner. "Well, my buddies are deserting me, so I guess — "

Jenner cuffed him in the chest with the back of his hand. "You can come with me."

Kate interrupted. "Look. Alex is waving."

The men turned. On the other side of a battery of metal detectors, Alex stared at them with a faraway look on his face. Around him, people scurried to put on their shoes and collect their valuables. A Homeland Security guard motioned for Alex to move along, but he ignored her. The guard motioned again. When he didn't respond, a police officer, her hand on her gun, stepped in front of him and ordered him to move. He nodded, looked over her shoulder at them, then picked up his bags and disappeared down a long corridor.

CHAPTER ELEVEN

Brian woke up the next morning in New York City. Whenever he visited his family in this hustle-bustle metropolis, he felt like a deer crossing a highway. This morning was no different. Sounds of taxi horns and garbage trucks blasted him awake. The smell of car exhaust seeped in from the street. A pigeon roosted on the windowsill and stared at him. Its head bobbed back and forth, mocking him.

Brian smirked. What can I tell you, my feathered friend? My family's here. Now, Kate is too.

Kate was staying with friends in an overcrowded apartment, so yesterday evening he sheepishly showed up unannounced at his family's apartment in the Chelsea neighborhood of Manhattan. He offered to crash on an air mattress in the living room. But his sixteen-year-old sister, Amanda, said she'd consider it an insult if he didn't sleep in her room. So, on his second night back in civilization, the combat-hardened veteran slept in a canopy bed with pink sheets and pillowcases.

The family was happy to have him, even on such short notice. Brian knew his father, sister, and stepmother expected him for breakfast. He vowed to put on his game face and get through the meal and small talk to avoid any conflict with his father. They could always discuss the weather. He heard on a BBC radio program there was never bad weather in England, only inappropriate clothing. Funny always works, he mused. He'd put on a cockney accent and make his family laugh. They'd feel relieved, comforted by laughter, familiar food, light streaming in from the kitchen window, and the return of the prodigal son.

Brian sang a verse of the Irish drinking song, "Wild Rover," as he sauntered toward his sister's bathroom.

> *I'll go home to me parents,*
> *Confess what I've done*
> *And I'll ask them to pardon their prodigal son.*
> *And when they have kissed me as oft-times before,*
> *I'll never play the wild rover no more.*

Brian suddenly stopped singing and stared at a photo of himself on his sister's bulletin board. His mother had taken the picture ten years ago. It showed him smiling into the camera before his first deployment, wearing a University of Maine sweatshirt and blue jeans. The snapshot captured the visage of the man he had once been — a man he no longer was — a naïve enlistee untouched by war, taunting him now with his former innocence.

Brian thought of his men. He tried to picture Alex and Jenner set loose in America. Having fun. Winding down. He imagined Alex getting his head together in Montana, communing with nature, and making friends wherever he went. He saw Jenner on his Harley, racing down the main street of some far-flung town, itching to raise Cain. His two friends deserved whatever America could give them. For others, it was too late. Some came home broken, some numb, some dead, some searching for the home and life they left, but not knowing how to find it. They deserved something more than a medal and a thank you for their service.

"It's no good thinking about this stuff," Brian muttered and entered the bathroom, where he splashed cold water on his face. He watched as the water ran down his forehead, off his cheeks and chin, and darkened the top of his tee shirt. The cold water invigorated him. It reminded him of how much he loved diving into the frigid ocean waters off Ogunquit, Maine when he was a boy. He loved Maine, its winters, the mild summers, the craggy coves, the lobster boats, and the cotton candy at Palace Playland. In his heart, Maine was still his home. He knew it, and it claimed him, a native son.

So, what was he doing in this strange city?

Somewhere far away, Alex and Jenner were probably just waking. He didn't expect Alex to call and let him know how he was faring. Alex never did. Brian would need to call him. But Jenner could storm through some god-forsaken shit hole in Texas, hooking up with anything that wasn't wearing a chador or Ugg boots, and he would still take the time to call him. He'd boast of his latest exploits, proclaiming his right to a world that sent him into battle. Brian had no idea when Jenner would call, or from where, but he knew he could count on him.

***

Bill McEnroe observed his son through the partially open bedroom door. He didn't want Brian to catch him spying, but he couldn't look away. Damn it, he thought. He is my kid. If he's struggling, I want to know it.

Bill's time in Vietnam left him with a first-hand knowledge of what signs of trauma to expect. Last night, he stood for a half hour outside this door listening for the panic attacks or night terrors confirming his worst fears.

But he heard nothing of concern.

He took one last look at his son and tip-toed back into the kitchen. As he entered, he turned to his daughter, who was emptying the dishwasher. "Amanda, go tell your brother to come to breakfast."

She groaned. "I thought you were going to do it. You told me to put the dishes away."

"Did I now? I thought you agreed to empty the dishwasher as a gesture of family solidarity."

"Get real, Dad."

"My darling daughter, remember what your mother used to say, 'If you keep making that face, it will stay that way.'"

Bill took the dinner plate out of his daughter's hands and gave her a playful push toward the hallway. "Now, go get your brother, and don't make him feel bad about the mess in your bathroom."

Amanda rolled her eyes. "I wouldn't say anything to Brian. You know I don't care about him using my room."

Bill chuckled. "Oh, now you're lying. But I love you for it. If I only had a sister growing up, I might have turned into a civilized man."

"Now it's too late, Amanda," Gretchen said, as she swept into the room. "Your mother and I tried. But with men, you need to start early, before the Neanderthal trait gets hard-wired into their brains."

She wagged her index finger at Bill. "Where's my coffee, Mr. Cave Man?"

Bill slapped his forehead and turned on the coffee grinder. As he poured the grounds into a filter, he again directed Amanda to summon Brian to breakfast. The teenager groaned again and headed down the hallway. Bill watched her go as Gretchen wrapped her arms around him from behind.

"Are you worried?" she asked.

Bill turned to his wife and held her. "I don't want to be."

"But you are."

"I am. But Brian looks fine. He has his mother's resilience."

"Emma was a strong woman, but I see more of you in Brian."

"Jesus, I hope not." Bill said and pulled away from his wife abruptly.

"Bill . . ."

Without looking at Gretchen, Bill held up his hand. "Stop."

"I just wanted to —"

He turned to face her. "We talked last night. I don't want to get into it again."

"We didn't talk last night. I tried. Remember?"

Bill didn't answer.

Gretchen moved closer. "I just want to help. When Brian is over there, I know it's hard for you. But he's home now. And safe. So, what's going on?"

Bill didn't answer.

"You can't shut me out of what you're going through."

Bill didn't turn around. "He's my son."

"We can talk about it."

Bill exploded. "He's *my* son."

"That's not fair!" Gretchen said and stepped back. When he didn't respond, she dismissed him with her hand and left the room.

Bill scanned the empty room. He had wanted his son's homecoming to be perfect, but he didn't anticipate old feelings reemerging like this. How long ago did he return from war? Fifty years? More? His reaction to Brian's visit troubled him. Gretchen didn't deserve his hurtful remarks. She was Emma's best friend when Emma got sick. She was there for her friend, the kids, and him. Until the end. And after. Gradually, their friendship had grown into something more. He loved her. She had rescued him and helped him reclaim his soul.

Just then, Brian and Amanda entered the kitchen, and Gretchen returned a few minutes later. While Bill served coffee and prepared breakfast, the family seated themselves about an oak table with four claw-footed legs.

"So, Dad, do you love it?" Brian asked.

Bill glanced over at his son. "Love it? What?"

Brian nodded his head to his stepmother. "New York City. Gretchen told me all the things you've done together. Sounds like fun."

Gretchen stared at Bill. "I think your father would still rather be living on Penobscot Bay."

Bill flinched. "You're mistaken."

"But you love Maine."

"May I remind you that, long before NYU offered you a teaching job in its psychology department, I had lost all desire to lead new expeditions in Maine for screwed-up teens? I was ready to sink one of those pulling boats with all-hands-on-deck."

"But New York City? And uprooting Amanda? And leaving the house where you grew up?"

"I needed a change."

Bill held his hands out, palms up. "And I love being here in New York City with you."

Gretchen's face softened. "You always know what to say."

"It's the Irish in me."

Brian lifted his coffee mug. "Here's to the Big Apple."

They clinked their cups and drank.

Bill leaned forward and grasped his son's wrist. "So, what's on your agenda for today?"

Before Brian could answer, Bill added, "I took the day off and thought we might do some rock climbing."

"Where?"

"Near New Paltz. The Shawangunk Cliffs. It has some nice sheer rock faces."

Bill studied his son's face as Brian mulled over his offer and realized his likely answer was no. The thought disappointed him. Brian's guarded emails and phone calls from overseas revealed little about his Afghan experiences. A day of hiking and climbing might facilitate the heart-to-heart talk he desired. Ever since Brian was old enough to talk, he rarely talked much to him unless he was in motion.

Brian shook his head and pushed his chair back from the table. "Sorry, but I promised to meet Kate this morning. We're going to spend the day together. Maybe some other time, Dad."

Brian walked over to Bill and massaged his shoulders. "But Kate's busy tomorrow, so I'm all yours. Maybe we can go bowling or take in a 'guy' movie."

Bill stood up and faked a punch to Brian's midsection while Brian responded as if the blow landed.

Brian glanced at Gretchen, who was placing her cup in the sink. "Of course, you're invited as well."

"Not in a million years," she said. "I'd rather go through a two-hour bikini waxing than sit through a shoot 'em up action film."

Brian chortled and turned back to his father. "OK, then tomorrow it's you and me. Right, Pops?"

Bill gave him a thumbs-up sign as his son left the kitchen.

Gretchen put her hand on her husband's cheek. "You may be looking for something that isn't there."

"What do you mean?"

"Because you came back from war with PTSD doesn't mean your son will."

"But how can I be sure?"

"You do what you can."

"And what's that?"

Gretchen kissed Bill on the cheek and handed him a dishtowel.

"You watch and wait."

CHAPTER TWELVE

A s he left the kitchen, Brian's cell phone vibrated. It's Jenner, he guessed.

It was.

"Greetings from the Ganges, Homeboy. It's Icarus, your fly-fuckin', rim-running, biker brother from Fort Bragg, home to the Delta gods."

Jenner was shouting over the roaring engine of his Harley Davidson.

Brian waited until he shut the bedroom door before responding. "It's hard to hear you even with your Bluetooth headset. Turn off the road. And shut down your egg beater."

"Negative, Team Leader. This beast has a mind of its own."

"Where are you?"

"I'm shooting for Yellowstone, expected arrival 0600 hours tomorrow. After that, I'm off to California. Bike Week's happening: twenty-five thousand bikers, shots of tequila, Five Finger Death Punch, and naked girls with pearl studs in their tongues."

"Sounds like your kind of vacation. Keep your head down."

"Roger, Falcon."

"Have you heard from Alex? He's not returning my calls or texts. I left him a message that I was in New York and he should get in touch right away."

"I've no news from the Hammer," Jenner said. "He's fucking up his mind somewhere."

Jenner always sliced problems into easy-to-digest pieces.

Terrorists attack the United States? Kill all the bad guys. Recover from the fallout of war? Ride a motorcycle cross-country. Can't contact your war buddy? Consider him wasted.

"I'm worried about Hammer. He's not himself."

"He's OK."

"I just have this feeling he might do something."

"Hammer? No way. He's a warrior. A screwed-up warrior, but a warrior. He'll snap out of it."

Despite Jenner's assurances, Brian couldn't shake the feeling that Alex was at risk. Since September 11, more than four times the number of former and current service members had perished by their own hand than had died in combat or during training activities. Brian knew several. Most deaths caught him by surprise. Most had used firearms, but others used drugs, car crashes, poisons, ropes or cords, or long hoses stuck into car exhaust pipes. The Army offered counseling services, then gave mixed messages to those who considered them. Like him, they all attended workshops, received pamphlets, and watched videos designed to help them recognize warning signs in themselves and their fellow brothers-in-arms.

"I hope you're right, Jenner, but if you're wrong . . ."

"Listen, if it makes you happy, I'll skip Yellowstone, cruise north on I90, and check on our boy in Kalispell."

"That would be great."

"I was thinking of making the trip before you called."

"You're worried too?"

Jenner laughed. "I've just never seen Big Sky Country, Dude."

Brian wasn't convinced.

"But forget the Hammer for now. Because you're the smartest guy I know, I have something sweet for you. It's a quiz

I made up based on this outstanding book I skimmed through while visiting my sister in St. Louis."

"I didn't know you could read," Brian said, though he knew Jenner was plenty smart.

"I googled the book's title," Jenner said, "and came across this amazing nugget of information that wasn't in the book and probably isn't even true. It's a newspaper ad recruiting men for a dangerous journey. So, here's the challenge. I recite the ad, and you try to guess the journey. Get it right, and you earn ten points. Fall asleep while I'm talking, and you get zip. Are you ready?"

Of course, Brian was ready. Between missions, he relied on mental jousting with Jenner to break the monotony. The contest's outcome was less important than their back-and-forth forays. Gamesmanship was everything. The timing of their moves provided the sweetener.

"Wait a minute."

Brian sat down on a white wicker chair and propped his feet up on the bed.

"Before we start, let me ask you something. Since you're talking to me on your cell phone, does that mean you're steering with one hand?"

"One hand? Are you crazy? I'm holding a bottle of beer in my other hand, so I'm using my knees to guide this beast."

Brian knew Jenner was joking but still pictured him barreling down the highway, daring the road or the three Sisters of Fate to take him down.

Jenner pressed on. "You ready for my quiz?"

"Do I have a choice?"

Jenner snorted. "You kill me. Here goes: 'Men wanted for hazardous journey, small wages, bitter cold, long months of complete darkness. Constant danger, safe return doubtful. Honor and recognition in case of success.'"

Brian did not answer.

"Well?" Jenner paused, then filled in the silence. "I love the 'constant danger, safe return doubtful' part. Sounds like us, except we don't get honor and recognition in the end. A raw deal, don't you think?"

Brian hummed as if he had bitten into a juicy hamburger. "Your quiz is too easy. People say Sir Ernest Shackleton placed the ad in the London newspapers to recruit seamen for his expedition to cross Antarctica. But, as you pointed out, that ad is almost certainly apocryphal."

Jenner groaned. "I can't believe you got the answer."

Brian chuckled. He knew all about Shackleton's expedition and the hardy men who undertook it. At the onset, an ice pack trapped and crushed the ship. For almost a year, the explorers faced death from sub-zero temperatures, ice floes, and starvation. They endured the worst weather on earth. Finally, six men in a lifeboat crossed eight hundred nautical miles of dangerous sea to get help. Not one man died. All returned home.

"I'm not done, Alex Trebek. I bet I know the author and title of the book you read. Alfred Lansing, an American, wrote the best account and titled it *The Endurance*, the name of the ship crushed by the ice."

Jenner whistled. "You earn an extra ten points!"

"I own the book, Fool. Bought a first edition for a dollar at a school fair."

"You know, you're wasting your life as a warrior. You could be the next Jeopardy champion and hook up with starlets at the Sundance Festival. Why are you wasting your time talking to me, you smart son-of-a-bitch?"

Brian felt a tinge of resentment whenever Jenner called him a warrior. He was a soldier. He didn't love war like Jenner. His friend's concept of a warrior centered on power, ferocity, and whatever it took to kill the enemy. If the Special Forces Command threw Jenner out of the military, Brian could see him working happily as a paid contractor or mercenary if the adrenaline addict wanted to stay on board the thrill ride. No, Brian was not Jenner's warrior nor the psyche-wounded warrior his dad feared he might be. Neither Jenner or his father — blinded by their own perceptions — could look past their own war experiences to see him as he was.

"Do you feel weird being back home?" Brian asked.

"Of course, bro. Home is what it is. That's why Alexander the Great fought his way through Afghanistan into India and would've marched into the Pacific Ocean if he hadn't died. He never planned to go back home."

"But what about you?"

"Why come back to the ants and their little ant hills in the dirt? My sister's husband, Geoffrey, the Trader, goes to work, drives home, and eats Cheese Doodles every night in front of his big-screen TV. The most excitement he gets is when he brushes the orange crumbs off his crotch. That's home."

Brian laughed at Jenner's hyperbole. Jenner could make a scab look like Ebola. For Brian, however, being home was like gathering his chute after a jump. All he had to do was go through the motions because the hard part was over. He liked returning to normal.

"My battery's dying on me. Call me when you get to Alex's mother's place and tell the bastard to answer my texts."

"Roger, Falcon."

Brian's cell phone beeped and powered down. He would

charge it before he called Kate. Maybe he would try to get some scalped tickets to a Knicks preseason game or two orchestra seats for an off-Broadway show. There were a million things to do in New York if you had a mind to explore it. If Kate was going to live in New York, he had to be open to the City's seduction.

After plugging his phone into the charger, he kicked off his shoes and fell back on the bed, sinking into the foam mattress. His eyes surveyed the room, decorated in the please-notice-me way teenage girls accessorize their bedrooms. Posters of cute boy singers plastered the walls. Photos of Amanda with her friends, making faces for the camera, covered a corkboard. Stuffed animals and little vials of makeup and glitter populated a vanity table. In one corner of the room, on a plump upholstered chair, was a bright violet pillow with the words "Live well, Laugh often, Love much."

Brian was feeling anxious, so he picked up his phone and tapped a key. The phone on the other end rang four times, then answered with a recording of a familiar voice announcing he wasn't available. The voicemail prompt signaled him to record.

"Alex, it's me again. Where are you? Call me ASAP."

CHAPTER THIRTEEN

Teresa Vilanova recognized the familiar voice of her son singing Ry Cooder's hit song "Little Sister" outside her door.

Teresa joined in the singing, flung open her door, and threw her arms around her son. "Alejandro!"

She squeezed Alex, peppered him with kisses, and breathed in the menthol scent of his aftershave. Her fingers sensed the strength hidden beneath layers of fabric. She leaned back and looked up at him.

"I didn't expect you, *Niño*."

She suddenly realized that her apartment was in complete disarray and smelled of stale pizza from the Three Brothers pizza parlor downstairs.

"You fool, you should have called."

Her only child chuckled. "And miss the look on your face when you realized it wasn't Ry Cooder outside your door?"

"You are so bad." She pushed him back into the hallway.

"Wait right there," she said and raced over to the ashtray on the table by her lone window. Stubbing out her cigarette, she placed her hand on the table to steady herself. "Excuse the mess, Sweetheart."

She dumped the ashtray's contents into a bulging trash container, then checked her appearance in the microwave's reflection. After taking a reproachful look at the mess she had left in the sink, she danced over to the doorway and pulled Alex inside.

"Let me look at you."

The young man twirled slowly, as a model might.

Teresa inspected him. He was not conventionally handsome. From his parents he had inherited what Teresa believed were their worst features: Bernie's unruly hair and her pug nose. But her son had a kind face with what she called "feeling eyes." And everything about him signaled strength from his wide shoulders to his sinewy arms and enormous hands.

"How did I ever get you for a son?"

"I guess you hit the lottery."

She guided him to the couch and helped him take off his backpack. "That's heavy."

"Has about everything I own that's not Army issue."

They sat down. Teresa gazed at her son while Alex scoped out his surroundings. His mother had abandoned clothes in every corner of the living room. Rings of coffee stains and smudges of food sullied the glass coffee table. A brown shag rug partially covered the painted pine floor. Behind him, on walls in desperate need of repainting, two adornments interrupted the pale green expanse: an Indiana Jones movie poster, and a framed photo of Alex in uniform.

"Are you going hiking in the park?" Teresa asked, as much to distract him as to get information.

"I figured I'd do some backcountry living for a couple of days in Glacier, seeing that you're just a bull's rump away. It's medicinal to bushwhack through mountains where no one is shooting at you."

"Too late for that." Teresa giggled, poking him like he was a child. "You can carry guns in the national parks now."

Alex threw up his arms in mock dismay. "No."

"It's true!"

"Damn, where is it safe anymore?"

Alex leaned back against the lumpy sofa cushion and relaxed, fighting the desire to nod off. Most of last night he had spent in bars a few blocks away. When they closed, he walked the streets, slipping into dark doorways to avoid police patrols. He thought about knocking on his mom's door but was not prepared to face her. Now, in the day's light, he could see the reason. She looked so worn out. She was only forty-nine, but her once-coal-black hair was mostly gray and wound tight in a ponytail accentuating her sunken cheeks and smoker's mouth. An Old Navy t-shirt swamped her thin body and extended almost down to the knees of her faded blue jeans. As a child, Alex boasted that his mother was the prettiest woman in the neighborhood, but that was before the toll of Bernie Vilanova's fists reached a tipping point.

When Alex turned seventeen, he chased his father from the house with a samurai sword, and his father went to prison a short time later for violating a restraining order. But Bernie's imprisonment came too late to save Alex's mother.

Teresa patted his hand and frowned. "If you go backpacking, will you have any time when you come back to spend with me?"

He hugged her tight and told a lie to protect her. "Once my head has cleared, you and I are going to rock this state."

Her eyes widened. "Really?"

"I promise, little sister," he teased, touching her pug nose with his index finger. It was something he learned to do from his mother when just a toddler. It connected them.

Teresa reciprocated, then laughed.

"Are you hungry? Can I fix you something to eat?"

"Sure, what do you have?"

Alex saw the pained look on his mother's face and imagined he would find nothing but a six-pack of beer if he opened the refrigerator.

"I can fix you a sixteen-inch pie with pepperoni and extra cheese straight from the ovens of the pizza joint downstairs. And I have some beer in the fridge. How does that sound?"

Alex unlaced his boots and sighed.

"Sounds perfect, Mom."

As Teresa walked toward the phone to call downstairs, Alex's eyes followed her. He was glad to see her one last time before he did what he came here to do. Growing up, his mother never had much to give him in the way of worldly things, but he never doubted she loved him with a fierce and total love. And he loved her in the same way. They were always so close, maybe too close. He didn't want to cause her heartbreak, but he had no choice. She would miss him. Terribly. Forever. The loss might break her. He wished he could make her understand his reasons for going to Glacier, but he knew he couldn't do it. She'd blame herself for what he was feeling, and he couldn't stomach that. He had to make sure only he was accountable for his actions. That's why he wrote the letter he carried in his pocket. And why he would take it to Glacier.

CHAPTER FOURTEEN

Jenner never intended to bike to Yellowstone.
He lied to Brian. A small lie, but one escaping his mouth as naturally as spent breath. Jenner skirted the truth to savor the pure pleasures of deception. The more untruths he told, the more outrageous the falsehood, the more people believed him, and the prouder he felt. He loved when artifice collided with a person's reality: What did he just say? That can't be true, can it? Maybe it is. Damn, that's amazing. The trick was to tell a lie as if it were the solid gold truth. Don't flinch, don't smile, just aim, and fire. Keep repeating it until the sucker believes you.

True, there was always the risk some skeptic would uncover the falsehood, but it was a risk he gladly took for a shot of adrenaline. In some ways, only fighting a battle gave him a bigger thrill. "Damn right, I'm going to Yellowstone," he shouted into the wind.

Jenner had no desire to see geysers or hot mudflats. The only thing he wanted to do was to visit his grandfather, who lived alone in a cabin near Cody, Wyoming. Other than his sister in St. Louis, his grandfather was all he had left in the way of family. Jenner knew this might be his last opportunity to see the old contrarian. The old man was ninety-two years old and terminally ill, but still as rough as the bark of a Monterey pine.

When Jenner phoned him yesterday, Frank Chapman swore at his grandson and told him to stay away. "I can die just as well alone, thank you."

The air turned frigid as Jenner rode the fast lane on

Interstate 70, leaving the traffic out of Saint Louis far behind. He congratulated himself for attaching a windshield to his Harley before he escaped from Fort Bragg. Riding in chilly autumn weather in North Carolina was one thing; riding the frozen plains and mountains of the West was another. Dressed in layers, wearing a black watch cap under his helmet and a heated Gervin vest under his wind stopper, he felt ready for the cold weather ahead.

When Jenner was growing up, his grandfather, a retired policeman, often took him on winter camping trips in the woods. His grandfather fashioned himself as an outdoorsman and loved passing on the backwoods knowledge he had soaked up during the Great Depression when, as a hard-to-handle teen, he worked in the Civilian Conservation Corps.

Jenner recalled a night when he and his grandfather sat around the campfire they built together in the woods behind the family's home. "Young man, there's nothing like the outdoors," his grandfather pronounced. "I told you about my time in the CCCs, didn't I?"

"Yes, Grandpa," Jenner answered as he stoked the fire.

"Yes, I guess I have. I was fifteen years old, a city kid, all snot and piss, and my father signed me up even though seventeen was the minimum age. The camp was in Northern Idaho. The place scared me, but within a month, I was at home in the woods. Six months later, Pearl Harbor came. The older guys left to join the war, and the government shipped me back to Chicago, as unhappy as a tree frog in a desert. I couldn't wait until I was old enough to enlist."

Jenner's grandfather rubbed his chin. His grizzled face was so close to the fire he looked like a ghoul, with light and dark shadows playing off his deep-set eyes and boney cheeks. He poked at the fire with a stick, then flung the stick over Jenner's head into the dark.

"After the war, I didn't know what to do. Go back home to Chicago or chuck it all and move to Idaho? I don't know why, but I wound up in Chicago and then Los Angeles. Cities pack you in tight, my boy. They make you into something less than human, so you need cops . . . lots of cops. So, I always had a job. But I couldn't do this." He gestured around him. "This. You know what I mean?"

Jenner knew. He knew even before his grandfather said it; before he had the words to say it himself. For as long as he could remember, Jenner craved a different way of living. His childhood was a good one, by all objective measures. The boy's parents were loving — his father was a teacher and his mother a nurse — and he had lots of friends in their suburban neighborhood east of Crescent City in Northern California. His neighborhood was a place without crime, mean streets, or anything else that would tarnish its picture book image as a late-twentieth-century Utopia. It even abutted Jedediah Smith Redwoods State Park, so the family faced no danger of being surrounded by what his grandfather called "undesirables."

But Jenner didn't fit in, nor did he want to. He felt that what his parents called the "perfect place to grow up in" was a slow poison, killing whatever life dwelled within him. As a boy, he fantasized about the men portrayed in western movies on TV every Saturday morning. In Living Technicolor, restless men like Hondo, The Man with No Name, and Ethan Andrews rode across prairies and mountains, living in open country, creating their own laws, and hunting down and killing any man who dared to cross them. God, how he loved those fictional characters. But he also admired the real adventurers like Jim

Bridger, Kit Carson, and Liver-Eating Johnson, and devoured their stories in paperbacks hidden in the textbooks he carried to school.

He suffered through classes, performed well on school athletic teams, tested his libido in high school, and felt unfazed by it all. He drifted along because everyone else seemed to do the same. When he graduated, he applied to Redwoods Community College and hoped his life would miraculously change. But two weeks before classes began, he left home and hiked the length of California on the Pacific Crest Trail, trekking on through Mexico and into Guatemala. There he lived for a year in the jungle in a Mayan village, occasionally serving as a white-water guide to English-speaking tourists. When asked, he told the tourists that his birth name was Liver-Eating Johnson, which earned him big laughs and tips.

***

By the end of the day, Jenner approached the outskirts of Cheyenne. A sign warned the bridge ahead might be icy. The Harley's tires had no studs, but Jenner didn't slow down. His friends called him crazy or suicidal for riding his bike fast on slick roads, but Jenner figured after fighting terrorists in shitholes across the world without a scratch, Fate was on his side. *When Hell freezes over, I'll be biking full throttle,* he thought as he rocketed over the bridge.

He had ridden for twelve hours and needed food and rest, so he took the ramp off Interstate 80 and rode into the heart of downtown Cheyenne. On his left, he spotted The Historic Plains Hotel, which reminded him of the elegant hotels sprouting up in the West when cattle barons and their crews drove their herds to the Union Pacific railroad terminals. Jenner pulled into the parking garage, took his ticket, unloaded his bag, and removed his helmet, watch cap, and gloves before he strode into a grand two-story lobby mezzanine. He appraised the stained-glass skylight and an enormous chandelier with wild buffalo bronzes circling its glass dome and guessed the room rate might cost him dearly. Still, he reasoned, he deserved a little luxury after sleeping all those nights on rocky ledges in the Hindu Kush.

"I want to book a room for the night," Jenner said to the bespectacled man in the dark suit behind the marble counter. "I'm here doing advance work for a movie we're filming out at Fort Laramie and the territorial prison."

The assistant manager's eyes opened wide and inspected the bearded, red-haired man dressed in what resembled a black spacesuit. "Really? Well, we do have rooms available. Are you traveling alone?"

"Yes, the studio hired me to scout locations and arrange accommodations for the cast and crew. But this needs to stay confidential until they get here."

"Of course. I can give you a queen if that will be all right."

"And the rate?"

"Sixty-eight dollars plus tax."

"That will be fine." Jenner slid his credit card across the counter.

As Jenner filled out the paperwork, the assistant manager inserted his hand into his inner pocket and extracted a business card. "My name is Brody Hynds, and I'd be happy to work with you and your company when your people are ready to choose a place to stay while here in Cheyenne."

Jenner palmed the card and smiled. "Thank you, Mr. Hynds. Now, where's a good place to eat?"

Mr. Hynds smiled back. "Our Capital Grille serves a fine steak, and I'd be happy to give you a meal voucher if you'd care to dine with us tonight."

Jenner picked up his bag and accepted the offer. "Brody, it's nice doing business with you. I'll let Mr. Spielberg know what a fine hotel you have here."

Brody Hynds didn't say a word. His face said it all.

***

After taking a long hot shower and dressing in jeans and a flannel shirt, Jenner found his way to the restaurant off the main lobby. The Grille was a typical hotel bar and restaurant with red leather booths near the bar and wooden tables and chairs near the street windows. As he slipped into a high-backed bench at the far end of the room, he thought: Eight o'clock on a Saturday night, and this place is only half full. Either Cheyenne's full of morning people, or the food here tastes like crap.

He asked a passing waiter to get him a beer and a menu. When the waiter returned, he placed the items down and said with a smirk, "Your waiter will be with you in a minute. I'm waiting on those tables over there."

Jenner scoffed. "Suit yourself, wise ass. You just lost a big tip."

The waiter opened his mouth to reply, then turned and retreated to the kitchen. A moment later, a young dark-haired man in a white dress shirt and a black tie glided over to the table. "I am Youssef, your waiter. Welcome to the Capitol Grille. Would you like to hear our specials?"

When he looked up from his menu, the sight of the waiter startled him. The server was a dead-ringer for the Afghan soldier he last saw in Bagram the night he returned from the village. The man was lying face-up on the street, unconscious, severely beaten, and close to death.

Seeing Jenner's reaction, the young waiter stepped back.

"Sir, can I help you?"

Jenner shook his head. "No . . . Excuse me, I was just thinking of someone you look like."

He stared at the man's face, amazed at the likeness: the same chiseled jaw and bone structure, the same bushy eyebrows. The waiter could have been a twin.

Jenner pushed the menu toward the waiter and placed his hand on his heart. "Are you Afghan? Speak Pashtun? Dari?"

Youssef looked puzzled. "I'm Moroccan-American. I speak only English and French."

Jenner lowered his hand and nodded. "My mistake. I'm sorry if I upset you. Really."

For a moment, Youssef seemed to consider Jenner's apology, then held out his order pad and retrieved a pen from behind his ear. "No problem, sir. You're not the first to mistake me for someone else. Do you want to hear our specials for tonight?"

Jenner shook his head. "Forget the specials. I'll have the pot roast and another Pullman Porter."

The waiter jotted down the order and walked away until Jenner called out his name.

He turned. "Yes?"

"Are the specials any good?"

Youssef raised one eyebrow and grinned. "Not really. Stick with the pot roast."

"*Merci.*"

"*De rien, Monsieur,*" Youssef said and disappeared into the kitchen.

CHAPTER FIFTEEN

Early the next morning, Jenner rode out of Cheyenne and headed toward Cody. His GPS marked the distance to his grandfather's cabin at three hundred ninety-two miles, with a traveling time of almost seven hours. But Jenner figured he'd make the trip in five and a half to six hours if the state troopers looked the other way. If not, he'd let slip that he was a soldier just back from defending America against blood-thirsty terrorists. Patriotism in Wyoming trumped all speeding violations.

He wondered what his grandfather might do when he showed up on his doorstep. Jenner was pretty sure Frank Chapman would lambaste him with profanities. He was a hard man who didn't ask for anything and gave little in return. But Jenner knew there was a thread binding them together despite the physical and emotional distance between them. That thread might be history, blood, DNA, or kinship, but whatever it was, it was infrangible and tugged at him like a cord made of sinew.

The front tire of his Harley suddenly wobbled, and Jenner eased off the throttle reluctantly. His brain snapped to full attention whenever he tested his control over the unruly monster beneath him. He prized speed, ripping wind, and the drumbeat of tires on the road. Unlike civilians in their comfortable steel-and-glass sealed vehicles, he welcomed the shock of cold air as he rocketed across the Big Horn Basin's high desert landscape. For miles, all he could see was an empty highway, sagebrush, and arid land, beautiful and forbidding, its expanse treeless as if an angry God had swooped down and snatched up anything that dared to reach toward Heaven.

Jenner never figured out why his grandfather settled in this harsh land. He always thought the old outdoorsman would wind up in Idaho's dark forests. But ten years ago, without explanation, the recluse sold his home in California and moved to Wyoming. A few months later, he sent Jenner and his sister postcards with a photo of Butch Cassidy and the Sundance Kid on the front. On the back was the following transcription:

I moved to Wyoming.

Take care,

Grandpa

His grandfather didn't write a return address, but Jenner's sister tracked him down. And every Christmas, she flew him to St. Louis, where Jenner would join them whenever he was in the States. No one had much to say to each other. They told the same stories each year, laughed at the same jokes, and argued about the same issues. If one of them strayed too far from the script, the other two steered the trespasser back. They guarded their real selves like hoarders. In that regard, Jenner thought they were like other families.

When Jenner reached Cody, he stopped for gas at a Maverick station. He filled his tank and strolled into the convenience store. "Do you have Slim Jims?" he asked the gap-toothed teenage boy behind the counter.

The teen pointed to a tall jar filled with sausage sticks. "That's a nice bike you have. What is it?"

Jenner pulled a handful of Slim Jims from the jar, unwrapped one, and stuck it in his mouth. "It's a 2008 Harley-Davidson Night Train with an electronic fuel-injected, rigid-mounted 96B V-Twin engine."

The teen's eyes opened wide. "I'm going to get me a Harley

someday."

Jenner slapped a twenty down on the counter. "Is the New Fork Highway nearby?"

"Not far. You turn left on Sheridan and keep following it till you see the signs."

Jenner scooped up his change and handed the teen a Slim Jim. "Take this. Harley riders all eat Slim Jims."

The teen reacted as if Jenner had given him a million dollars. "Thanks, Mister."

Jenner winked, pocketed his change and the remaining sausages, and exited the store.

***

Frank Chapman's cabin was ten miles out of town. It lay off a dirt road at the base of a gnarled mountain in the Wapiti Valley, surrounded by burnt-out hackberry and cottonwood trees. It had a stone chimney and a small covered porch with about a half cord of firewood stacked to the left of the front door. An old red Ford F-100 pickup, pockmarked with dents and faded paint, blocked the three steps to the porch.

Jenner gingerly lifted his leg off the bike and took off his helmet and gloves as he inspected the Ford. The smell of rust and burnt oil was robust. He guessed it was his grandfather's truck and wondered how the old man could drive such a wreck, especially in winter. Jenner had passed a ranch further down the hill, hoping the owner or ranch hands would likely look in on their elderly neighbor occasionally. But westerners will give a man — even a ninety-two-year-old — enough rope to tie up his loose ends or hang himself.

Jenner squeezed between the pickup and porch railing and climbed the stairs leading to the front door. The stairs creaked, and Jenner wondered if his grandfather heard the noise. But there were no windows on this side of the cabin, so Jenner couldn't tell if anyone inside had stirred. He heard no sounds. Out of habit more than fear, he moved to the side of the door before he knocked and yelled, "Grandpa, it's me, Jenner. Open the door."

No one answered, and Jenner hit the door harder with the edge of his fist: once, twice, a third time, harder and faster. He tried to open the door, but the lock was on. "Open up. You hear me? This is your grandson."

Jenner stepped back from the door. Maybe he wasn't home, maybe someone picked him up and left. Or maybe he's inside and can't answer.

Jenner kicked the door and shouted, "Grandpa, can you hear me?"

The door was sturdy, and Jenner found nothing he could use to breach it, so he circled the cabin to find a window or other access. He found a small screened window at the side of the cabin and peered in. A lit table lamp projected shadows around the room, and Jenner could make out a few pieces of furniture, a wood stove, and a small open kitchen braced against the back wall. But he couldn't see his grandfather. He was about to move away from the window when a dark, crouching figure shuffled across the room and opened the back door. Jenner sprinted around the cabin and spotted his grandfather trying to escape from the back porch.

"Grandpa," he yelled, and the old man turned to him. "It's me, Jenner."

"Go away," his grandfather said in a raspy voice. "I told you not to come."

Jenner hardly recognized his grandfather. His upper torso bent over at the waist, and he was so thin his collar bones stuck out from his shoulders like tent poles. He wore a brown stocking hat, canvas carpenter pants and shirt, and a quilted vest with rips at both pockets. His face was unshaven, and his skin was the yellowish-brown of an over-ripened pear.

Jenner positioned himself at the foot of the steps. "I told you I was coming. Why didn't you believe me?"

The rheumy-eyed man looked for ways to flee but then slumped down on the bench perched by the back door. He didn't look at Jenner as he spoke. "You shouldn't have come. I told you not to. Why did you?"

Jenner followed his grandfather's gaze out to the stream casually flowing down a slurry of rocks thirty yards from the porch. The sharp *kik, kik, kik* sound of a prairie falcon pierced the stillness. In the distance, the sun was a spent flame sinking below the purplish peaks of the Absaroka Range.

He turned to look at his grandfather. "I wanted to see you."

Frank Chapman didn't blink. "I have cancer and am half-blind, you know."

"Sheila told me."

"Cancer began in my prostate, but now it's in my liver and spine and brain."

"Yes, I know."

The old man grimaced, and Jenner wondered if his grandfather's reaction stemmed more from Jenner learning his secrets than from his physical pain.

"So, why did you come? You can't do anything for me, and I can't do anything for you."

Jenner looked away. "I understand that, Grandpa."

The elderly man's hand trembled badly as he touched the side of his head and turned to his grandson.

"I have everything I need here: food, water, a woman your

sister hired to visit me every day to see if I'm still breathing and taking my painkillers. And I have a rifle, a rifle for when I can no longer crawl out here to look at the stream or put food in my mouth. This cabin and what's left of my life are too small for company. I hope you can see that."

Jenner felt the doors of his mind shut and lock. "I guess so. I just thought I'd take a ride. As they say in the movies, get out of town. So, I headed west. No big deal. I need to catch up with an Army buddy in Montana, anyway. He had a hard time in Afghanistan. A friend died. Killed by a man he trusted, who was like a father to him."

His grandfather put his hand on Jenner's shoulder. "Sometimes you can't save anyone but yourself."

Jenner scoffed. "Like my parents?"

Frank Chapman dropped his hand from his grandson's shoulder. "No one could save them. Not you, not your sister or me, not before the fire, nor during it. No damn rain the whole summer, and everything dry as a bone. The winds were strong and blowing in the wrong direction. It's Fate. Nothing or no one is pulling some lever and making things happen. Isn't that what I always taught you?"

He stretched his arm out to the hills before him. "There's just this."

Jenner leaned over and put his elbows on his knees. "Maybe so. You know, I'd be in the Hindu Kush mountains on patrol, and we'd take a break. I'd sit down on a rock and imagine myself being born there; raised in a tribe. I'd believe the world spun out in circles: my family, my clan, my tribe, my country, and the rest. If that were me, I'd be shooting American soldiers."

Jenner straightened his back. "But I don't belong to a tribe. I'm an American. I spent all those nights with you when I was a little boy in front of a fire in those California woods, thinking there wasn't anything that can hurt me."

Jenner's grandfather winced and shriveled in his skin.

Jenner held him. "Is the pain bad?"

His grandfather didn't answer.

CHAPTER SIXTEEN

The only solace in Teresa Vilanova's hard life arrived in the half-hour slice of the day when the setting sun met the mountains. Once, she tried to describe a Montana sky to her sister in Baton Rouge. But her words failed to capture the purple clouds stretching like a shimmery blanket across the horizon.

"Send me a picture," her sister, Louise, suggested.

"A photo doesn't do it justice," Teresa replied, unwilling to admit she didn't own a camera or a cell phone that took decent photos.

As she gazed out her window, she took a drag of her cigarette and traced the last fiery sliver of light across the horizon with her finger. "Lovely," she said under her breath.

The nightly sky show made it almost worthwhile to live in Montana. Almost, she thought. For Teresa, the Big Sky State had little else going for it. As she got older, she turned into an indoor girl — in the mall, the dance hall, and the beer joint. Venturing into the mountains to hike or ski held no allure. She traveled outdoors only to reach her car, office, or nearby Walmart. No friends or family lived in Kalispell, and she had no use for her neighbors. Only one radio station played Ry Cooder, and that one wasted air time trying to sell her Jesus, exercise machines, and sure-fire ways to get wealthy working from home. Aside from the sky at dusk, Montana meant a steady job paying $16.40 an hour with benefits processing medical records for the local hospital. That, and the belief Bernie, her ex-husband, wouldn't think to look for her in Kalispell, sixteen hundred miles northwest of Texas.

When the sun finally set, Teresa switched on the table lamp next to her chair. She looked at the framed photo of her son in uniform and took another drag of her cigarette. Her son's face and the way he stood in that uniform said all's right with the world. She recalled the same look in his high school graduation photo and his picture with his Pop Warner football team. He projected such a pure expression of pride and satisfaction that she wondered where such confidence came from. Not from me, she thought, and certainly not from his father.

The morning her son set out for Glacier National Park, he put on a Texas Rangers cap, a blue polar fleece jacket, tan multi-pocketed pants, and ankle-high hiking boots. She hadn't bothered to ask him how long he'd be gone, assuming he'd be backpacking for two days at most. But that was three days ago. She knew it was silly to worry. He had survived his time in Afghanistan without a scratch. He could survive Glacier. She figured he had just lost all track of time in the wilderness. It happens. The solitude, getting high on nature, all of it. That's all. It was good for him. But she felt cheated because she knew the Army wanted him back soon. The Army always wanted him back.

How many days did he have left on his leave? She hadn't asked him that, either.

She took another drag of her cigarette. Something's wrong, she thought.

***

Alex had just lit the campfire when two strangers approached, struggling under the weight of overloaded backpacks. He did not expect or want company. Annoyed, he hoped they would pass by the campsite without stopping or saying hello. He pulled down his cap and pretended not to notice them heading his way.

The strangers were young, probably in their early twenties, and their Eddie-Bauer-style clothing was perfect for a stroll on local trails but not for Glacier backcountry. The woman led the way. She was tall with long arms and legs, a freckled nose, reddish-brown hair, and full lips nesting on a decisive chin. He was smaller, frailer, with darker hair and thick eyeglasses bridging a long witch's nose. They spoke to each other in what sounded like German. Her tone rang with the confidence of youthful invulnerability, while his tone was wary.

"Hello," the woman said in English. "That's a good fire."

Alex didn't respond. Walk on, he thought. It's not the summer, for chrissakes. It's late October. Plenty of empty campsites.

She walked to a spot in front of the fire opposite Alex and extended her gloveless hands to warm them. "I'm Petra. My friend's name is Leo."

Her voice only hinted at an accent. She motioned for Leo to come closer to the fire. "We've been hiking for two days. Tonight is our last night in Glacier. We didn't expect it would turn so cold, so fast."

Alex placed another dead branch on the fire. "In the mountains, you can't predict the conditions. One moment, it's warm and sunny. The next, you're in a blizzard."

Petra dropped her pack on the ground and squatted, looking Alex square in the eye. "What's your name?"

Alex pointed up the trail. "You still have some daylight left. You can make it to the next campsite if you hurry."

Petra pursed her lips as if deep in thought, then let out a

bemused chirp. "We could, I guess, but we have reservations for this campsite for tonight. The Ranger said this site holds up to four people: Leo, me . . . and you? That's three. What do you say? Are you alone?"

"Yes."

"Did you have a reservation?"

"No."

"You're a walk-in then?"

"I guess."

She smiled. "Good. We love company. What shall I call you?"

Alex took a good, hard look at the couple. He guessed that the man would happily move on if Alex got surly. But he wasn't so sure about this woman, this Petra, not the way she had stood in front of her friend to protect him, not the way she stared at him now, expecting him to do the right thing and share his name.

"My name is Alex," he said as he stood up. He figured he could collect his belongings and be on his way in about five minutes if he wanted to. But there was something inside him begging to stay. He came to Glacier to let Fate take its course. Tonight, Fate chose this spot for the three of them. Tomorrow morning, he would leave the trail and disappear into a million-plus acre wilderness. These two strangers were probably the last vestige of humanity he would ever see.

He pointed to a clearing about twelve feet from the fire. "I'm just staying the night myself. There's a site for your tent over there."

"Thank you," Petra said and stood. Leo rushed over to the clearing to unload his backpack.

Petra took two steps in Leo's direction but then turned back to Alex. "You don't have a backcountry camping permit, do you?" She asked like she already knew the answer.

Alex smiled. "How did you know?"

"You're traveling alone. You light a wood fire on a campsite where it's not permitted. And I didn't see your name in the Ranger's permit book."

Alex nodded. "You're clever."

Petra snorted as she broke into laughter. "Me? Leo is the smart one, a genius. He won all the honors in school and someday will be a professor of physics. I will be a clown in the circus."

"A clown? Really?"

"No, I will be a pirate captain in the waters off Sumatra."

"Right."

She grinned. "Maybe you should unclench your fists now. We're going to be friends."

Alex looked down at his fists and unclenched them. He felt embarrassed. He was awkward with women, especially attractive young women like Petra. Brian and Jenner always seemed to know what to say and do around women, but not him. For them, small talk felt as natural as breathing. For him, a conversation with a pretty woman was akin to holding his breath underwater. It made no sense to open his mouth.

"Well, I guess I should go help Leo pitch the tent," Petra said, then turned away.

"I can help," Alex called out and followed.

***

After they set up the tent, Alex and the young Germans huddled around the fire, mesmerized by the dancing blue and yellow flames and swirling smoke. At first, Petra and Leo did most of the talking. Petra told stories interspersed with comic asides while Leo interjected wry comments and snippets of Johnny Cash songs in a thick German accent. As the night wore on, Alex grew more comfortable and joined in.

"Tell us a story about where you came from," Petra said.

"About cowboys and Indians." Leo tittered at his suggestion.

Alex poked at the flames with a stick and rubbed his chin with his other hand. "The only cowboys I know play professional football in Dallas. But when I was a kid, I went to Apache powwows with my best friend, who is half Apache and half Mexican. Heard lots of stories. Want to hear how humans discovered fire?"

"Wonderful idea," Leo said, then turned to Petra. "Wouldn't you wish to hear it?"

Petra winked at Alex. "Of course. Please, tell us your story."

Alex withdrew his stick from the flames and held its glowing tip in front of him. "Well, sit back a moment and stare at the fire."

He waited for several seconds before continuing. "We rarely think about it, but fire is truly amazing. It heats our homes, cooks our food, and lights our nights. But it wasn't always so. Long ago, humans possessed no fire. Not until a lowly coyote stole it for us."

Leo's eyes sparkled. "A coyote?"

"The Apache called him the Trickster because he was so sneaky, greedy, and willing to break any rule to get what he wanted. But for all the trouble he brought to humans, he still felt sorry for them because they had no fire. Only the Gods possessed such power, and they would not share it. So, one night, Trickster crept into the Gods' village and raced around their campfire. Round and round he went until his tail caught fire. The Gods tried to catch him, but the coyote ran too fast and he escaped."

Alex threw the stick into the flames with a theatrical flourish. Sparks flew up, then floated into the night. "As he fled across the world, he brushed his tail against thousands of trees, igniting them; teaching our ancestors how to start a fire. Why, even today, if you peer into a wood fire, you can sometimes still see the coyote running through the flames."

He pointed his finger at the blaze. "Look closely."

All three stared into the fire.

"I see it," Petra said, jutting her chin over Alex's outstretched arm.

"I can't see it," Leo cried, leaning so close to the flames that Alex prepared to rescue him.

Petra directed Leo's head with her finger. "There's the Trickster! By the log on the left. It's jumping"

She pointed again. "There's its tail."

Leo shook his head. "I can't see it."

Petra giggled and turned to Alex. "I don't think he knows what a coyote looks like."

Alex patted Leo on the back. "It's OK, Leo. The damn thing ran away. . . Listen, have you ever heard a coyote howl? Robin Williams, the comedian, once described coyotes as 'dogs on crack.' It's the most goddamn awful sound. Here goes . . . "

Alex unleashed a wild howl. "Ahwooooooooo!"

Leo, then Petra, joined him. Again, and again.

The three dissolved into hysterical laughter. When the merriment subsided, Alex glanced at his watch. "Man, oh man, you two are funny. Thanks for a great night, the stories, and the laughs. But I best put the fire out. I'm heading out early. You two had better get some sleep."

Petra and Leo stood up and brushed themselves off. She

whispered something to Leo, then stayed behind to throw dirt on the fire while he lurched to their tent.

"Thank you for not chasing us away tonight," she said to Alex as she sat on her haunches next to him. "I know you wanted to."

Alex tilted his head toward her. "As you know, I don't have a backcountry permit, much less any hold on this site."

"Thanks, anyway."

Alex touched her forearm, then withdrew his hand. He wanted to ask her questions about her relationship with Leo and learn more about her, but it was late. The air was bitterly cold, and the embers were dying. In the silence between them, he could hear the night sounds: the wind, a distant howl, a closer and shriller yipping, and the gurgling of a nearby stream. Perhaps coyotes prowled nearby. The world of humans and gods seemed far away.

CHAPTER SEVENTEEN

Alex slept like a she-bear in winter until he heard something stir in the darkness. He sat up and focused his eyes in the sound's direction. Slowly, he withdrew his Yarborough from its scabbard, though the knife wouldn't do much good if the intruder were a grizzly. As quietly as he could, he rose on his hindquarters and peered into the pitch black. He heard something, a shuffling sound. He moved closer.

He heard Leo's fearful whisper. "What's that?"

As Alex's eyes adjusted to the dim light, he perceived the hunched figure of Leo following a cat-sized creature as it slowly circled the campsite. Alex moved closer, holding his knife.

"Stop chasing it, Leo."

Leo answered in a frightened voice. "What is it? It woke me up."

Alex realized Leo was without his glasses. "Don't move."

But the nearsighted German didn't listen. He continued tailing the animal.

"Leo, stop moving."

Leo paid no attention. Each time he crept closer to the animal, the dark creature crawled ahead a few feet, thus keeping its distance. When Leo moved faster, the animal kept pace. When he slowed, so did the animal. They looked like two partners in a strange dance

Alex inched closer, careful not to trigger the creature's fight-or-flight reflex. What he could not understand was why the critter made no effort to escape. Most animals avoided humans, but this one appeared unafraid. Why? If he could just get closer to it before Leo did something stupid, maybe he'd find the answer.

Just then, Alex saw the white stripe. "Leo, watch out! It's a skunk."

Instead of freezing, Leo reared back like a frightened horse and fell backward, sending the skunk scurrying into the woods. Spared the indignity and embarrassment of getting sprayed, Leo broke into laughter interlaced with German obscenities and spasms of coughing and gasping.

Unable to resist, Alex broke into laughter. He sat down in the dirt, roaring, and rolled over on his right side, arms crossed in front of him. The more Alex looked at Leo, the more Alex thought about the skunk, and the more he laughed. He was in free fall. He heard Petra in the background shouting, first to Leo, then to him, trying to find out what had happened. Then she too began laughing, not at the thought of the skunk but at the two crazy men laughing uncontrollably in the middle of a wilderness.

After things settled down and Leo and Petra returned to their tent, Alex lit his lantern and looked at his watch.

A half-hour before sunrise, he thought. Better get ready.

Alex needed to get back to his mission. Triple Divide Peak waited for him. The mountain stood as one of the few places on earth where the water falling on top flows into three oceans. Ever since he first climbed the summit thirteen years ago, he knew he'd return one day. He was a teenage vagabond then, traipsing from one national park to another, picking up seasonal jobs, hitch-hiking mostly, sleeping out in the open or in the guest rooms of kind strangers. In Grand Teton National Park, fellow climbers urged him to thumb his way to Glacier and visit Triple Divide. They joked that the climbing sucked, but promised that the vision quest to the mountain's summit would change him forever. Great Spirits dwell on top of Triple Divide, they said. The next morning, Alex set out with fourteen dollars in his pocket and great expectations. When he entered Glacier, he chose a circuitous route to the peak to give him time to cleanse his body and soul. After ten days of fasting and soul-searching, he summited Triple Divide Peak, then spent the next day and night taking stock of his life. He was alone, but not lonely.

On the last day, he envisioned himself finishing his GED, joining the military, and living a life that meant something. For years, he followed that path. Life, at first, was good. He loved Army life, the discipline, the honor of serving, the comradery of his fellow soldiers. But the endless war and the death of his friends had blindsided him. In the Fayetteville motel room, he intended to blast away the despair suffocating him like a chokehold. Only the memory of Triple Divide prevented him from pulling the trigger. It was his last hope. If he summited the peak one more time, the spirits might give him back his life, or, at least, let him die in peace.

A life without meaning is not worth living, he thought. He remembered an Afghan proverb, "A broken hand can work, but a broken heart cannot."

Alex dragged his bedroll and possessions out of his tent and deposited them on a flat surface near the fire pit. He picked up and carefully evaluated each item and sorted them into three piles. By dawn, his task remained unfinished.

Alex slowly took off his watch. "Unnecessary baggage," he muttered and dropped the timepiece onto the pile on his right.

The morning air was frosty and damp. Alex wondered if Petra and Leo were prepared for such a sharp change in the weather. He glanced over at their tent. The memory of Leo blindly following the befuddled skunk around the campfire, one more near-sighted than the other, made Alex smile. Then he remembered Petra leaning against him to search for the coyote in the fire. Her eyes were bright with wonderment and her face glowed like a Botticelli angel.

The image of her left a dull ache in his chest.

I must go, he thought.

It was getting late. Alex wanted to leave the trail before Petra and Leo stirred from their sleeping bags. But his mind failed him. His decision-making should have been easy and fast. After all, he brought to Glacier only a small number of possessions. But hopelessness had sucked the life out of him like a scorching-hot, August-in-Texas day.

"Decide," he muttered, then inspected his piles. The small one on his left included all the possessions he intended to bring with him on the last leg of his journey. Every item he intended to leave at the campsite was in the pile on his right. The pile in the middle, the biggest of the three, comprised everything he couldn't decide what to do with. He called it his "Fucked up Pile" because the items in it should have been in the other two piles already, but his emotions had messed up his mind too much to think clearly. Something had to give for him to move forward.

"Alex?"

It was Petra. She stood behind him, shivering in her fleece pajamas. He felt sorry for her. If he had time to spare, he'd gather wood and light a fire.

"How long have you been awake?" she asked, bending

down on one knee to look him in the eye.

Alex didn't answer. Instead, he studied her U-shaped face, punctuated with green eyes and lips upturned on one side into a half-smile. So pretty and full of life, he thought. It was a face untouched by horror.

"You're cold," he said. "Maybe you should go back to your tent."

"I'll get dressed," she said and rushed back to her shelter, only to emerge moments later with her arms filled with a change of clothes. She placed the clothes on a tarp.

"I don't want to wake Leo," she said. Unembarrassed, she pulled herself out of her fleece, changed her underwear, and hopped into a pair of Levi's, a torn T-shirt, socks and boots, and a quilted tan jacket.

Alex stared at her the whole time. To him, Petra's nonchalant nudity was not erotic. He attributed her lack of guilt to parents who raised her in a less-uptight culture than his. For most of his thirty-one years, he lived in small towns where narrow-minded citizens would misinterpret behavior such as Petra's as a sin, a come-on, or an excuse for sexual violence. Many of the good folks he knew growing up sang in church on Sundays and lusted after their neighbor's spouse the rest of the week. Worst of all was his father, who never let a pretty woman pass him on the street without remarking. Even with Alex's mother by his side, Bernie Vilanova would snigger and turn to Alex with a wink and a conspiratorial smile.

Alex watched as Petra came to him. Maybe, if he had been born in Germany and they had met in school, he might have had a chance for a different life. But nobody gets to choose where and when they are born.

"Today is going to be colder than yesterday," he said.

Petra's lips quivered at the thought. "I'll make Leo walk faster."

"Tell him a skunk is on his tail."

Petra gazed at him with a questioning look, but then brightened. "That's good!" She said and slapped her thigh in appreciation. *"Das Stinktier ist hinter dir, Leo. Das ist so lustig!"*

"I agree with whatever you said."

Petra nodded. "I said, 'The skunk is behind you, Leo.' And I thought that was funny."

Alex chortled.

"I like you, Alex. You have a good laugh,"

The compliment surprised Alex. A few minutes ago, he was wallowing in self-pity. Now he was laughing.

"You and Leo make me laugh."

"That's good, isn't it? Laughter makes the best sound. You were too quiet when we first met."

"Quiet?"

Petra moved closer. "You seemed sad."

Alex looked away, and Petra moved so close to him he could smell her musky scent.

"At first, you didn't answer when I asked if we could share your campsite. You just stared at us. But I saw the pain in your eyes."

Alex turned back to Petra. Unexpectantly, he longed to tell her about Afghanistan. About the team, the village, the raid, Hector's death, the moment he saw Aarmaan pointing a gun at him, and all the nights he woke up in the middle of the night dreading the return home.

Petra put her hand on his arm. "You shouldn't be alone today. Why don't you hike with Leo and me?"

Alex gazed at Petra's hand on his arm, then at her face. "I'm traveling alone, but thanks anyway."

He swept his stringy hair back from his unshaven face, bent over, and shoved the Fucked-up Pile to his right, adding the items to the stack of things he intended to leave behind.

Noticing, Petra pointed to the two piles. "What's this?"

"This . . . " Alex paused, picking up the items in the pile on his left and stuffing them into his Dap pack. "This is what I'm taking with me from here on out."

Petra pointed to the remaining pile. "And this?"

Alex rubbed the back of his neck, searching for a name. "That's the Lost and Found."

"Lost and Found?"

Alex hoisted his rucksack over his shoulders. "Yes. The lost left it, and you found it. It's all yours if you want it."

Petra bent down and scooped up Alex's wallet. She held it in her hand and turned it over before she opened it to inspect the contents. "This is your wallet. My God, everything is still in it: your money, your ID, your credit cards, everything."

"So?"

"But, I —"

"Take what you want and leave the rest."

"This makes little sense."

"That's just the point. It doesn't need to make sense to anyone but me. I came to Glacier because I have something I need to do. And no one else needs to make sense of it but me."

Petra held out the wallet to return it to Alex.

"I can't take your wallet."

"Then leave it. The next person who runs across it won't have the same reservations."

Petra continued to press the wallet on Alex. Their voices

rose until Alex knocked the wallet from her hand.

"Listen," Alex said with an intentional sharpness. "I appreciate your concern, Petra, but trust me, I know what I'm doing. I'd rather you take this stuff than some stranger. Where I'm going, I won't need it."

Petra shook her head and picked up the wallet. "Where are you going that you don't need what's in this?"

Alex didn't answer.

The young German woman stepped closer until her face was only inches away from Alex's, so close he could see his face reflected in the pupils of her eyes. He sensed that if he did not look away at that moment, he would stay. He averted his eyes.

"I must go," he said.

"Wait till Leo gets up. We'll have some breakfast together. Yes?"

"No, I need to go."

"Let me wake Leo," she said and turned toward her tent.

Alex grabbed her arm and pulled her back. "No, let him sleep. Please."

"But —"

"Please, Petra."

Petra shrugged her shoulders and sighed. She looked like she might cry, then smiled with resignation. "All right, I'll let him sleep."

"Leo didn't sleep so well last night," Alex joked.

They both smiled. Petra kissed Alex on his left cheek, on his right, and again on his left. "You are a crazy American."

"Goodbye, Petra. *Sei freundlich zu Leo.*"

Petra's eyes widened. "'Be kind to Leo.' You know German?"

"Not much."

"*Sei freundlich zu dir selbst,*" Petra said, then translated: "Be kind to yourself."

Alex dropped his hands from Petra's shoulders. He took a moment to study her face one more time as if he were attempting to imprint the image in his mind, then walked away. After taking several steps, he stopped and turned around. He removed an envelope from his breast pocket. He looked at it, then at Petra, before shuffling back to her and placing the envelope in her hand.

"Petra, take this letter. I want you to do me a favor. I was going to bring it with me, but maybe you could mail it when you leave Glacier. It has no postage. Use the money in the wallet to buy a stamp and drop the envelope in a mailbox. Use the rest of the cash for whatever you damn well please."

Petra took the letter. "I'll mail it for you."

"Thanks."

"But I won't use your money."

"Then give the money to Leo. And tell him I said goodbye."

"I will."

"Thanks."

"Before you leave, tell me where you're going."

Alex gazed at the mountains, whose peaks rose like ancient towers forming part of the Continental Divide that split the country like a giant zipper. The Blackfeet called the mountains a name meaning "The Backbone of the World." Layers of ice and snow carpeted the higher peaks. Smaller pinnacles flaunted blue-gray rock streaked with gold from the rising sun. Below the mountaintops, blankets of green forest covered the slopes and descended into lush valleys. As far as he could see, Glacier's peaks stretched before him and called to him like the mountains of the Hindu Kush.

Alex pointed at the string of mountains. "I'm going out there."

"But Alex —"

"Goodbye," Alex said, then disappeared off the trail.

CHAPTER EIGHTEEN

Teresa had labored for hours, trying to make her dingy, cramped apartment feel more like a proper home. She cleaned the place from top to bottom, bought new sheets, and prepared meals for later reheating. By the end of the day, the apartment resembled a reasonable facsimile of a home.

Suddenly, she heard steps on the hall stairs. Thinking it was her son, she rushed toward the door and swung it open just as a young couple was about to knock. Her disappointment showed on her face. "Can I help you?"

"Do you know Alex Vilanova?" the young woman asked in a slight accent.

"I'm his mother," Teresa said. "And you are?"

"My name is Petra, and this is Leo. We're friends of Alex."

"Oh," Teresa said, then smiled an apology. "Why don't you come in?"

The young couple entered the room, but Teresa didn't shut the door behind them. Instead, she straddled her doorstep. "Alejandro . . . Alex . . . is hiking in Glacier."

Petra turned back. "We know. We were with him yesterday morning. It's why we're here. We backpacked in the park and met your son at our campsite."

"Was he alone?"

"Yes."

"Yesterday morning?"

"No, the night before. We were cold. He had a fire. At first, he didn't want us there."

"I thought you said you were friends?"

"Yes, but please, let me explain. We're from Germany and had never been to Glacier Park before. We were a little scared. Alex helped us. That night, we became friends."

Teresa found it hard to swallow the young woman's story. She believed Alex had helped them. Her son had a good heart. But why were they here, in her home? And how did they even know where she lived? For all she knew, they came here to scam her.

"Listen," she said, her arms folded across her chest. "I don't want to be rude. Can you get to the point? What are you doing here?"

Petra glanced at Leo. He seemed hesitant to speak so Petra continued: "When I woke up yesterday morning, Alex was sitting on the ground sorting all his things into two piles. I asked him, 'What are you doing?' He explained he was leaving and taking only the smaller pile with him. I could keep everything else."

Teresa fidgeted. "He gave you some of his gear. So, what's the big deal?"

Petra pulled Alex's wallet from her coat pocket. "He left this with us. Why would Alex leave his wallet with me? The other things, perhaps, but not this."

She opened the brown leather wallet and placed the leather billfold in Teresa's hands as if it were an offering.

Leo said, "I told Petra we should give everything to the authorities."

Petra interrupted. "But the Rangers didn't seem interested. Alex didn't have a backcountry permit. And even if he did, they don't send out a search party every time a hiker goes off the trail unless they have reason to believe the person is in danger. They said they would wait a couple of days to see if he came in."

Teresa brushed back her hair. "I don't understand. He just walked off; left the trail? The rangers aren't searching for him? None of this makes sense. Why would he leave his wallet with you?"

"I'm not sure. Your name and address were inside his wallet. Since you have the same last name, I thought you might be his wife, sister, or mother. The rangers told me I should give his wallet to you. They want you to call them."

Petra handed Teresa a scrap of paper. "This is their number."

Petra took a step closer. "I had to talk to you."

"This doesn't add up."

"I know."

Leo interrupted. "Tell her about the letter."

Teresa turned to him. "What letter?"

Petra answered for him. "There was a letter in an envelope. Alex asked me to put a stamp on the envelope and mail it when we got back to town."

"And?"

"I mailed it earlier today," Petra said. "I sent it Priority Express."

"Was it addressed to me?"

"No."

"Then who?"

Petra withdrew a small yellow notebook from her jacket. She thumbed through the book and stopped on a tagged page. "Alex addressed it to Brian McEnroe, to an address in New York City."

She handed the book to Teresa. "Is he a relative?"

"No," Teresa said, wiping a tear from her eye. "He's a soldier."

CHAPTER NINETEEN

W hen Brian emerged from the Chambers Street subway station, he stepped into what resembled a zombie movie. Hordes of tourists, shoppers, and commuters swarmed across each other's paths with such intensity that Brian momentarily froze at the top of the subway stairs. He wanted to get his bearings and make sure he faced in the right direction, but people behind shouted at him.

"Whaddya doin'? Keep movin'."

"C'mon, keep walking."

"Get the hell out of the way, asshole."

Someone pushed him forward, and he stumbled into the swarm. Hands, shoulders, forearms, elbows, and hips pressed against him, and almost in self-defense, he walked straight ahead. In his entire life, he had never had to navigate through such a mob.

He was going to be late.

Kate told him to meet her at the 9/11 World Trade Center Memorial in downtown New York at 10:30. He didn't bother to get an exact address because he figured he could find one of the most famous places in New York City and spot the love of his life with little difficulty. But he hadn't counted on this crowd.

"Excuse me, sir," he said as he tapped the shoulder of a man in front of him. "Is this the way to the 9/11 Memorial?"

The man recoiled at Brian's touch. "The Memorial? It's that way."

The man had pointed in the opposite direction. Brian cursed

under his breath and halted, prompting pedestrians to detour around him. Again, he heard angry comments. Again, passersby pressed against him. He wondered how Kate could tolerate this madness? He would have preferred going to Central Park and finding a quiet spot to picnic and talk. But Kate loved the crowds, the confusion, and the over-the-top bustle of the city.

According to his phone, he was still several blocks away from the Memorial so he had to move fast. Fighting his way across the stream of people heading north to join the people pushing south, he hit Kate's number on his speed dial. Just then, he bumped into a flustered older woman who unleashed a series of Spanish curse words with the firing speed of an AK-47.

"*Lo siento mucho*," Brian said to the back of her disappearing head.

Kate's voice on his phone was a life preserver thrown into the raging waters. "Brian? Where are you?"

"I'm on West Broadway heading south, I think. The crowds and traffic are terrible. The natives want to throw me in front of a bus."

"Hurry. Our reservation is for 10:30. If you're late, I don't think they'll let us in."

"I know. I'll hurry. But where exactly are you? I looked at directions on my phone, but it would help to have your exact location."

"I'm at the entrance to the Memorial. It's at the intersection of Liberty and Greenwich Streets. Walk down West Broadway till you get to Greenwich and follow the signs."

"There are signs?"

"Of course," Kate said. "You can't miss them."

"Of course," Brian mimicked, less playfully. "I'll be there

as soon as I can."

Brian slipped his phone into his pocket and followed the masses moving south. Because of his size and agility, he made good progress, weaving past ogling tourists and stragglers. As he did, he scanned the faces of pedestrians passing him in the opposite direction. As each person approached — young or old, man or woman — the hair on the back of his neck stood up. Unconsciously, his training for walking in Afghanistan had kicked in: inspect everyone who wore a heavy coat or loose clothing; who carried a large backpack or talked on a cell phone, or hid their hands in their pockets. Even a seemingly pregnant woman or an innocent-eyed child might wear an explosive device. A child's toy might contain three-inch nails, screws, ball bearings, or odd bits of broken machinery mixed with homemade explosives. A smile might suggest an anticipation of paradise.

Brian knew that the civilians presently swirling about him would call him paranoid if they knew what he was thinking, but what appeared abnormal to them registered as normal to him. To him, behaving as if the world were a safe place was insane, even suicidal. Somalia, Iraq, and Afghanistan had taught him that the civilized world, where the rule of law prevails, is an aberration. He assumed violence could strike anywhere, anytime. He knew that, even in America, human beings had murdered almost twenty-five thousand victims in the past year. How safe are we? he thought. Illusions of safety are for children and fools. His vigilance in war zones had kept him and his men safe, and he couldn't turn it off instantaneously like a light bulb. It might take weeks, years, or a lifetime.

A tall, stocky man with a heavily tattooed and pockmarked face hurried toward him, wearing a puffy brown jacket a size too large. Brian made eye contact, sized him up, and watched his hands for any hint of wire snaking down his arm. The man was probably harmless and on his way to the subway, but Brian's mental alarm sounded, anyway. As he moved closer, the man stared back at him as if he too were assessing risk. At the last minute, Brian stepped aside, then brushed against the man's torso to assure himself the man wore no explosive vest. The man reacted by brushing off his coat as if bees were attacking him.

A suicide bomber if I ever saw one, Brian joked to himself as he hurried on.

When he reached Greenwich Street, Brian ran into the street rather than trudging through the crowd. Traffic snarled the lane, so he didn't worry about a moving taxi or bus striking him. He darted into the grid-locked mess and made progress, but narrowly missed slamming into a bicycle messenger who swerved in his direction.

He shouted Kate's name when he saw her waving to him from a long line spilling out onto the sidewalk.

"Brian," she shouted back, holding up two tickets in her hand.

He rushed toward Kate and noticed how she stood out in the line. Taller than most of the ticket holders, including the men, she wore a short, squash-colored wool dress that showed off her beautiful legs and generous curves. Around her neck, a long, crocheted red scarf contrasted perfectly with the rose tint of her cheeks and the lush purple of her knit cap. Her wavy blonde hair flowed down her face and spilled over her shoulders. Every time he saw her, he grew more mesmerized.

When he reached her in line, she grabbed his jacket lapels, kissed him lightly, and took his hand. "The line just started to move," she said.

The ticket-holder line proceeded with a level of efficiency and respect that surprised Brian. At first glance, he attributed the crowd's civility to the presence of heavy security. Armed guards checked photo IDs and searched through all bags. Anything more substantial than a tote, they confiscated. Along the way, attendants channeled everyone past various checkpoints hemmed in by rope lines or steel walls. But, as he looked around, he saw the truth. The somber faces and hushed whispers of the humanity on the line revealed a collective awareness that they had entered hallowed ground.

Kate pulled on his arm. "I hope you don't mind coming here. The last time I was here, I was a child. This was all just a big pit."

Brian squeezed Kate's hand. Central Park could wait. It didn't matter where they went if they were together. Reaching out and touching her, watching her face, or hearing her voice meant everything. He just hoped they could be alone for a while. He needed to talk with her in private.

The line ended at a large plaza surrounded by a fence.

"Oh, my God," Kate said in a hushed tone when she saw the memorial.

Two enormous, man-made waterfalls cascaded down into one-acre reflecting pools built on the footprints of the fallen towers. The rushing water drowned out street sounds and sent a fine mist sailing off in the slight breeze. Around the perimeter, people prayed, took photos, or simply stared into the reflecting water. Stone masons had carved the names of those lost on 9/11 on the parapets. A green area with grass and hundreds of sweet gum and swamp oak trees provided refuge on one side of the plaza. On the other was a sleek glass-and-steel museum.

A large group of children — fourth-graders, Brian guessed — clustered with their teacher and chaperones thirty feet in front of them. The teacher motioned at something behind her as she spoke, but Brian couldn't see what it was. Kate suggested they look. By the time they reached the spot, the group had moved away, and they could discern the object of so much interest.

A small pear tree.

"It's the Survivor Tree," Kate said in awe. "It's the only tree that survived the fall of the Twin Towers. Authorities dug it up, replanted it elsewhere, then brought it back after they completed the memorial."

"It's a tough son-of-a-gun," Brian said.

"When I watched the towers fall, I couldn't imagine anything surviving."

"Firemen pulled people out of the rubble. They survived."

"How?"

Brian shook his head. "I don't know. There's no explanation for it."

"There must be."

Brian didn't want to explain to Kate that sometimes there's no rhyme or reason for one person dying while another person lives. Sure, there's cause and effect. One guy drives over a bomb; the other doesn't. But there's no purpose; no point to it. No use trying to find meaning in it. Why couldn't people accept the simple truth? In battle, many men, women, and children died, some friends, some enemies, and too often innocent civilians in the wrong place at the wrong time. Enemy combatants should have killed Brian many times, but something always saved him. A bomb fuse faltered. An AK-47 jammed. A woman carrying her daughter stepped in front of him just as a sniper pulled his trigger. Brian couldn't explain it. Was it luck or Fate? How do you explain when no reasonable answer existed?

"Let's walk," he said.

Kate and Brian walked around the North Pool and gazed at the names honoring the dead, most of whom died in the North Tower. A few names they recognized from news specials. But most of the names were just names, without faces or voices. A guide told them that computers at the visitor's center could link up names with photos and bios, but Brian told Kate he viewed such a search as an invasion of privacy. He was a stranger here to honor strangers. To go beyond that felt wrong to him, but he knew Kate or others might feel differently. Grief, he knew, flowed from many tributaries.

"I don't want to go on a computer either," Kate said.

She led Brian to the South Pool, where they watched the torrent of water rushing down the glistening grey walls and contemplated the names inscribed on the bronze parapets. Visitors had wedged small yellow flowers and tiny flags into some inscriptions. A family knelt at the section for first responders and said a prayer. An elderly man in a woolen overcoat told Brian and Kate that authorities had kept the names of friends and colleagues together on the parapet. Thus, flight crews and engine companies, and workers in the same office remained connected in memoriam as they were in life. Kate thanked the gentleman, then stood with Brian as he lingered at the section honoring the 125 men and women killed when Flight 270 crashed into the Pentagon.

"Do you know any of these people?" Kate asked.

"No," Brian said. "But it still feels personal."

Kate looked up at him. Her face showed concern.

"Are you OK? We should go."

Brian shook his head "We just got here. You wanted to see this place. I'm fine."

"No, you're not fine."

Kate took his hand and pulled him behind her toward the exit gate.

CHAPTER TWENTY

Brian and Kate walked for almost a half hour without saying a word until they found an empty bench in a park bordering the Hudson River. The wind sweeping off the river chilled them, so Brian opened his jacket to let Kate nestle inside. He peered across the river to New Jersey, where new high-rise luxury apartment buildings anchored the shoreline. A large clock four or five stories high, a remnant of the long-gone industrial waterfront, faced him. Small ferries and tugboats plied the waters and seagulls soared overhead. The air smelled like the sea. The sky was darkening.

"Looks as if it might rain," Brian said.

Kate didn't take the bait. "Are you OK?"

"Me? Of course."

"Don't 'Of course' me, Brian. I know when something is bothering you."

"I'm fine."

"No, you're not. I saw it in your face at the memorial. You're not fine."

"Listen, when I say I'm fine, I am."

"There's no reason to get angry."

"I'm not angry."

"Then why is your mouth so tight and your eyes all squinty-like? Are you suffering from constipation?"

"Funny, Kate."

"No, you're funny, telling me you're not angry with that Elmer Fudd face."

He laughed as he pictured the Looney Tunes cartoon

character. Kate could always make him laugh.

"It's just that a lot of things keep going through my head."

"Like what?"

"Nothing special. I —"

Kate interrupted him with a sharp elbow to the ribs. "Elmer Fudd."

"Ow!"

"Tell me."

Brian rubbed his palms together, embarrassed that his facial quirks had blown his cover. "It's nothing new. You went through this with me the last time. That's why it's so frustrating. I come home and I feel like an alien in a foreign country. OK. Everyone is so nice to me. Too nice, if you ask me. Yet they don't know what to say. They don't know how to act. There's just this awkward silence. They don't understand. And I don't expect them to. But they're more uncomfortable than I am. It's weird."

A young skateboarder flashed by. Brian noticed that the teen's neck sported a tattoo of a winged dragon whose tail whipped up the back of his shaved head. The kid jumped up in the air, taking his board with him, and did a 360-degree turn before landing back on his board. The boy pushed off and skated their way. He looked up and gave Brian an all's-right-with-the-world smile. Then the boy spun around and skated away with a fluidity and grace Brian admired.

He didn't hear what Kate had said. "Can you say that again?"

"I said it's not weird to feel uncomfortable coming home after what you've been through. It's normal. You know that. It just takes time."

Time? he thought. In less than two weeks, I'll be back in training for a new mission.

He wished he could trade places with the skateboarder. "This time it's different. I don't know how to explain it."

"Do you mean because of what happened to Hector?"

"Maybe, but I think it's more than that."

"It's only been a few days since you came home."

"I guess. Maybe I'm making too much of it."

Kate shook her head. "No, you're not. You said this time was different. What makes it different?"

Brian squirmed on the bench. Kate always told it like it was. She never tried to bull-shit him. If she felt he was hiding something from her, she was relentless. In that respect, she reminded him of her father, a no-nonsense Charleston lawyer who pulled Brian aside to interrogate him the first day they met. He wanted to know why a college graduate like him settled for being an enlisted man. Brian didn't have a well-thought-out answer then, and he didn't have one now.

"I don't know," he said to Kate. "In less than two weeks, I train for another mission. We'll have a new member of the team. Then we go back overseas, maybe to the Hindu Kush or some new hot spot. All I know is that my reenlistment date comes up soon, and it worries me. How long before I lose Jenner or Alex or the new guy? No amount of re-up bonus money could make up for losing another friend."

Brian had mulled this decision over in his mind most of the night. After college, the military molded his entire adult life. Leaving the Army would be like tearing a piece of flesh from his body. He could request a non-combat position, but the military would put him where it needed him. The Army offered no guarantees, and besides, it would be better for him if he made a clean break from the military while he was healthy and relatively young. He could go to graduate school or get a job doing consulting or intelligence work.

And then there was Kate. He had thought so hard about her last night. Recently, she refused his marriage proposal because she didn't want to be married to the Army. She wouldn't have any excuse if he were free of the Army. Would she marry him then? Insist they live in New York City? Be willing to live somewhere else? He recalled a ninety-year-old Afghan tribal chief named Zamai telling him he was proud of each of his eight wives, but his favorite wife's voice made his ears deaf to all others. It was that way with Kate. She made his ears deaf to everyone else.

"I feel so foolish, Kate."

She gave him a look that always made him feel like jelly: those brown eyes drinking him in, watering, resonant with emotion. Her lips quivered, and her eyebrows lifted.

"Brian," Kate said, and stroked his cheek with tenderness.

Brian sat up and slid his hand underneath Kate's hair and caressed the back of her neck. With his other arm, he drew her closer. "I missed you so much."

Kate's eyes closed and her mouth opened fully as Brian leaned over and kissed her, softly for the first time, then harder and harder. She pressed against him and made the soft moan he loved.

Brian shuddered with longing. "I need you," he pleaded, and inserted his hand between her thighs.

"Oh," she sighed, restraining his hand at the same time she opened her legs so slightly. "Someone is likely to walk by."

"Let's go back to your place."

Kate groaned. "My roommates are home. What about your apartment?"

"With my little sister watching?" he asked, realizing how

ludicrous their situation was.

Kate laughed and sat up. Her cap had fallen off, and her long hair fell across her face. "Look at me. You're a wild man, Elmer Fudd."

Brian zipped his jacket to hide the effects of their groping. "I can get wilder."

Kate rested her palm on the bulge in his pants. "Tomorrow night, my roommates will all be out. I'll order Chinese food, and you bring the Bass Ale."

A biker flew by and whistled at them.

Kate removed her hand and spoke in a husky, full-throated voice. "Is it a date?"

"How could I say no?" Brian answered, still feeling the sensation of Kate's hand on him. Making love with Kate always made the battlefield seem far away. It was the ultimate act of coming together, of healing — an antidote to the poison of war. In her caress, he could walk away from the emotional minefields and mental walls he built to defend himself. He saw redemption in her eyes. He found courage in her arms. For a short time at least, she made him whole again. All the psychiatrists and all the drugs in the world couldn't do that.

He suddenly wanted to ask Kate to marry him, but resisted the impulse. What's she thinking right now? he wondered. Why didn't she say more when he mentioned his misgivings about reenlisting? She knew what that might mean for them. Why didn't she make more of it? Perhaps the Army wasn't the only obstacle for her. Maybe she didn't love him enough. Perhaps she was afraid.

A grey pigeon cautiously pecked at their feet. Brian flicked the pigeon away with his foot, but the bird approached again. Brian stood up and chased it away, but it returned once more.

With a shout, Brian jumped up, raised his arms, and rushed forward until the bird took flight, and left him alone at the railing overlooking the Hudson.

Kate followed him and put her arm around his waist. "My hero."

"That's me," he said, still looking straight ahead at the ships in the harbor.

They stood there for a few minutes before Brian broke the silence. "I was at the Memorial reading the names of those who died and thought of Hector. He should have his name carved somewhere, not just on his tombstone. Someplace surrounded by waterfalls and trees, with a museum so Marianna and the kids could see him honored."

"That would be nice."

Brian's voice rose. "That would be right."

"Brian!"

Brian's face softened. "Sorry. Way out of line."

"I understand."

No, Brian thought. You don't understand. You can't, not unless you've been there, done the things I did, saw the things I've seen. Even you, Kate, even you, can't begin to understand.

He took her hand. "When we were at Marianna's, you stayed inside the house while Jenner and I went outside."

Kate looked bewildered. "Yes?"

"What did you say to Marianna after you closed the door?"

"Not much. I made her a cup of tea and then I just listened. She said little. Mostly about the kids and how they missed their father. She wasn't angry anymore. She was just very sad."

"Can't imagine," Brian said, then paused, not knowing what else to say. "I don't want you to be one sitting in your living room alone like that. I'm quitting the Army."

"I don't want you to give up the Army for me."

Brian shook his head. "I'm not leaving the Army just because of you. It's me too. I don't want to leave any more men behind."

Kate touched Brian's face and wrapped her arms around his neck. He lowered his head and whispered, "I love you, Kate."

Kate stroked his hair. "And I love you. More than anything."

For a moment, Brian considered taking the next step and asking Kate to marry him, but he held off. It can wait, he thought. Don't want to spoil things. Let my decision to leave the Service sink in first. There's time before I leave for training.

He grabbed her by the hand. "Let's walk. I don't care how cold or rainy it gets. Let's walk around this whole damn island: North, South, East, and West."

Kate looked at him as if he were insane. "So, now you cotton to New York?"

He picked her up and swung her around, singing the chorus from the jingle, "I Love New York."

Kate squealed at the tune. "You're a maniac."

"I Love New York, I Love New York, I Love New York."

"A maniac!"

Brian let her down and held both her hands. "Are you ready to hit this town?"

"You're on, soldier. I have my running shoes on."

"We'll go up to the Village, then onto the High Line, up Broadway to Times Square, hike up to Washington Heights, and then we'll figure how to get back because, by that time, I'm completely lost. How does that sound?"

"Wonderful."

"And I'll buy bagels. Lots of them. As many as you want."

"And pizza?"

"Real New York City pizza, with lots of cheese and olive oil dripping down your chin every time you take a bite."

Kate wiped her lips with her tongue. "Yummy."

"Are you ready?"

"Try to keep up with me, Mr. Fudd."

Kate sprinted ahead, and Brian raced to catch up to her. They meandered uptown, making stops along the way. They gazed into store windows in Soho, ate lunch at an outdoor hot dog stand in the West Village, gaped at the Empire State Building, watched street performers in Times Square, strolled in Central Park, stood reverently at the entrance of the Dakota, perused a flea market on the Upper West Side, and fell more in love the farther they walked.

They were on Riverside Drive, near Grant's Tomb, when Brian's cell phone rang.

He let it ring.

"See who it's from," said Kate.

He showed Kate his screen. "Gretchen, my stepmother."

"You should take it."

"No, it can't be anything important."

The phone stopped ringing.

"You see."

The phone rang again. "She probably wants us to come to dinner."

"Then you must answer her."

Brian shook his head. "I don't want to go to dinner."

"Then tell her no, but answer her."

Brian saluted. "Aye, aye, sir."

Kate pointed at the screen. "Answer it."

He held the phone to his ear. "Hello, Gretchen?"

Gretchen's voice was firm. "Come home."

Brian looked at Kate as if he were saying, I told you so.
"I can't. I'm with Kate, and we are —"
Gretchen cut him short. "It's your friend. Alex."
"Alex?"
"His mother called."
"Why?"
"He's in trouble."

CHAPTER TWENTY-ONE

Alex notched a small piece of aspen with his knife to construct a hearth board for his hand drill. With the drill, he produced a lump of bright, shining coal. The hot coal lit the kindling and ignited the blaze. Within minutes, the fire's warmth erased the chill of the mountain air.

Alex inched closer and held out his hands to warm them. After tonight, no more fires, he thought. Tomorrow, he'd switch to evasion mode. He'd move only at night, using the day to rest and hide.

But for tonight, at least, he reasoned that the park rangers had not yet formed a search party. They had better things to do than look for a crazy soldier who walked off the trail, especially when they thought he'd show up in a day or two. Sure, his violation of their rules would irk them, but budget cuts and frequent wildfires annoyed them more. If the missing person were a child, a celebrity, or the Chairperson of the House Appropriations Committee, the rangers would swarm over these mountains with dogs and helicopters. But he was a nobody. Just a speck on the wall of humanity.

Of course, he could not be one hundred percent certain no one was looking for him. After all, his mother was probably frantic by now, and a mother afraid for her child was a relentless force of nature. Pity the ranger who said no to Teresa Vilanova. If the Federales didn't respond, Alex pictured his mother emptying every bar in Kalispell and Whitefish to form a rescue party. That is why he had erected a Dakota Fire Hole for his fire. The

Fire Hole, a recessed fire pit with an upwind air shaft, flamed mostly underground, which made it hard to detect.

Can't be too careful, he thought.

Because he had no appetite for food, Alex only wanted the fire for heat. He knew a human being could live a long time without food and saw no need to make snares or weapons for hunting. Water was more important. He carried purification tablets for several days' worth of water in his pack. He could boil water after he ran out. If he was still alive.

Before joining Delta, he had learned the elements of survival at The Army Ranger School, and the training was still second nature to him. He had memorized all eight elements with the acronym for SURVIVAL:

S   Size up the situation, your surroundings, physical condition, and equipment.
U   Undue haste makes waste. Plan your moves.
R   Remember where you are in relation to enemy units, location of friendly units, water sources, and good cover.
V   Vanquish fear and panic.
I   Improvise.
V   Value living.
A   Act like the natives; watch their daily routines.
L   Live by your wits. Learn basic skills.

All good dictums, but the "value living" element meant little to him now. And without that, all the rest crumbled like dikes during a flood. Life just promised more nightmares, terrible memories, and suffering. Death didn't have any great attraction, but it might be better than living like this.

Night in the mountains posed the toughest challenge. He knew trekking in the daylight was safer, but he wasn't interested in playing it safe. His night training taught him to walk slowly, stop regularly to listen, and look to the sides of objects rather than straight on. But he intended to cross rugged terrain rather than the open country. That went against his training. If clouds blocked light from the moon and stars, he could easily fall and break a leg. And he was much more likely to cross paths with predators like bears and cougars that hunted mainly at night.

Other dangers faced him, as well. The threat of an avalanche or landslide was omnipresent. Lightning strikes and wildfires posed additional problems. In the eastern part of the park where he was, strong winds blew down shallow-rooted lodgepole pines that killed more people than all the grizzlies and fires combined. Killer trees never made the tabloids, but Alex respected their reputation.

***

Long into the night, Alex sat in front of the fire, peering at the sky. A half-moon and a stenciled blaze of stars lit the heavens. Gazing at the sky brought him comfort. The flickering lights reminded him of when he and his mom sat on the porch at the ranch and gazed upward. She called the night sky, The Big Show.

"Millions of stars out tonight for my little boy," she crooned as her hand swept across the celestial array. "The Big Show coming straight from Heaven and brought to you by the fine people at Purina Puppy Chow."

No matter how many times he heard her spiel, he would always giggle and search the sky for a shooting star, which seemed to arrive on cue. One night, when the sky was crisp and clear with approaching winter, his mother led him by the hand to the thin strip of blacktop in front of their property.

"Alejandro, let's lie down in the middle of this road and

watch The Big Show. The surface is still warm from the sun, and we can look up and see nothing but the sky."

"But the cars, Momma," Alex said, dithering. It wasn't unheard of for a car or pickup truck to pass by at night on the way back from town.

His mother patted his head. "We'll hear them coming, honey, and besides, we'll feel the road tremble before we hear them."

It made sense to a six-year-old. He lay down and imitated his mother when she spread out like a snow angel on the warm blacktop. Together, they marveled at the heavenly bodies dangling above them in the sky. Every few minutes, they looked at each other with wide eyes, forgetting the sad house behind them. He loved his mother's face so much at that moment. It was a girlish face, giddy with delight, so unburdened he thought her whole body could float if she willed it. That night she poked him and giggled, then touched him on his forehead with her index finger.

"Store this memory right here, baby. Our show, just yours and mine. No one else in the world can see these stars the same way we can from this spot. You keep a picture of these stars in your head so you'll never lose it."

As he recalled his mother's words, Alex heard a small creature scurrying in the darkness. He listened as its sound retreated into the woods. Intrigued, he riveted his attention to other night sounds: The wind hummed. A waterfall drummed in the distance. Animals and insects stirred and called to each other.

Aarmaan taught him that the night sounds were the mountains speaking to each other. "They tell stories to pass the time of a million nights with no place to go," he said. "If you listen to them at night, you will learn a great deal. When my sons are old enough, I will take them into the mountains to learn how to survive with courage."

Now, as Alex warmed himself by the fire, he listened to the mountains, eventually drifting into a dreamy state between wakefulness and sleep. His mind wandered. Images flashed to life, though they made little sense. He saw a dog he loved as a child, a stray half-coon, half-lab, asleep on a hot slab of concrete. A smiling flight attendant reminded him to buckle his seat belt. The face of his first girlfriend transformed into his grandmother, then his father. The visages blurred and darkened.

The fire spat sparks into the air that flickered across the dark emptiness. The flames reminded Alex of demons, arms outstretched, motioning, demanding. He squeezed his eyes shut. The sound of charred wood, crumbling, morphed into distant mortar fire. He pictured Jenner and Brian taking small arms fire. Behind them was a dark shadow: Hector hunched over like a grotesque gargoyle, his arms wrapped around his legs, his head perched low over his knees. In the outer perimeter, other men, bearded men with loose-flowing garments, scurried behind rocks. They rushed toward him, hunched low, weapons in their hands, and surrounded him.

Alex trembled. He opened his eyes. No matter. The enemy was already inside his head.

CHAPTER TWENTY-TWO

When Brian and Kate entered the apartment, they heard Gretchen and Bill talking in the kitchen. As soon as Gretchen saw them, she rushed toward them with a white envelope. "This just came. A hiker he met in Glacier mailed it for him."

Brian tore open the priority express mail and extracted a one-page letter written on blue-lined paper. His frown betrayed him as he read it.

"What does it say?" Kate asked.

Brian's voice caught in his throat. "I need to call his mom right away."

Before he could pull out his cell phone, Gretchen thrust out her landline phone. She had saved Teresa Vilanova's number on the device and had turned it on speaker mode so she could listen to the conversation.

Brian nodded and took the phone. He counted on his stepmother's skills as a pyschologist to come to the rescue. He pressed the call button.

Teresa answered on the second ring.

"Hello, Mrs. Vilanova. This is Brian McEnroe, Alex's team leader."

The voice sounded strained. "I know who you are. You got a letter from my son?"

"I just opened it."

"Read it to me."

Brian hesitated. Long ago, Alex had confided in him that

doctors had hospitalized his mother for manic depression. Brian didn't want to trigger a relapse. He looked at Gretchen, who motioned him to continue.

Brian read slowly.

Brian,

If this letter gets to you, it means they found me in Glacier National Park and took this off my dead body. I'm sorry. I let you down, but better here and now than in the Hindu Kush.

I've not been thinking straight for some time. I'm an albatross to everyone. You tried to help me. Now, only God can.

Would you do me a favor and call my mother at 406-554-3212? I want her to hear from you about what happened to me. Tell her I love her and I died after seeing the headwaters of three oceans. Tell her I died looking up at the stars. I saw The Big Show. She would appreciate that.

Brian choked up. His eyes watered, and he took a deep breath to steady himself. The man he fought alongside, the friend he treasured, had written his obituary.

Teresa's voice shook. "Is that all?"

"No, there's more."

You have been my brother, a good friend, and the best soldier I've ever known. I'd follow you into battle anytime, anywhere, but this time you can't save me. It's better this way for my mother, for you, for Jenner, for everyone.

I tried to be a good soldier, a good Ranger, and a Delta warrior, but I failed. The Ranger creed says, "I will never leave a fallen comrade to fall into the hands of the enemy, and under no circumstances will I ever embarrass my country."

But I dishonored my country. I left Aarmaan. Back in Bagram, I didn't act with honor. I let things happen and told no one. Now, I'm cleaning the slate.

I have paid the ultimate price for failure. Keep yourself safe.

Your friend,

Alex

"The letter ends there," Brian said.

Brian heard choked sobs on the other end and cursed himself for reading the letter. "Mrs. Vilanova . . . Mrs. Vilanova?"

Teresa's voice returned, sharp and direct. "Do you think he's dead?"

"I don't know."

Brian waited several moments for her to respond, to no avail.

"Mrs. Vilanova?"

Her response burst forth, rapid-fire, and explosive. "You know my son. He was over there with you. You know how he thinks. What he will do? Dammit. Answer me. Is he dead?"

Rather than blurt out an answer, Brian did what the Army trained him to do. Consider the facts. Analyze everything he knew about Alex. Forget what he wanted to believe; what others wanted to hear.

"Is my son dead? For God's sake, tell me."

Brian heard the fear in her voice. How could he explain his

reasoning so she would understand? He weighed the words in his mind before he spoke.

"Is Alejandro dead?"

"No, Mrs. Vilanova, I don't think so. He's not dead. Not yet. I'm not certain, but Alex wrote, 'If this letter gets to you, it means I'm dead.' He thought the park rangers would find the letter on his body. But instead of taking it with him as he planned, he asks another hiker to mail it to me. Why? Knowing him, I believe it's because he's not ready to give up just yet. He's struggling, but Alex is a fighter. Part of him doesn't want to die."

Teresa gasped.

"Your son is my responsibility. I knew he was hurting. But I didn't see this coming."

"I didn't see it either, and I'm his mother. It's my fault."

There was silence on both ends of the phone until Gretchen spoke out.

"Teresa, this is Gretchen. Are you there?"

"Yes."

"We know all this is a shock, but you need to be there for Alex right now. Did you call the ranger headquarters?"

"I did. I told them what you told me: that Alex is a soldier, just back from Afghanistan. He's depressed and not thinking straight. And he's out there with no food or equipment. They promised me they'd mobilize a search party."

Brian rubbed his face. Glacier's an enormous park with rough terrain, he thought. It takes time to round up experienced searchers. And they're up against a Delta warrior who is an expert at evasion.

Brian bent over the phone's speaker. "I'll find him, I promise. As soon as I can, I'll leave for Kalispell. If the Park

Rangers don't find him, I will."

A familiar voice interrupted on the other end. "I'll find him for you, Falcon."

"Jenner, is that you?"

"None other. I arrived here about twenty minutes ago. As promised, I came to Kalispell to check on Hammer, only to find out he's lost in Glacier."

"Thank God you're there."

"I didn't know what was in the letter until you read it. Now that I know what he is planning, I'll track him down before he hurts himself. A couple who met Hammer in Glacier gave Mrs. Vilanova a topographical map. They marked the location where he stepped off the trail."

Brian picked up a pen from the counter and tore a piece of paper from a notepad. "Give me the coordinates."

Jenner snickered. "Why? By the time you get here, I will have found him."

"Give them to me."

"Suit yourself. Longitude -113.50192, Latitude 48.65602."

"Wait for me, Jenner. We should do this together."

"Sorry, Bro', but I can't wait. Not after hearing what he wrote in his letter."

Brian's jaw clenched at the thought of Jenner going it alone without him. "I'll be there in Kalispell ASAP. I want you to be there when I arrive. Do you understand? That's an order."

There was no response.

"Jenner? Jenner?"

Teresa's voice interrupted him. "Your friend just left."

Brian threw back his head and groaned. He looked at Kate and shook his head. He could not read her expression, but he felt he had somehow let her down. He was leaving her again.

"Are you still coming?" Teresa asked.

"Yes, I'll be there as soon as I can."

"Call me when you know your plans."

"I will."

Gretchen interrupted. "Teresa, I'll call you later."

Teresa hung up without answering.

Brian took Kate's hand. "Wait for me in the living room while I make a plane reservation, then we'll go to the airport together."

As Kate left the kitchen, Bill stopped Brian from proceeding.

"You're joining the search party?"

Brian didn't answer.

"It's a lot of country out there to search on your own, trust me."

"I don't have time. I need to book a flight. Will you drive me to the airport?"

"I'll take you," Bill answered. "And I have outdoor gear and clothing in the storage closet if you need them."

"Good. I don't have any time to spare."

Brian rushed down the hallway, and Bill and Gretchen watched him go.

"I'm sorry," Bill said to Gretchen.

"For what?"

"For what I said this morning. I mean, about Brian being my son. It was a rotten thing to say."

"It was, but it didn't stop me from putting my two cents in."

"I'm worried about him. War does strange things to you."

"He's strong, like his father."

Bill hung his head. He had put Emma, his first wife, through hell when he returned from Vietnam. He couldn't keep a job and drank too much. His wife and family had never signed up for the heartache they suffered. For a moment, he relived the guilt he had felt.

Finally, he lifted his eyes. "Soldiers bend in war, even if they don't break."

"You survived. So will Brian."

Bill nodded, then noticed Teresa's letter in Gretchen's hand. "Let me see the letter," he said, his hand out.

Gretchen looked down at the letter, then at Bill. "Why?"

"I just remembered something important."

***

As he searched the Web for flights to Kalispell, Brian called Jenner on his cell phone. He needed to reach him before he left for Glacier. They would find Alex together. They lived by a code that said no man gets left behind. The brass called it unit integrity, but the term didn't capture the way men like Jenner and he lived it. They would rather die than abandon their brothers. No, Brian thought, wherever Jenner is, he'll meet me at the airport.

Brian left a message. "Icarus, Falcon here. Call me. We need to do this together. I'll call you again in about a half hour to give you my flight info."

He expected Jenner to call back soon, probably before the half-hour was up. As unpredictable as Jenner could sometimes be, he always returned his calls. In his head, Brian had already worked out a plan involving the two of them: He would book a helicopter to take them from the airport to Glacier. They would trek to the spot where the German couple had last seen Alex. There, Jenner would do his thing. Comanche-like in tracking skill, Jenner would find Alex's trail and follow it until they caught up with him. Then they'd bring him out of the wilderness alive.

"Damn it," Brian muttered. There were no direct flights to Kalispell from New York. Finding Alex in time was fading.

Brian booked a flight with one connection and a short layover. When he finished, he made a list of the things to bring with him. He and Jenner would travel as light as possible. When his dad walked into the room, Brian handed him the list. "Dad, do you have any of this?"

Bill perused the list. "I have it all."

"Great. Can you put it together for me while I try to book a chopper ride from Kalispell to Glacier?"

"Brian?"

"Yes?"

"I'm going with you."

"Like hell you are."

"Listen —"

"You'll slow me down. You're —"

"Seventy years old. I know what you're thinking. Give me three minutes to explain why it's a good idea. If you're not convinced, I'll take this list, pack the stuff up, keep my mouth shut, and drive you to the airport. How's that sound?"

Brian sat back with arms crossed over his chest. "Three minutes."

Bill sat in front of Brian and made his points, enumerating each with the fingers of his right hand.

"First, you're searching for someone who is not likely to leave many tracks. If you move fast, you'll miss the few signs he leaves. Therefore, I don't need to reach your maximum speed to keep up. And besides, you know I'm in better shape than most guys thirty years younger. Second, when I was with Outward Bound in Colorado, my friends and I backpacked many times into Glacier. I know the place. You don't. And knowledge of the terrain is crucial in any search. Third, you may find your friend, but what will you say and do when you find him? Have you ever dealt with men with PTSD, ever talked somebody out of suicide? I have. And my last argument is that Alex has too far a head start on you if you plan to follow him. But what if I knew exactly where he was going, and I could lead you there?"

Brian sat up. "You know? How?"

Bill held out Alex's letter. "Your friend told you. When he wrote this letter, he thought he'd be dead when you received it, so he didn't mind telling you. I didn't get that when you read the letter on the phone. But then I realized something. It was in a sentence I just passed by when I first heard it. Remember, he wrote 'Tell her I love her and that I died after seeing the headwaters of three oceans.' There's only one place in that part of the world where the rainfall flows into three oceans. It's called Triple Divide Peak. I can lead you there."

Bill waited while his son mulled it over. Finally, Brian said, "Pack the bags. I'll book another ticket."

CHAPTER TWENTY-THREE

When Jenner left Teresa's building, he glanced over his shoulder at a painted sign in the window of the Three Brothers pizza parlor. The bold lettering beckoned travelers to explore Glacier National Park. Jenner considered it an omen.

A slight change in plans, he mused, as he slipped on his riding gloves.

Jenner made a mental list of what he wanted to bring to Glacier. Like Alex, he'd travel light. He had already strapped his cold-weather trappings and his snivel gear to his Harley. Now, he needed to rent a four-wheel-drive vehicle and find a garage to store his bike. Whatever else he needed, he could pick up at the Walmart just outside of town.

"What I don't need is Brian staring over my shoulder," he murmured. He checked how many text and voice messages he had on his phone. "Fourteen, and they're all from him, I bet. Well, I'm not answering, homey."

He smirked. He felt a special bond with the men he locked shields with. They were his brothers. But like stags in a rut, tensions sometimes grew between them. Jenner normally channeled that aggression into fighting the enemy. But this was not the Hindu Kush. Give all the orders you want, Jenner thought. I'm not listening. I'm on a solo mission now.

Jenner powered down his cell phone and shoved it into his pocket. He would leave it behind. The last thing he wanted was to carry a device the government could use to track him down.

***

A half-hour later, Jenner had convinced a garage owner that it was his patriotic duty to store his bike for free and give him a forty percent discount on a Jeep Grand Cherokee rental with a V8 Hemi engine and twenty-inch wheels. On his way to a nearby Walmart for supplies, he spotted a thirty-foot fiberglass cowgirl twirling a lariat around a sign that read: BUSTER'S — Best Steaks and Beer in Kalispell. The prospect of squeezing his next few days' meals out of cans and tubes made a porterhouse with fries and a pint of brown ale sound enticing. With a squeal of his Jeep's tires, he swerved into the crowded parking lot.

When Jenner shouldered through the swiveling glass doors of Buster's, a hostess in a gold cowboy hat and a buckskin vest smiled a greeting. Before she could speak, Jenner pointed at the long mahogany bar spreading across the right side of the spacious building. "I'm in a hurry, *Senorita*. Can I get a steak at the bar?"

The cowgirl with the pasted-on grin handed him a menu. "The bar menu is on the back, Bronco Bill."

Jenner beelined toward a stool in front of the beer taps at the center of the bar. As he crossed the dining room, he noticed all the two-fisted beer drinkers, with their humongous bellies sitting on their laps, their necks bigger than their heads, guzzling beer while wolfing down bloody-red bison steak. What a beautiful sight, he thought.

The restaurant boasted of its meat-driven existence. At least ten stuffed heads of bison, bear, elk, mountain goat, cougar, mountain boar, and — incongruously — a circus clown hung from the walls. Animals' skins stretched like trophies on either side of a gigantic oil painting of Blackfoot Indians hunting buffalo with lances and bows and arrows. Light poured out of ceiling lamps with shades featuring stencils of mountains, pine trees, and antlered moose. Above the mirror behind the bar, a life-size cutout of a steer, with its assorted cuts of meat drawn and labeled in red enamel, supplied information to the unschooled carnivore.

The carnal display reminded Jenner of a Nairobi restaurant he visited, where waiters carried around a roasted zebra on a pole and carved slices with a sword. The allusions to meat made him hungry, which was the idea, he supposed. He pulled off his jacket, draped it over his stool, climbed aboard, took a quick look at the bar menu, and slapped it down on the granite-top bar. A young bartender wearing a black Stetson, a white shirt, a black string tie, and red suspenders chatted with an older couple at the end of the bar. To Jenner's right, two burly gentlemen in sharp-cut western suits and thin ties argued over commodity prices. When Jenner turned to his left, he caught the eye of two young women several stools down. They wore stylish black dresses and leather boots and drank from tall tumblers filled with a lime green concoction.

He smiled.

They smiled back.

Friendly place, Jenner thought.

Whenever he ate at a bar and was in a hurry, he sought a stool in front of the beer taps which bartenders frequently returned to for refills. The strategy bore fruit right away.

"What can I get you, Mister?" the bartender asked, as he pulled the lever for a draft of Pig's Ass Porter.

"I want a porterhouse, rare, with fries and a pint of Moose Drool Pale Ale on draft. And could you put the order in right away? I'm military, and I have a plane to catch and don't want the Army calling me AWOL. We're shipping out tonight."

The bartender put the other glass down and filled a glass with

Moose Drool. "Sure thing," he said, and placed the brimming glass on a coaster in front of Jenner. "Let me see what I can do."

He came back a minute later, swooped up the other customer's beer glass, and bragged, "Your order's in. Anything else you need, just give me a shout."

Jenner almost blurted out: I'd love to hear Mumford and Sons, drink Kamikazes, and get laid. Can you help me with that?

But he refrained and shouted, "Any peanuts?"

"I'll get you some," the bartender shouted back. Jenner hoped against reason that the man had read his thoughts and the Mumford and Sons song, "I Will Wait", would play, and the girls next to him would strip. But he knew the best he could expect was a bowl of Planter's salted.

The soundproofing in the cavernous dining area seemed nonexistent. The din of diners and the clatter of overworked staff cleaning tables reminded him of the racket in Camp Braggs' mess hall. As he downed his beer, he tried to block the clamor by humming and drumming with his fingers the marching song he had learned in his Ranger training:

> *Somewhere there's a mother*
> *She's crying for her boy*
> *He's an Airborne Ranger*
> *With his orders to deploy;*
> *Don't you cry for him*
> *He don't need your sympathy*
> *He's an Airborne Ranger*
> *That's the best that you can be.*

A bowl of peanuts appeared before him while he hummed and drummed the next stanza. The hand holding the bowl bore only three fingers, each of which looked like the cigar-shaped stumps kindergartners roll out of pink clay. When Jenner looked up, he saw a smiling face that was a ghoulish mask of angry scars, watery green eyes, and a misshapen mouth. Jenner guessed that a skillful plastic surgeon had reconstructed the chin and nose and inserted the unblinking glass eye.

The face startled him. In Afghanistan and Iraq, he witnessed many burn victims with horrendous injuries — some worse than this — but that was a different world. That was a world where humans expected horrors: grotesquely disfigured men and women walking down a dirt path or peeking out from a stone hut; children without limbs carried by mothers to the marketplace; young and old, enemy and ally, without minds, speechless. In that world, war broke so many people, physically and emotionally, that the sight of someone untouched seemed an oddity. But that was over there, not here.

"Tommy told me you're in the service," the man said, not seeming to notice Jenner's reaction. "Can I pour you another beer on the house?"

Jenner looked down the bar at the bartender, who observed both men with keen interest. He saluted him, then turned back to the disfigured man. "A free beer? Sure. Thanks."

"And the steak dinner is on me, too. Tommy said you were shipping out tonight. First time?"

"Not a chance. I've stopped counting."

"Let me guess, Afghanistan?"

"Yep."

"A lovely place."

"You were there?"

The man slid his fingers over his hairless head, as if he were pushing back a pompadour, and then saluted. "Combat engineer, 4th Combat Brigade, 10th Mountain Division, deployed 2011 in Wardak Province, a lovely place if you don't mind enemy combatants shooting at you every day. Not even God, or your first sergeant, could save you there."

Jenner knew Wardak well. In 2012, coalition special forces flew in to root out the hard-core Taliban fighters who infiltrated the area in numbers. Some of the old-timers in his unit were the first to go in. It was bad.

"I guess you got waxed pretty hard."

The man leaned back with a look of bewilderment. "What?"

Jenner held his palms up. "I mean . . . your . . ."

The man chortled. "You mean my burns? No, no, no."

"I'm sorry."

Laying his hand down on Jenner's forearm, the man interrupted him. "No offense taken. I didn't get my scars in Afghanistan. I was one of the lucky ones. Didn't even get a razor cut over there. This is all homegrown, a bus accident."

"Sorry."

"Shit happens."

One of the burly men in western suits leaned over, with one arm leveraged at a right angle on top of the bar. "What he didn't tell you was that it was a school bus, and he charged into it after it caught on fire. He saved twelve kids. The man's a hero."

The scarred man shrugged. "Any person would have done the same."

The burly man sat back down. "The hell they would. But he did it. Won the Soldier's Medal for it."

The scarred man ignored the praise and turned to the bartender. "Tommy, see what's happened to this soldier's steak."

"Yes, Sir, Mr. Wright," the bartender answered and left the bar.

Mr. Wright made a clicking sound and looked out beyond Jenner's shoulder. "The place is pretty busy," he apologized.

He scanned the bar. "Anyone need anything?"

A few hands shot up, and Wright strode over to serve them. Jenner observed how the customers reacted to him or did not react in the way Jenner thought they might. They showed neither fear nor disgust, and they lit up when he bent to listen to their every word. Across the bar, Wright's deep voice rumbled. He sprinkled his conversation with first names and inside jokes. Folks seemed to gravitate to him. To watch him take orders and mix drinks was like contemplating a magician working his audience as he pulled rabbits from a hat.

His body was short but wide, with no neck. His broad shoulders and thick thighs bulged from his denim shirt and corduroy jeans. Despite his bulk, he moved with a defining grace, and, as he glided, he bantered with patrons:

"You wanted an Old Fashioned, didn't you Burt? Like the drink, I work best with a little bourbon."

"A Stolichnaya and soda? My dear, if you can say it, I can make it."

"Take pity on me, folks. I'm only subbing for Tommy. I'm just the lowly owner of this beer joint."

"Ah, here he is. Tommy, take over before my wife finds out I'm working."

Tommy scooted over to Wright's side with Jenner's steak platter in hand and passed it off to his boss, who presented it to Jenner with a flourish. "Here you go, soldier. Grass-fed beef, tender as a baby's bottom, and so succulent, you'll wish you were staying in Kalispell another night."

"Mmm," Jenner murmured as he cut into the thick slab of steak. "It smells delicious."

"Tastes even better."

Jenner chewed on the sweet purple-red meat, crusty on its surface with a sauce redolent of white wine vinegar, butter, and peppercorn. The meat smothered his tongue with a savory smoothness.

"Well?" Wright asked.

"Excellent," Jenner said. "I'm impressed. So, you own this place?"

"My father owns the title, but he's retired. I run it."

"Is he Buster, or is that you?"

The man offered his hand. "I'm Buster. My father named this place after me on the day I was born, thirty years ago this past July 7th."

Jenner shook Buster's hand. "Pleased to meet you. I'm Jenner."

Buster raised his glass of bourbon neat. "To the U. S. of A."

"To the U. S. of A."

They clinked glasses.

"You won the Soldier's Medal?"

Buster sipped on his drink. "They pinned it on me after I came out of the hospital. I'm no hero. I woke up the next day feeling the same way about myself as I did the day before. Like I said to Burt, I was just doing what anybody would have done if they drove by, saw that bus, and those kids."

Jenner understood completely. He guessed that, when Buster heard those children screaming, he didn't wait to see if others would get out of their cars and rush into the bus. Something kicked on inside of him and he acted. He didn't stop to think.

In his mind, it was the only thing to do.

Jenner knew what it was like to have people call you a hero. Whenever he had to wear his dress uniform back home, people would look at his medals and fawn all over him. "I just did my job," he would tell them. Those medals on his chest could have gone to plenty of guys and women in the Kush who did more than he did, but nobody was watching. Maybe the commanding officer didn't like the soldier, or forgot to write the commendation, or it lay forgotten in a desk drawer.

"Just the same," Jenner said to Buster. "You paid a heavy price."

"Three months in a burn center in Seattle. Thirty percent of my body with second-and-third-degree burns. They put me in a coma for a while. Operated on me twenty-eight times. The plastic surgeons still have more work to do. But this community was always behind me. It kept me going. Them and my wife and kids. The only hard part is when some stranger from out-of-town stares at me with a look that says, 'if it were me, I'd blow my brains out.'"

Jenner shook his head. "Assholes."

"I love to tell them, 'My face is not so bad. I was uglier before the fire.'"

Jenner snorted and bumped fists with Buster.

Buster finished his drink. A dribble rolled down his chin, but he did not wipe it. Jenner guessed because he couldn't feel it.

"You know, Jenner, I'm a lucky guy. I was in Wardak Province, and God spared me. He let me live so I could come home and drive down that highway and witness that truck slam into the back of that school bus."

As Buster placed his empty glass on the bar, Tommy walked over. "Mr. Wright, Luis says we have a delivery."

Throwing his arm over Tommy's shoulder, Buster pointed at Jenner and said, "Give this soldier anything he wants."

To Jenner, he said, "Be safe, soldier."

Jenner gave him the thumbs-up sign. "Charley Mike."

The bartender watched Buster walk away and then said, "Can I get you anything?"

"Just the check."

"Mr. Wright said no check."

In another bar, in another place, in another time Jenner would have accepted the freebie, chalked it up to his finesse, and traveled on, but he didn't feel right about taking advantage of Buster. The man was a hero, a warrior, a brother.

"Listen, Tommy, I'd like to pay my tab, but I don't want Buster to know. So, give me the check and keep this between us."

Tommy pushed back the brim of his cowboy hat and pondered his choices. "Sure, if you say so."

After the bartender walked off, Jenner wolfed down the rest of his food. He was eager to start his search. He was feeling a little guilty for enjoying the steak and beer while Alex was alone in Glacier.

Tommy shuffled over with the check, and Jenner counted out several twenties which covered the bill and a hefty tip. "Say goodbye to Buster for me."

"Will do and thanks," the bartender said, then scooped up the money.

Jenner rose from his barstool and tipped his cap at the commodities traders on his right who raised their glasses.

"Hey, join us for shots," one shouted.

Jenner raised his palms in surrender. "Can't. I'm going hunting."

CHAPTER TWENTY-FOUR

As he made his way out of Buster's, Jenner eyeballed the two young women in black dresses who had smiled at him when he sat down at the bar. One was voluptuous with raven black hair and dark olive skin, while the other was rangy with reddish hair and a milk-white complexion. They fingered their touchphones, chatting back and forth with each other and their wi-fi friends, and Jenner was about to look away when the rangy one threw back her head, laughed, and muttered something in German.

Jenner froze. He remembered Mrs. Vilanova's description of the couple Alex met in Glacier. They were young Germans. One was a tall woman with red hair. What were the odds of hearing German in Kalispell, in October, when few tourists, domestic or foreign, would brave the bone-chilling weather? How many redheaded fräuleins could there be besides the one who befriended his comrade in Glacier?

He scoured his memory for the name Alex's Mom had given him.

"Petra?" Jenner asked, taking a step in her direction.

She turned and looked at him with a puzzled expression. He had guessed right.

"I'm Alex's friend, Jenner."

Wide-eyed, Petra stared into his face, then jumped from her seat and scanned the restaurant. "Is Alex with you? Is he here?"

Jenner shook his head and inched closer. "He's still in Glacier. I'm going there to find him."

Petra took one step towards Jenner, then halted. "Can you find him?"

"I will."

Petra gritted her teeth and turned to her friend, who scrutinized Jenner with alcohol-clouded eyes. "This is Marta. I'm staying with her for a few days. My other friends flew to California yesterday."

Marta and Jenner acknowledged each other with slight nods.

"I hoped Alex would come home," Petra said.

Jenner looked at his watch. "I don't have much time. I need your help. His mother told me everything you told her, but I have questions."

Petra raised her eyebrows and sat down. "I know nothing."

Jenner placed his left hand on the bar and leaned in, creating a human wall between Petra and her friend. His left hand gripped the back of Petra's stool. "You think you don't, but you're the only one who saw him leave the trail. You were the last person to speak to him."

"What do you want to know?"

"Can we go outside? It's so noisy here."

Petra hesitated. She studied Jenner's face, then bent over the bar to address her friend. "I'll be right back."

Marta pushed her stool back and half-heartedly tried to stand. "Do you want me to come with you?"

"No, I'll be fine."

"Whatever," Marta mumbled, and lifted her cocktail from the bar.

Jenner helped Petra with her coat and escorted her outside. They hurried from the entrance to a truck unloading site about thirty yards away. Three halogen lamps mounted on the roof of the restaurant lit the area. Jenner stopped in front of a yellow step van with a steer's head stenciled on the side panel.

"We can sit in my car and put on the heat if you prefer," Jenner said.

Petra bundled herself up and crossed her arms. "No. This is fine."

Jenner blew on his hands. He noticed how naturally pretty Petra was. She was just the type of girl Hammer would get weak-kneed over. The kind any man might find easy to talk to. Even me, he mused.

"I want to know if Alex told you anything at all about what happened in Afghanistan."

"No, I didn't even know he was a soldier until his mother told me."

"Are you sure? Did he say anything about a village raid or the day he returned to base?"

"No."

"Did he say anything about me?"

"I don't understand why you're asking these questions."

"Are you telling me the truth?"

"Of course. Why would I lie? Maybe I should go back."

Jenner lightly touched her arm. "Sorry. No offense. I'm just trying to get inside Alex's head. Maybe it will give me some clues. Alex has a lot on his mind. Do you understand how important it is that we find him, and soon?"

"Of course."

"Good. Now, tell me. Did he mention my name?'

Petra noticed Jenner's hand on her arm and pulled away. "No, never."

"Nothing about a raid or what happened afterward?"

"No."

Jenner shook his head, then looked up as if he were trying to decide what to do next. A boisterous group of five men dressed in black western-styled suits and alligator cowboy boots passed them. Two of the men sniggered and motioned to Petra to come with them. Jenner glared at them. The taller of the two stopped to face him. Jenner slid his right foot back and blew the man a kiss. The tall man's friend pulled him away.

Jenner turned back to Petra. "Sorry about those goat-ropers. Now that the stare-down at the OK Corral is over, tell me the reason Alex gave for going off the trail."

"He just said he needed to do something, then pointed to the mountains."

"This was at dawn, right? Where was the sun when he pointed? Was it in front of him, behind him, to the left, or right? This is important."

"Let me think," she said.

She closed her eyes, and Jenner studied her face as she tried to retrieve her last moments with Alex. He could tell how hard she worked to summon the memories. Her eyelids fluttered, the muscles around her mouth and jaw pulsed, and her lips pouted and puckered as her mind's eye cast pictures unseen by anyone but her. He liked her face. It was strong, yet vulnerable. It reminded him of the faces of other women he had known, yet he found hers unique in ways he couldn't explain. The skin wore the thinnest layer of makeup. Her eyelashes were long and spread out like an artist's brush. Her mouth curved like two rose petals barely touching. A warm yellow light with a blueish tint reflected off her face.

Petra opened her eyes.

"The sun was on his left. I'm sure it was on the left."

Jenner nodded. "That's very helpful."

Petra smiled. "Good. I hope it helps you find Alex. Please

call me when you do. I'll be in town for a few more days. I'd like to see him — at least talk to him — before I go."

Jenner shrugged. "Sure. Give me your phone number."

"Do you have a pen and paper?"

Jenner tapped his right temple. "I have a photographic memory."

Petra hesitated, but then recited her number.

They said goodbye to each other, then Jenner watched as Petra walked back into the restaurant. The thought that Alex had a woman like Petra, who obviously cared so much about him, filled Jenner with envy.

Jenner turned around and headed to his Jeep, parked five spots over. The talk with the German woman was useful. Not the part where Petra told him that Alex faced south when he stepped off the trail. That fact might save him a few minutes at most before he picked up Alex's tracks. That difference made no difference. He had asked the question to obfuscate the real intent of his other questions. He wanted to know if Alex had told Petra anything about the night after the team came back from the village raid. Alex had never mentioned Jenner. And he had never revealed what he and Jenner had done with the Afghan soldier.

Now, all he had to do was to find Alex before anyone else did.

CHAPTER TWENTY- FIVE

The Brooklyn-Queens Expressway morphed into a Walmart parking lot on Black Friday. Snarled traffic clogged six lanes of traffic heading east and west. Drivers of cars and trucks blasted their horns. Exhaust pipes spewed clouds of noxious fumes. Vehicles lurched forward a few feet, braked, and waited for the next opening.

Brian leaned forward from his back seat and gripped the sides of the driver's seat. "Dad, we're not going to make our flight,"

"I know," Bill answered while scanning the adjacent lanes for an opening. "I've never seen such bumper-to-bumper traffic."

"If we don't make it to LaGuardia in time, we'll miss our connection to Kalispell. There isn't another one until tomorrow. If we're going to find Alex, that's too late."

"I know. I know. What do you want me to do?"

"Something . . . anything."

Gretchen pulled her phone from her clutch bag. "Let me see if there's another way."

Brian thrust himself back in his seat and stared out the window.

Bill glanced at his son through his rearview mirror. "Any luck with Jenner?"

"He's not answering his phone."

"He'll call," Kate said, folding her hand in Brian's.

Brian peered at three SUVs, a Greyhound bus, and a tractor-trailer as they squeezed into the merging lanes of a feeding ramp. Car horns blasted him from all sides. He looked again at his phone to check if Jenner had left a text. Despite all his concerns about his wild friend, Brian knew Jenner added incredible assets to a search. He couldn't say the same about his father.

Gretchen stared at the GPS on her phone. "If we get off at the Northern Boulevard exit, we'll make better time on local streets."

"I'll try anything short of murder," Bill said.

Gretchen scoffed. "No violence, please. Just follow my directions. Take the next exit on the right."

Moving over to the right lane would not be easy, however. A slew of drivers illegally used the right shoulder to squeeze by the crowded right lane. In response, frustrated drivers in the right lane steered their cars back-and-forth between the shoulder and their lane, determined to block anyone from taking advantage of them. Bill inched his Chevy toward his right. A moving van pushed him back.

"Let me in, goddamn it." Again, he tried to maneuver into the right lane, but a Toyota Tundra nearly side-swiped him. "We're going to miss our exit."

Abruptly, Brian leaped out of the Chevy and darted in front of a tow truck moving alongside. When the tow truck lurched forward to intimidate him, Brian slammed his hand down on the hood and then held it up, palm outward, like a traffic cop.

"Stop!" he shouted.

"Get the fuck out of my way, you douchebag," the burly truck driver yelled. He revved his engine as a warning. Horns blasted from behind.

Brian didn't flinch. He fixed his eyes on the man and held his hand steady. The driver's head and arm popped out the driver's side window, his hand holding a large wrench. Spittle sprayed out of his mouth. "How about I come out there and smash your pretty-boy face in?"

Holding the palms of both hands out to his sides as if he were a supplicant, Brian answered in a matter-of-fact voice. "It's your life, sir. Don't waste it for six feet of space."

The man pondered his options, then pulled his head and arm back into his truck's cabin. He gave Brian the finger but didn't utter another word. As soon as Bill steered the Chevy into the right lane, Brian dashed over to the exit lane and shoulder to repeat the process. When the car was safely on the exit ramp, Brian sprinted to the back door, flung it open, and dove inside to a blast of car horns behind him.

"God, it's wild out there. And I thought a soldier's job was dangerous."

Kate nudged him. "You're crazy, you know?"

"But he'd make one great traffic cop," Gretchen said.

Brian chortled. "You think?"

"Absolutely."

"No, thanks."

When they hit the local streets, traffic moved along at a better clip. Even with the occasional red light and double-parked car, they made good time. The sidewalks teemed with shoppers of all colors and ethnicities. Signs in Spanish, Korean, Vietnamese, Arabic, Italian, and many other languages splashed across storefronts of faded aluminum and safety glass. One large store caught Brian's eye. Its goods spilled out of the remains of an old Woolworth's five-and-dime store. On the sidewalk, families dressed in traditional Afghan and Pakistani garb milled around pungent bins of colorful spices and fruit. To

Brian's eye, it looked like a typical market in Kabul. The scene transported him back to the dusty streets, where he calibrated himself to every smell, sound, and sensation.

To divert his mind, Brian tapped Gretchen's shoulder. "You're a psychologist. Do you think Alex has gone crazy?"

"Crazy?"

"You know what I mean. Is he sick? Does he have a disorder like depression?"

Gretchen pinched the bridge of her nose. "I think he's depressed, but I wouldn't use the terms 'crazy' or 'disorder'. Those words paint an ugly picture. Let's frame Alex's state differently. Think of it in terms of his adaptation to trauma. Some psychologists hypothesize that depression may have evolutionary advantages."

Brian thought of how Alex looked after he came back from the mission. "I don't see any advantages in being depressed."

"Think of it this way. Our human ancestors were weak and slow compared to the predators hunting them. They survived because they solved problems better than the other species. But as human communities grew, problems grew more complex. Depression evolved as a way for human beings to cope when things went out of control. Food, sleep, and sex hold no interest when you're depressed. You focus only on the obstacles you face. Suffering is a rite of passage. You work through the obstacles and come out the other side, stronger and wiser."

"And if you don't?"

Gretchen smiled as if she knew the question was coming. "Then someone must rescue you. In remote Puerto Rican villages, for example, natives called the depression *ataque*. You usually see it develop in women overburdened with work, poverty, and childbearing. A woman may sit silently for days, oblivious to family, friends, and even the weather. The villagers just wait, because they know one of two things will happen."

Bill chuckled. "Either she'll swallow Zoloft or buy new shoes."

Gretchen gave Bill an admonishing look and turned back to Brian. "Either the woman will deal with her problems or she'll have an *ataque*. The poor woman will go 'crazy', as your father might say. She'll cry, scream, and attack others. When that happens, all the village women carry her home and tend to her every need night and day."

Brian pursed his lips. "And it works?"

"So they say. If someone acts that way in our culture, we quickly drug them. We have no village."

Brian wrestled with what Gretchen told him. In Afghanistan, he learned the importance of the Afghan notion of the village. Every Afghan had a place they could go home to, no matter what. This deep sense of belonging enabled Afghans to endure nearly forty years of war. Brian always admired the ability of the men he fought against to persist despite the hardships they faced. After defeat or injury, they dragged themselves back to their village. There, everyone embraced and honored them. But when American soldiers came home, they rarely received such a welcome. Most Americans wanted nothing to remind them a war was going on.

Kate announced their arrival at LaGuardia which pulled Brian out of his woolgathering. Their car joined the merging lines of traffic entering the airport. Within minutes, they pulled over to the curb at the Departures Terminal.

Bill leaned over and kissed his wife. "Thanks for navigating."

Gretchen looked worried. "Take care of this old man for me, will you, Brian?"

"You can depend on it," Brian replied.

He turned to Kate. "I don't know what to say."

"Say nothing. Find Alex."

Bill slapped the seat of the car and advised his son. "Kiss her already. Best get moving."

Kate pulled Brian's chin down and kissed him.

The four exited the car and transferred the bags and equipment to a platform luggage cart. Brian gave Kate a bear hug. A Port Authority policewoman blew her whistle and motioned for them to move the vehicle. Bill flipped the car keys to Gretchen, who caught them, then ran to the driver's side.

"Call me as soon as you land," she said.

"I promise," Bill said.

Gretchen slipped into the driver's seat while Kate slid into the seat beside her. The car pulled away from the curb.

Bill waved, watched them go, then grasped the handles of the luggage cart.

Brian removed his father's hands, stepped in front of him, and pushed the cart toward the doors of the terminal.

"Oh, this is going to be fun," Bill said, then rushed to catch up.

"We have no time to spare," Brian said.

The men had an hour to check their bags, go through security, and board their plane. They were cutting it close.

CHAPTER TWENTY-SIX

Hemingway was right, Jenner mused. Men who hunt other men and love it find no other hunting as satisfying.

Jenner Chapman was a manhunter, trained and certified by the Army, or, to put it more accurately, by a former Rhodesian Army commando under contract to the Army at Fort Huachuca in Arizona. Technically, the U. S. military certified Jenner as a combat tracker. But, because he always tracked men, he called himself a man-hunter when asked about his set of skills. It had a nice ring to it. Man-Hunter, a true *nom de guerre.*

"Alex, I can't believe it." Jenner gloated as he snatched a three-foot-long twig off the ground. Someone broke the twig in two places, the break the size of a man's foot. The end of each break was brown rather than white. No animal made this break, he thought. The discoloration told him that whoever broke the twig was long gone.

"Hammer, you're making this too easy."

Jenner stood and resumed his slow cross-hatching movement, canvassing the area, then moving on. He checked every inch of ground for spoor, or tracks, as some civilians called them. In one direction, the area bore a thick carpet of creeper cedar sloping to the left. In the other direction, a football-field-size patch of bear grass ended at a stand of Western Larch trees. He breathed in, trying to detect the unmistakable scent of a campfire. His ears tuned into any unusual sounds. Every few minutes, his mind made itself available to any information lurking beyond his consciousness.

Jenner tried to put himself in his quarry's head. "Which way would I go if I were Alex?" He muttered. "How would I trick those searching for me? Would I walk forward or backward? Would I go through the cedar or the bear grass?"

With that last question, Jenner dropped to one knee. He turned his head to the side and gazed at the bear grass so the angle of sunlight delineated any irregularity in the field's symmetry. Several feet away, he noticed something odd. A few inches of flora appeared lighter than the rest. A man — probably walking with pieces of cloth tied to his boots — had bent blades of bear grass as he walked by. The grass blades pointed toward the forest of gold-leafed larch.

The discovery flummoxed Jenner. A warrior with Alex's training and expertise would not leave such telltale signs if he knew someone was following him. Hammer had excelled in Fort Bragg's Survival Evasion Resistance and Escape training, known to soldiers as SERE. Alex's evasive strategies would normally switch on in situations like this in the same way people automatically move to the back of an elevator and face the front. He'd wipe away his spoor, hide his steps in the middle of animal tracks, and create false trails almost without thinking. Yet, here in Glacier, he made careless mistakes Jenner could only explain in one of two ways. Either Hammer wanted searchers to catch him or he had become so addled he forgot his training. Either way made Jenner unhappy. Where was the challenge?

He cupped his hands on the sides of his mouth and yelled as if he were playing a children's game of hide-and-seek. "I'm coming for you."

At that moment, the sound of a horse and rider on the trail above startled him.

Oh shit, he thought. At this distance and angle, a person looking down from the trail above could see him. Without hesitation, he raced behind one of the three medium-sized boulders bordering the cedar carpet.

"Who's down there?" a deep voice bellowed. "Come on up here. I know you're down there somewhere. This is the park police."

Jenner didn't budge. Based on the ranger's words, he figured the man hadn't seen him. But he also knew it wouldn't take long to flush him out.

Jenner scolded himself under his breath: This is a total goat-fuck. I should have kept my mouth shut. Now, I need to embrace the suck and make the most of this situation.

The ranger was alone, probably scouting out the area for a search party. Jenner figured the lawman was on guard, knowing he had no backup, and was about to confront a distraught, possibly suicidal soldier on the loose. He would want to know if Jenner was that soldier, and if not, why he was there without a backcountry permit. Jenner could lie or make a run for it. But the probability of getting away with either tactic was dubious.

Whatever he did next had to work, or his search for Alex would end here. Can't let that happen, he thought, and removed his gun and holster from the small of his back and placed it on the ground under his pack. He coiled himself tight and low and waited for the ranger's next move.

"This is the police." The ranger's voice boomed. "Show yourself."

The horse snorted. Jenner heard its rider spur the animal to leave the trail and step over the rubble along the side. The sound of the horse's hooves changed as it descended onto the grassy area and swung over toward the boulders. As the horse and rider came closer, Jenner made out the subtle sounds of the ranger's pants rubbing against the horse's flanks and the horse's flickering tail. The awareness made him wonder if the Ranger could hear him breathing. With practiced exertion, he slowed his respiration.

"This is the police. Show yourself. You can't hide."

Jenner stepped out from behind the rock with his arms outstretched in surrender. "Hello, Officer. I was just taking a piss."

"Why didn't you respond when I called out?"

"I'm sorry, Officer, but I was hoping you'd pass by if I kept quiet. It was stupid, I know."

"Let me see your backcountry permit."

"I don't have one, I'm afraid. I'm looking for my friend, a soldier like me, who just came back from hunting down terrorists in Afghanistan. He's out there somewhere in those mountains, and I intend to find him."

The man positioned his horse to control Jenner's movements. "Let me see some identification."

Jenner made a quick assessment of the ranger. The officer carried a holstered Smith and Wesson 9mm, a Taser gun, and a radio, and his bearing screamed ex-military. His Park Service standard green uniform barely concealed a powerful frame. As he leaned forward, he tilted his round-brimmed, beaver-felt hat to conceal his eyes. The ranger was a worthy adversary.

Jenner slowly reached for his wallet. "I have my military ID right —"

The ranger's right hand unclipped his holster. "Hold it! Put your hands behind your head and turn around slowly."

Jenner followed the ranger's instruction, but the officer's voice remained tense. "Now, lift your coat real slow."

Jenner lifted his jacket and lowered his voice to assure the ranger. "I'm not carrying any weapon, Officer. I only want to reach into my pocket and pull out my wallet."

"All right, take your wallet out slowly with two fingers."

Jenner slid his billfold from his pocket and lifted it above his head. He kept his hands visible to the ranger while he extracted his ID.

Behind him, Jenner could feel the horse's breathing. Out of the corner of his eye, a hand withdrew the ID from his fingers.

"Jenner C. Chapman. All right, Sergeant, turn around and lower your hands."

Jenner turned and faced the muzzle of the large chestnut brown horse. Its nostrils spewed flumes of whitened steam, and its enormous hazel eyes glistened a foot from his face. Its musky scent exuded power.

Jenner stepped back. "Thank you, Officer."

The ranger patted his mare and kept its head down so its gaze fixed on Jenner. "So why didn't you sign up for the search party, Mr. Chapman?"

"I figured I could make better time on my own, sir. I've done a lot of combat tracking in mountainous areas."

"I bet you have. But you can't go out there on your own. Go on back to the ranger station and volunteer. Put your expertise to best use."

Jenner clasped his hands together in front of him and bit his lip. "I hear what you're saying, and it makes sense, but let me ask you something. If you were me, and your brother-in-arms had lost his way out there, would you walk back to the station?"

The ranger bent his head so that his beaver-felt hat obscured his face. For a moment, Jenner considered rushing the man and pulling him off his horse. He was an imposing man, but

Jenner could lock him in a rear-naked chokehold in seconds. Squeezing on his carotid arteries would cut off thirteen percent of the oxygen going to his brain. In nine seconds, he would be unconscious, without his weapons, and unable to stop Jenner from escaping.

I could do it, he thought. But he heard a voice in his head whispering: It's too risky. Don't do it.

It was Brian's voice.

The ranger lifted his head and shifted his weight in his saddle. "I plan to scout out the area just above here. When I come back, I expect you to be gone, maybe to join up with the search party. You understand me, Sergeant?"

Tipping his cap, Jenner smiled. "You won't see me here, sir. I swear."

"Take care, soldier," the ranger said, and winked. "I hope you find your friend."

He wheeled his mare around, and, without looking back, cantered to the trail and out of sight.

"Thanks," Jenner shouted after him, then rushed behind the boulder to retrieve his 9mm Beretta and holster. He fastened the holster and inspected his pistol before concealing it under his jacket.

He had little time. The ranger would return soon. Hoisting his pack onto his shoulders, he glanced once again at the telltale blades of bent bear grass. Alex must have gone that way, he thought. I've got to find him.

Within minutes, he was deep in the forest.

CHAPTER TWENTY-SEVEN

Alex adjusted his pack as the cloud floated by and revealed the moon.

Take advantage of the moonlight, Alex thought, and peered down at the rock formation in front of him. Slippery moss and lichen streaked the rock face that descended at a steep ninety-degree angle for over three hundred feet.

"This will not be easy," he muttered. But Alex was born to climb. Not long after he started walking, his parents let him scamper on the boulders near his home. At age seven, Alex belayed teenagers twice his size. While in high school, the Texas chapter of the American Alpine Club sponsored his climbing trips to Hueco Tanks, Yosemite Valley, and the Colorado Rockies. By the time he turned twenty, the climbing prodigy had free-climbed the Bugaboos in British Columbia and Charlotte Dome in the Eastern Sierras. He possessed unusually muscular hands and arms, and he could swing out into space, supporting his entire weight with two fingers while grasping a crimp in a rock six feet away.

He was a fearless climber, but not foolish. On every climb, he gauged the risks in an ascent or descent, judging if the margin of error fell within his abilities. Thus, he took careful stock of the problems posed by this rock face. Poor lighting. Loose sedimentary rock. Patches of slick moss. The biggest challenge, however, was the necessity of making an on-sight descent, finding handholds and pitfalls as he went. Unknown obstacles always posed the most danger.

"You can do this," he said, half-convinced.

He focused on the rock face below him. The way down offered hope for some respite from the demons torturing him. He understood the soul-soothing power of climbing. All one's attention and strength fixed on the moment, with no past or future, no memories or dreams, no regrets or hopes. Only the next handhold to reach. Nothing else mattered. Every inch of hard surface presented a crucible. Another way down the cliff probably existed, but he never considered it.

Alex looked up at the moon. It hovered silently over him. As a five-year-old gazing at the moon, he imagined a kind man's face watching over him. And even now, the shimmering orb seemed to smile on him and illuminate the dark. If God exists, Alex thought, he lives in the mountains bathed in the lunar light. He had grown up a fervent believer, but he didn't expect God to help him climb down this rock surface. He often heard politicians and athletes boast that a divine higher power helped them to succeed, but Alex only hoped that God provided some insight or direction in a world he helped blow to pieces.

And if no God existed, he thought, then let me die here on this rock.

Alex dropped to his knees and draped one leg over the cliff's edge. His foot tested a crack. It held, and he lowered his other leg. Test, test, test, backtrack, test, descend, test, move right, test, move left, descend. The progress took on a certain rhythm that Alex felt in his very core. He felt the adrenaline. It seemed like the climb tested every one of his six hundred muscles, firing or relaxing, contracting or lengthening, tensing or flexing. The face of the rock lay before him like a book in Braille, legible to his fingers. Every crack voiced a poem; every bulge told a story.

About halfway down, the route ahead appeared devoid of handholds or footholds. That left him with two choices. He could climb back to the top of the cliff and find a different way down. Or he could take his chances with slopers — grooves in the rock surface too shallow for holds but possibly adequate for providing enough friction for his feet and hands. With the right balancing and subtle shifts in positioning, he might make it down to the ground, or, at least, to a place offering better purchase.

He took his chances with the slopers. He stretched out to his left to find some friction for his left foot. The surface gave way to a mini-avalanche of pebbles and powder falling to the bottom.

In his head, he heard Aarmaan.

Be careful, my friend. Even rock can crumble.

I can't turn back, Aarmaan.

You can. There's another way to go.

Not for me. I must keep going.

Then be careful. Test the rock before you trust it.

I will.

Do you want a hand?

Sure.

Here's mine.

Alex reached out, but the hand disappeared.

"Aarmaan?"

No one answered. Alex put his palm against the rock where Aarmaan's hand had been. There was a small nub of coarse stone that he could use.

Slow and careful, he told himself. He placed his toes and palms against the rock as he inched downward. Keeping his body centered and balanced over points of contact proved difficult. Several times he came close to "barn dooring," or swinging away from the rock and falling. As he continued, moonlight reflected off the coarse rock and cast flickering shadows that made reliance on sight dangerous. Instead, Alex used sensations transmitted from his feet and hands to "see" his way down. The changeover helped as he descended another thirty feet to a spot next to a large crack, or chimney, about five feet to his left.

The crack appeared large enough to fit in and perhaps lead Alex to the bottom. It was worth a try to reach it, but a slight overhang jutted out between the chimney and Alex's position. To get across to the crack, he must cut loose from the cliff and spring across the divide. The maneuver, called a dyno, posed major challenges.

"Not much to push off from," he murmured.

He feared he'd swing to the other side of the overhang, then find nothing solid enough to grasp on the other side. He looked down at a stone slab about twenty feet below where a dwarf birch grew from the rocky soil. If he fell, he'd hit the branches of the tree or the rock below it. Neither landing interested him. A quick death might be all right, but he dreaded the idea of breaking his back, then left half-dead for a search party or predators to find.

Alex leaned out from the rock face as far as he could to check out safer alternatives. *Nothing,* he thought. *Only this way.*

Facing the chimney, he gritted his teeth. He readied himself, then screamed an ancient Greek battle cry: "*Alala!*"

With that, he sprang sideways over the overhang and into the void. He reached back with his left hand and caught hold of the lip of the chimney. His body swung backward, and he locked his other hand on the other side to secure his position. But the rock crumbled in his hand, and Alex plunged. His arms flailed, clutching for anything to arrest his fall. Nothing but air passed between his fingers. He fell, smashing into the birch branches and snapping them off with sharp cracking sounds. The force of the blow shot stabbing pain through his back and propelled him over the rock outcropping. He landed on the softer ground below with a deep thud, the ribs on his left side taking the most direct hit.

"Ah!" he screamed. The pain was intense. He couldn't breathe and feared he had broken his ribs or collapsed his lungs. He gasped again, and again, and, finally, his lungs inflated. But every subsequent intake thrust a dagger into his chest.

He dreaded taking each breath. With great effort, he sat up, then stood.

"Sweet Jesus!"

If the pain didn't subside, he'd never make it up Triple Divide. His journey could not end here. He willed himself to walk.

The pain was severe. Alex paused and gritted his teeth. He focused on the goat path in front of him. Taking a big step, then another, he pushed through the pain. He wouldn't stop. Or go back. If death snatched him before he reached Triple Divide, so be it. In his mind, his only hope for redemption and a future life waited for him on the summit. While breath remained, he'd fight anything or anyone who tried to stop him from reaching the holy place where rain flowed into three oceans. Step by step, he moved forward, accepting the stabbing jolts in his side.

"Walk, Soldier, walk."

Like a drum major, he chanted the command repeatedly as he marched.

Soon the rock face and dwarf birch disappeared. Foot by foot, he moved closer to Triple Divide. As he did, his chest pangs lessened and became part of him. Like the beat of his heart.

His journey wasn't over.

"Walk, Soldier, walk."

"Walk, Soldier, walk."

"Walk, Soldier, walk."

CHAPTER TWENTY-EIGHT

As Bill and Brian entered the vestibule of Glacier Park International Airport, they noticed a scrawny woman holding a cardboard sign over her head with the name "McEnroe" scrawled in red ink. She sidestepped behind a small crowd of limo drivers waiting for disembarking passengers.

Bill pointed at her. "Son, did you arrange a car service?"

"No, I figured we'd take a taxi to where the chopper is."

"Well, that woman is waving at us."

"Gretchen must've called a service," Brian said. As usual, his stepmother was one step ahead of them. "Let's not waste time. If she's arranged a ride, let's take it."

As they approached the woman, she pushed her way in front of the other drivers. She waved again, and Brian inspected her. She had a sallow complexion, dark shadows under her eyes, and long gray-black hair pulled back into a ponytail. Her clothes stumbled over her thin frame: a blue and red Mexican-style blouse, a green faux-leather jacket, faded jeans, and a cheap pair of department store running shoes.

"Hey," she shouted, then rushed to meet them. "Are you the McEnroes?"

"We are," Bill said.

The woman dropped her sign, sighed, and then bent down to retrieve it. "Ah, thank goodness. I thought it was you, but I wasn't sure until you pointed at me. I've been waiting a couple of hours for your flight to come in. It's a little late."

"Are you with a car service?" Brian asked.

The woman shook her head and rolled her eyes. "No, I'm Alex's mom, Teresa Vilanova. Gretchen called and told me what flight you were on."

Bill moved in front of his son and took Teresa's hand in his. "I'm Bill, and this is Brian. It's nice to meet you."

Teresa frowned. "I'm sorry about the confusion, but I had no way of letting you know I was coming. I thought Gretchen would tell you when you phoned her."

Bill grunted. "Oh, I promised to phone my wife as soon as we landed. Excuse me."

He scurried toward an alcove near the restrooms.

Teresa fidgeted and turned to Brian. "They don't let you smoke cigarettes here. I'm dying for a smoke . . . Well, I rented a car, and I can drive you wherever you want to go."

"We need to get to the Kalispell City Airport right away. I hired a helicopter to fly us to Glacier."

"I know where the airport is. It's not far. I'll drive you."

Brian looked over his shoulder at his father before answering. "All right, thanks."

Teresa ran her tongue over her teeth as if lost in thought and let out a sigh. "I was kind of hard on you on the phone. I'm sorry."

"No problem."

"I'm crazy with worry."

Brian put down his two large bags. "Understandable. Have you heard anything about Alex?"

Teresa's eyes welled. "There's no good news. About an hour ago, I spoke to a Captain Russell. He said they're searching the eastern side of the Divide."

Brian forced a smile. "That's a start."

"What will happen when they find him?"

"That depends. Alex may just give up, but if rangers move in on him with choppers and dogs and lots of men, he might react. There's no telling what might happen if he feels threatened. The letter he sent, and his actions lately, convince me he's not thinking straight. That's why I must find him before the rangers do."

Brian wanted to say more, but he stopped. His training hard-wired him to keep the lid on any mission. He knew that the more people knew, the more information and misinformation spread. The wider the spread, the more likely the chances that bad things would happen. In war, loose talk led to ambushes and explosive surprise packages waiting at your destination. Maybe knowing what he knew about Triple Divide Peak would reassure Alex's mom, but it wouldn't help to find him. And it could hurt.

What were the chances this woman would keep it secret? Brian didn't want to find out.

Bill scooted in between Teresa and his son. "Well, everything's fine on the home front. So, what have I missed?"

Before Teresa could speak, Brian said, "I'll fill you in later. Right now, Mrs. Vilanova is driving us to the Kalispell City Airport."

"Well, that's great. It'll give us a chance to talk."

"We need to do that," Teresa said, then turned to the exit and motioned for them to follow. "I parked the car outside."

She strode towards the exit but stopped at the high-capacity revolving glass doors. "Wait a second," she said and lit a cigarette. The lines around her mouth tightened as she inhaled deeply and blew a long plume of smoke toward the ceiling while annoyed travelers skirted around her.

"All right, let's go," she said and entered the central shaft of the rotating doors.

Bill attempted to follow her but Brian grabbed his arm and pulled him back.

"Don't tell her about Triple Divide."

"Why not? It'll give her some hope. You see how she is, don't you?"

Brian squeezed harder. "I'm asking you. I don't have time to go through my reasons."

"But I don't see —"

"Dad!"

Bill stared at his son's face. "You're leading this mission."

Brian's grip eased. "Thanks."

Outside the terminal, Teresa knocked on the plate-glass window. With her cigarette dangling from her lips, she waved for them to hurry. Then she plucked the cigarette from her mouth and screamed, "Are you coming?"

People around her reacted to her loud voice with astonished or disapproving looks.

Bill shouted back as he and Brian hurried through the revolving door. "We're right behind you."

After stowing their equipment in Teresa's rented Ford Focus, Brian and Bill slipped into the car. Bill sat in the front passenger seat and Brian hunkered down in the back.

When Teresa put the transmission into gear, the car lurched forward. "The City Airport is south of here on Route 93, so we need to go through Kalispell to get there."

As the car exited the airport, Teresa steered onto the highway and cut off an airport van with the right-of-way. The van driver blasted his horn and swerved into the other lane.

"Calm down, why don't you?" she yelled, and turned to

Bill. "They drive too damn fast around here. It's why I don't own a car."

Bill noticed Teresa's breath smelled of alcohol, and she seemed more intent on looking at Brian in the rearview mirror than on the road ahead.

"Would you prefer I drive?"

"No, just relax. You had a long flight."

"Are you sure? I don't mind."

"No. Besides, I don't know if I'm covered if someone else drives this car and there's an accident."

When there's an accident, Bill thought as he watched the rental car veer slowly into the next lane. He jumped in his seat. "There's a car on your left!"

Teresa instantly pulled back into her lane and asked with a slight tremor in her voice, "Do you want the radio on?"

"No, thanks," Bill said, feeling uneasy about his prospects of making it to the city airport in one piece.

Teresa pulled her hand away from the dashboard and tried to rein in a stubborn strand of hair. The lit end of her cigarette came very close to her ear. "I listen to KDBR. It's a country station. You know, all crying, lying, meeting, cheating, loving, and leaving. They play mostly the new kids, but every month or so, they'll slip in a George Jones song just to keep us ex-Texans happy."

"What's the weather been like here?" Bill asked, hoping a little conversation would calm the jittery driver.

"Pretty cold, especially at night, but it's colder in the mountains. Lucky, we're in a dry spell, and the last I heard, there's no rain or snow for the next few days."

"That's good."

Teresa rubbed her mouth and chin, then took a long drag on

her cigarette.

"You're going to find Alex, aren't you?"

"I won't lie to you. It's a big country out there, and your son has a head start. But Brian and I are both military men. I served as a Green Beret at the end of the Vietnam War. And Brian is Alex's team sergeant, so he knows him better than probably anybody else in this world other than you. He knows how he thinks, acts, and maneuvers in rough terrain. I wouldn't have come out here unless I believed my son could find yours."

Teresa looked over at Bill and nodded. "I guess not."

Teresa's eyes returned to the road, and she steadied the car. Her fingers tapped the steering wheel, and she hummed a song just under her breath, ignoring the trailer truck wanting to pass her. Every few minutes, she muttered a drawn-out "shit" as if an alien thought invaded her musing.

Bill relaxed and stared out his window. He observed the green sign announcing Kalispell and the gradual shift from sparse terrain to congested urban sprawl. From his previous trips there, he knew Kalispell was the Squalish tribe's name for "prairie above the lake," an apt description for this town built on flat land surrounded by majestic mountains and Montana's largest lake. But gas stations, fast-food restaurants, chain motels, and Going-Out-of-Business signs scarred the route they traveled today. Bill felt pity for the beautiful town he remembered.

Bill closed his tired eyes. The flights had taken a lot out of him, and the day was not over. Despite what he had told Brian, he was concerned he might be a drag on his son. Increasingly these days, he felt his age. He sometimes suffered morning aches, slow-to-heal nicks and scratches, sore muscles after a day's work, impaired hearing, forgetfulness, and a litany of other insults to his self-esteem. Now, he felt his head drooping and his mind slipping into slumber.

Suddenly, he heard his name called.

When he opened his eyes, he saw Teresa staring at him. "Bill?" she said again.

Bill waited for the question, but when it didn't arrive, he asked, "What is it?"

Teresa gripped the wheel. "I was just thinking about what you said before, about finding Alex and all that. But, is there anything else you forgot to tell me?"

Bill removed his arm from the back of Teresa's seat and noticed Brian sitting up straight and staring at him. "What do you mean?"

"I don't know. Call it a mother's intuition, but you two seem so sure you're going to find my son. I know you must have a plan. After all, you rented a helicopter. You didn't contact the rangers. And when I asked my question a couple of seconds ago, your son sprang up quicker than a prairie dog spotting a coyote."

Bill fought the urge to turn and glance at Brian. "I don't know what to tell you."

"Try telling the truth."

Brian leaned over the opening between the two front seats. "Mrs. Vilanova —"

"You stay out of this. I was speaking to your father."

She added, "Mr. McEnroe, you're a parent. You know what it's like to be one. All I'm asking is for you to tell me the truth."

Bill hunched his shoulders. "Well, I don't know what you want."

Teresa stopped the Ford in the middle of the street. The drivers behind them waited a few cautious seconds, but then blasted their horns. Unfazed, Teresa directed her anger at Bill. "What are you trying to hide? What's going on?"

Bill pointed at the vehicles behind them. "But the traffic. . ."

"You think I care about those drivers? I don't care about anything right now but my son."

Bill shook his head. "I can't help you."

"Then, we're not moving."

"But I don't know what you want."

Teresa pressed back against her seat and crossed her arms.

Brian leaned over the front seat. "Mrs. Vilanova —"

"Stay out of this."

More horns sounded.

Brian leaned over his father's seat. "Tell her, Dad."

Bill twisted his body to face Brian.

The younger man's face was calm. "If the only way to get to the airport on time is to tell her, that's what we do."

The older man nodded. "Teresa, drive. I'll tell you everything."

Teresa put the Focus back into Drive and pressed down on the gas, only to apply the brakes again, curse, and put the transmission into Park.

"You drive," she said, then stepped out of the vehicle and stormed to the passenger side.

As the cars and trucks behind them resumed their horn symphony, Bill slid over to the driver's side and shifted into gear. When Teresa sat down next to him and slammed the door, he drove forward at a quick clip. He sped through a yellow light, hoping the furious motorists behind him wouldn't be able to follow.

CHAPTER TWENTY-NINE

S o, tell me what's going on," Teresa said.

Bill glanced at the rearview mirror and the image of Brian in the back seat staring out the side window. Bill's eyes returned to the road. "We think we know Alex's destination in Glacier. It's a place called Triple Divide Peak. I was there a long time ago. If I'm right, we can beat him to the spot and stop him before he does something stupid."

"How do you know he'll go there?"

"I don't, not really. But in the letter Alex mentioned he was going to a place where the waters of three oceans meet. That can only be Triple Divide Peak."

"You knew this, and you didn't tell me until I dragged it out of you. Why?"

Bill didn't answer.

Teresa would not relent, her face and voice growing more inflamed as she repeated her question several times.

Brian's commanding voice stopped her. "Because I told him not to."

Teresa's eyes shot to Brian's. "You did what?"

"He wanted to tell you, but I told him not to."

Teresa stared at him with fire in her eyes. "You told him not to tell me the truth? Who do you think you are? Why don't you want me to know?"

"I can't trust you."

Teresa looked pained. "I'm his mother!"

Brian shook his head. "I don't want to go there."

"Tell me."

Brian looked her square in the eye. "Mrs. Vilanova, you don't want to know."

"But I do. Tell me."

"Because Alex told me you have a drinking problem."

Teresa looked as if someone had sucker-punched her in the gut.

Bill leaned over. "I was wrong not to tell you."

She hung her head.

"I didn't mean to hurt your feelings, Mrs. Vilanova," Brian said. "Alex loves you. He told me lots of times how much you mean to him. But the rangers will question you. And you might say something that —"

Teresa interrupted. "You don't trust me. I get it. Maybe I deserve your suspicion. But I can help you. I want to."

Brian leaned forward. "You are. By taking us to the airport."

"It's not enough. I want to do more."

"Maybe you can. "

"Let me."

"OK. First, keep everything we've told you a secret. Whatever the rangers say to you, don't tell them about Triple Divide. The last thing we want is to have a bunch of strangers surround Alex on the mountain. It could be dangerous for both Alex and the rangers. And second, keep in touch with the rangers, find out what is going on with their search, and give us updates. We have a satellite phone so you can call us when we're in Glacier."

"I can do that. But will you keep me informed about your search?"

Brian hesitated before answering. "I will."

"No matter what happens?"

"No matter."

Teresa wiped her eyes, then placed her hand on Bill's arm. "Bill?"

"Yes?"

"You're going the wrong way. You missed the turn back there."

"I did?"

"Yes. Make a left here."

"Thanks." He chuckled. "I'm glad you told me."

"Thanks for driving."

"My pleasure."

On the last stretch of road toward Kalispell City Airport, Teresa and Bill carried on a conversation while Brian spread out in the back seat of the Ford. For several minutes, he reviewed his topographical map, then folded it and peered at his father. It had been years since Brian sat in the back of a car and closely observed his dad. His father had aged. A lot. His once imposing figure had grown smaller and frailer over the last several years.

Brian grew up believing his dad would never get old like his friends' fathers, who settled and sagged in their middle years like houses built on sand. He admired his dad; always aspired to be like him. His father was a man's man, a man of many skills, of character, who accomplished much, but always shared the credit. "If you need the applause, join the theater," was his favorite saying.

Now Brian saw his father in a new light and worried about putting his old man in danger on his watch. He had already lost one man, two if you counted Aarmaan. He'd risk his own life to save Alex's, but he didn't want to risk his father's.

The thought reminded Brian of something else. Where are you, Jenner? he wondered. Why don't you call back? Could've used you, you son-of-a-bitch.

Brian pictured Jenner just before he left Fayetteville on his Harley. He had that self-satisfied cock-sure grin of his. It was the same grin Jenner displayed in a team photo, taken back in August at their base in Afghanistan. The image showed the men smiling in the sweltering heat, posing with heavy weapons, their team unscathed after fifty missions. Jenner and Brian stood posing on opposite ends, the acknowledged linchpins of the best team in the Unit.

What happened to us? He thought. The incident in the village had thrown their world upside-down. It didn't seem real to him that one man was dead, one was bonkers, and the other was missing in action. The team had its heart ripped from its chest. How long had it taken? Seconds? Minutes? Aarmaan fired his gun. Hector fell to the ground. Jenner picked up Hector and ran. Alex leaned over Aarmaan and begged me to bring his body with them.

"Brian?" Bill called out.

"What?"

"I thought you said something."

"No. I was just daydreaming."

Bill pointed ahead. "You see those radio towers? That must be the airport."

When they reached the airport entrance, Bill made the turn and saw a sign for Hawk Aviation.

"Is that it, Brian?" Bill asked.

"That's it."

When they reached the building that housing Hawk Aviation, Bill stopped the engine and popped the trunk. While Brian pulled out their gear, Bill thanked Teresa for the ride.

"Here are your keys. Drive carefully."

"And you be careful. Take care of our sons."

She gave him a peck on his cheek, then skirted around the Ford to say goodbye to Brian. He promised he would keep her informed, and they exchanged numbers. Teresa hugged him awkwardly and hurried to the driver's side. She slid behind the wheel and started the engine.

"Bye, boys," she called out and pulled away with a tire-squealing exit.

"God help the pedestrians," Brian said in jest.

"She's all right," Bill said. "You never know how much steel is in someone's backbone until you put weight on it."

"Maybe. I just hope she keeps quiet about Triple Divide."

"She will."

Bill picked up a pack and slung it over his shoulder. "Well, it's just you and me now."

His father's remark made Brian think of Jenner again. Despite his hopes, his right-hand man did not show up at the airport, and he certainly wasn't here. From here on out, Brian would put Jenner out of his mind. It made no sense to dwell on what the mission lacked. He would go forward, alone, and concentrate on keeping his father safe.

The thought made him uneasy.

CHAPTER THIRTY

Jenner watched the distance evaporate between him and his prey. He estimated it would take him one day — maybe two — before he caught up to his comrade-in-arms.

But he needed to get some rest. Hunting humans demanded mental sharpness. Getting strung-out led to mistakes. Besides, changes in Alex's stride showed signs of an injury. From experience, Jenner knew that wounded prey lost ground no matter the terrain. The search party still posed a threat, but Jenner was not overly concerned about that point. He had covered his and Alex's trails and created many false trails. At this moment, rangers were probably scratching their heads. Unless they had dogs.

Experienced tracking dogs worried Jenner the most. In Hollywood movies, the fugitive hero always throws dogs off the scent, but Jenner was aware that a dog trained to track humans possessed abilities and traits that made evasion almost impossible. Though a dog's eyesight and stamina fared no better than his, and maybe even worse, its hearing and sense of smell performed far better. A dog's hearing surpassed a human's forty times over. Its ability to smell was at least a thousand times greater. A good tracking dog could detect and locate a human scent even when the search dragged on for days. And walking in a stream would not deter a good dog because it could sniff the air above the water for the minute skin particles humans shed all the time. And the breeds most used for tracking — labs, shepherds, and hounds — stayed naturally curious and eager to please, so evasion techniques that would frustrate and slow a human tracker only encouraged tracking dogs to try harder.

Jenner knew he could defeat even the strongest opponent by attacking its strength. Before he left Kalispell, he had purchased a package of copper sulfate powder in the garden supply section of the local Walmart. Most customers bought the powder to kill algae in their ponds, but Jenner knew that the potent emetic would stop dogs in their tracks when spread in places they were most likely to sniff, including tracks. The canines would vomit so fast, and for so long, the only thing to do was to take them back home to recover.

Take a good sniff, pooches, Jenner joked to himself and sprinkled powder behind him on the path.

He scanned the rocks until he found a shallow cave that would make a perfect camp for the night. He settled in and lit a small lantern to ward off the approaching darkness. In the light, he opened a zip-lock bag and poured a thin sliver of crushed green marijuana leaves and seeds onto a sheet of cigarette paper laying flat on his lap. He rolled the sheet and its contents, licked the ends, and sealed the joint. He lit the blunt, inhaled, held the bitter smoke in his lungs, and exhaled slowly.

"Too bad Hammer doesn't smoke this shit more often. He wouldn't have slipped off the deep end if he did."

His thoughts flipped to that night in the village. "Alex, Alex, the Hammer Man. You should've watched the terp. Or you should have let me know what was going on. You knew something was wrong."

Jenner accepted the fact that the team he loved was an artifact of the past. Hector was gone. The Army was bound to discharge or hospitalize Alex. New guys would take their places, but the team would never be the same. Their crazy string of successful missions, the bond they had — all gone. Dead and buried, like Hector.

In the past, he lived for his fellow warriors and was willing to die for them. He had tried to hold their broken team together, tried to pull Alex back into the fold, especially in the last days before they flew out of Afghanistan. But no matter how hard he willed it, he had failed. And he felt Alex deserved most of the blame.

But Jenner faulted Brian as well. He was like a brother to him, but, in Jenner's estimation, his team sergeant exemplified the by-the-book soldier who followed the rules of engagement like a lemming. What did the generals who make the rules know about this kind of war? Many were just pencil pushers. When they fought as young men, it was a different enemy, a different war. The enemy doesn't play by the rules, so why should they?

He held his joint up in the air as if holding a torch and bellowed the Army cry, "Hooah!"

In his mind, he was a far better leader than Brian. The Army should have selected him — not Brian — as team sergeant. No one meant more to the team's success. He took the boldest risks. When necessary, he had the guts to bend the rules to extract information from prisoners. And he was the guy who saved their lives more than once.

"Where would they be without me?"

Jenner took a deep pull on his joint, sucking the acrid smoke into his lungs, holding it there as long as possible, closing his eyes to heighten its effect, then expelling the spent air in a protracted, smooth release.

The dope was making him mellow.

CHAPTER THIRTY-ONE

The office for Hawk Aviation was at the end of a long, narrow corridor lined with black-and-white photographs of flying vehicles, ranging from hot-air balloons to stealth bombers. Above the glass entry door, someone had crudely painted a fierce bald eagle with wings and talons extended. The door creaked when Brian opened it, and as he followed his father into the room, the stale smell of cheap tobacco smoke assaulted him. The office was a large square with no windows. On one side, radio equipment, thick manuals, loose papers, and a half-dozen coffee cups nearly covered a long table. On the other side of the room, a dumpy green sofa and two metal chairs formed a less-than-inviting sitting area. Flourescent lighting cast a harsh light from the ceiling.

"Come in," a voice boomed from the back of the room where a burly man half-rose to welcome them. He reached out his hand to shake theirs, then invited them to sit across from him at a large, mahogany campaign desk.

"I'm Chet Hawkins, the owner and pilot. Which one of you is Brian McEnroe?" Hawkins asked. Before Brian could answer, Hawkins added, "I have the rental forms all ready for you, and I took the liberty of preparing your credit slip with the information you sent me. All you do is sign."

Hawkins pushed the unsigned credit card slip and pen toward Brian and drawled, "You boys aren't terrorists, are you?"

Brian examined Hawkins' bulldog-like face — the bloodshot eyes, the hanging jowls, the close-cropped hair, and protruding lower teeth — and questioned whether the owner of Hawk

Aviation was joking or not.

The man looked dead serious.

Hawkins leaned forward over his desk dressed in khaki cargo pants, a red sweatshirt, and a leather bomber jacket, waiting for his answer. Short and sturdily built, the man's fireplug body perfectly complemented his face.

Brian silently took stock of the helicopter owner, a surly bastard who expected answers to his questions.

Brian slid the signed merchant's copy and the pen back to the man. "Mr. Hawkins, do we look like terrorists?"

Hawkins placed the receipt in a desk drawer and pronounced, "You ask a tough question, son. If I were plotting something bad, I wouldn't send somebody who looked like Saddam Hussein, if you know what I mean. No sir. I'd send a little old lady or an All-American-looking man who looks like Channing Tatum. Somebody like you."

"And why would terrorists want to fly to Glacier Park?"

Hawkins chewed on Brian's question for a moment and let out a belly laugh. "You got me there, son." He paused and then continued. "But I guess that still leaves me with a puzzle. Why would somebody spend all this money to rent a chopper to take them to the outskirts of the park to get to a gravel road taking them to a campground that closed almost a month ago? It doesn't compute in my mind."

"You have the money, Hawkins. Does it matter why?"

Hawkins flinched. "Well, let me think about your question. The economy is rotten in these parts and business is slow. Few hunters nowadays have the wherewithal to pay high prices for easy access to the Bob Marshall Wilderness. And God knows tourism remains way off at this time of the year. My only income lately is for training lessons, and they come as infrequently as tax refunds. I already laid off two of my pilots. I guess I can't afford to lose the rental fee you agreed to pay."

Brian clasped his hands. "Well, good then."

Hawkins interrupted him with a self-satisfied snicker. "On the other hand, it's for good reason my wife complains I'm too damn nosey for my own good. It may not matter to you, but I have an FAA license. I need to be sure I'm not doing anything that will get me into any trouble."

Brian's mouth tightened. "My father and I are only interested in backpacking. We're not asking you to fly us into the National Park or break any laws. We're only asking you to fly us to a spot outside the park leased by a friend of yours from the Flathead Nation. You said he leased it for grazing cattle, and it's no problem for you to land there."

"That's what I said."

"So, how can you get in trouble?"

"I don't know." The bulldog's face scrunched into cascading folds of flesh. "Well, why are we going at night?"

Brian remained calm. He noticed his father standing behind Hawkins, gazing at one of the many photos of hovering helicopters nailed to the walls. "Let's just say we're in a hurry and don't want to wait till morning to begin our journey. If we weren't in a hurry, I would've rented a car at the airport and driven to Glacier."

"It's a long drive by car."

"Exactly. We're in a hurry."

Hawkins scratched his head and twisted his lips to the side as if he had bitten into something bitter. "And does this escapade have anything to do with that soldier the authorities are searching for?"

"Hawkins . . ."

"I mean, you look military, and you don't have any way to get back and —"

Brian barked, "Hawkins!"

The bulldog's eyes opened wide.

Brian leaned over the desk and pointed his finger at the man's chest. "Why we want to go into Glacier, and how we get back, doesn't concern you. We both signed a contract for this flight. Your only concern should be how to fly us there quickly and safely. Can we start on that? I mean, right now."

Red-faced, the copter pilot pushed back his chair and turned to Bill, who stared at him. He rubbed his mouth and turned back to Brian and stood up. "This way, Gentlemen," he said as he circled his desk and picked up two of his passengers' bags.

Bill and Brian followed Hawkins out the back door with the rest of their gear to a small landing pad where a sky-blue copter with red striping and lettering along its side waited. A bubble of what looked like tempered glass gave the cabin an open design, and the copter's long thin fuselage and cambered tail gave it the look of a huge dragonfly. Even more impressive was the chopper's pristine quality. It was as clean as Hawkins' office was dirty.

"That's a beautiful bird," Brian said.

"Thanks. It's my prize."

"It's a Robinson R44-II, isn't it?"

Hawkins registered both surprise and pleasure. "Ah, you know it?"

"I flew one in Lebanon several years ago. The Lebanese army uses them. They hold up and the fuel-injected engines perform almost as well as turbines."

Hawkins nodded. "It's a good bang for the buck and flies well at higher altitudes."

"How long have you been flying choppers, Hawkins?"

"Twenty-one years, mostly in Alaska. I moved down here and started this business five years ago when my wife's mother got Alzheimer's. It's tough sometimes."

Hawkins stowed the gear underneath the seats and opened the doors. "Who's going to sit up front with me? What about you, soldier?"

He was looking at Brian, who answered. "Sure."

Hawkins zipped up his jacket and climbed in. He waited for Brian and Bill to join him in the cramped cabin.

"I have a heater, but it still gets cold in the cabin, so I suggest you button up. And soldier, just a caution: Don't knock into the cyclic tube at your feet there. I once had a teenager pull up on it and ask, 'What is this?' He nearly killed his parents and me with that maneuver."

Brian said, "Maybe it was intentional."

Hawkins' bushy eyebrows lifted in surprise, but then spread when he got the joke. His belly laugh exploded against the windshield. "That's a good one. You got me there, soldier."

***

During the short flight, the men didn't attempt at first to speak over the loud beating of the rotors. Brian gazed at the rising mountains on his left and the limitless prairie on his right. The sky appeared a purplish canvas of light and dark shadows. They passed over two pockets of bright lights, and Brian surmised those were the towns of East Glacier and Browning. The only other lights he saw came from intermittent vehicles rolling down a desolate stretch of road leading to nowhere. He leaned back in his seat and listened to the beating heart of the copter.

Suddenly, Hawkins' loud voice punctured the drone of the

rotors. "We're coming in for a landing."

Brian peered downward at the darkness. "Aren't you going to turn on your landing lights?"

"No, I just use my navigation lights in this kind of darkness. The landing lights are so bright my eyes can't adjust quickly enough."

Brian deferred to Hawkins's judgment and relaxed, noticing how the wash of the chopper's blades kicked up the dust of the dry prairie. The copter landed softly on the parched ground, and the men waited while the rotors slowed and stilled. "Here's your landing zone, soldier. Good luck in whatever the hell you're doing."

He thrust out his hand, and Brian shook it. "Thanks. Where's Cut Bank Creek Road?"

"It's about fifty yards to your left. I would have tried to land on the damn thing, but it's too narrow. I'm a good pilot, but not that good."

As soon as Brian and Bill's gear were out of the way, Hawkins and his copter took off. The McEnroes picked up their bags and made their way to where the gravel road entered the National Park. They stood facing each other in the center of the barren lane.

Brian examined his father's weather-beaten face. "So here we are."

"Yep, I'm ready whenever you are."

"You know, I could do this alone. We could walk to the Ranger Station, and you could probably get a ride back to Kalispell tomorrow."

"I could, but I thought you wanted to avoid the rangers."

"I do."

"Then we keep to the plan. We follow the creek, circumvent

the station, hook up to the trail at the campground, and hike into the Pass where we spend the night."

Brian sighed. "Shall we go?"

"Just a minute." Bill reached into his breast pocket for a pen flashlight and a five-by-seven-inch wire-bound book. He lit the flashlight and randomly opened the book to a page. "Years ago, all the Outward Bound instructors at Hurricane Island got together and shared all the quotes we used over the years to inspire and sustain ourselves and our teams. We collected them into this little book of readings. It's a tradition to read one when we start a new expedition. What say we do that now?"

Brian looked out into the darkness. He wanted to get moving, but a couple of minutes wouldn't matter. "Sure."

His father looked over the opened page for a suitable quote and picked one by Jack London, which he read:

I would rather be ashes than dust!
I would rather my sparks should burn out in a blaze
* than it should be stifled by dry-rot.*
I would rather be a superb meteor, every atom of me in
* magnificent glow, than asleep and permanent as a planet.*
The proper function of man is to live, not to exist.
I shall not waste my days trying to prolong them.
I shall use my time.

Bill closed the book, shut off the light, and stuffed both into his pocket. "Enough said. Let's go, son."

CHAPTER THIRTY-TWO

Someone or something was tracking him.

Alex didn't see or hear anything out of the ordinary. He didn't know why the suspicion crossed his mind. But something lurked behind him in the dark. He felt its presence in his gut. His body screamed at him to act, to run. But something else, perhaps his Army training or his time in the Hindu Kush, warned the opposite. Don't run. Stop. Pay attention.

He stood still and gave himself up to his senses. He was on a goat path covered with smooth grey scree making the footing unstable in the night's darkness. A flagging breeze whispered. The smell of something musty and foul hung in the air. Muted, mixed, and foreign sounds surrounded him. He felt danger but couldn't identify its shape or proximity.

He wondered what he should do. He could run, but it was dark, and the path was treacherous. If an animal stalked him, running would only trigger a chase reflex. If it were a man, it would be best to meet him face-to-face in a place of Alex's choosing. Whatever's out there, he knew he had to wait for it.

In the moon's pale light, Alex searched for a spot from which he could see the goat path while hidden. Up ahead, he spotted a shrub oak growing out of a crack in the side of a ledge about twelve feet above the path. From that height, he could watch his surroundings while waiting for his stalker to show.

Though it hurt to do so, he hauled himself up to the oak. He took out his knife and placed it on the ground within easy reach. Quietly, he picked up two baseball-sized stones to serve as missiles. He held one stone in each hand. He was cold, exhausted, thirsty, and in pain, but he was alive. For the first time in a month, it felt good to be alive. He wasn't ready to give up or give in just yet. At the moment, he yearned for life.

"If you're tracking me, come, let's get it over with," he muttered under his breath.

For several minutes, he waited. Then he spotted a shadow creeping along the path. Whatever it was, it wasn't human. It stalked him, moving forward, then pausing, getting closer each time. When it was close, he still couldn't hear it. He sensed the beast heard or smelled him because it stopped moving forward and sank to the ground. It lay flat and lifted its head to sniff the air. As it did, Alex recognized what it was. A mountain lion poised to attack.

The cat crouched about twenty feet away, close enough to reach him in seconds. It pulled its ears back, and its eyes glowed in the moonlight. Its right eye was clouded over and hemmed in by a long, jagged scar. The animal made no sound. Its head flattened against the ground. Its sinewy shoulders tightened and prepared to spring. Alex realized the cougar had probably followed him for some time, intending to sneak up on him from behind and pounce. But it was face-to-face now with a large man and was wary.

But it was still hungry.

Facing death rarely terrified Alex. He had faced it so many times in the Hindu Kush that it had lost its power. But those threats emanated from an enemy who looked like him. This was different. The one yellow cat eye that stared up at him saw him as food, and the thought made Alex shiver.

Alex didn't wait for the cougar to attack. He rose to his full height, lifted his arms as high as possible to appear larger, then hurled a heavy stone at the cat while yelling "Ayala!" The projectile rocketed through the air and slammed into the animal's shoulder. Surprised, the big cat yelped, jumped back, and snarled. Alex roared back and threw a second stone, which missed its mark but caused a dust explosion in front of the angry mountain lion.

The cougar turned tail and fled.

Alex lifted his arms above his head and roared a guttural sound that was a mix of pain and triumph. His first throw had probably hurt him as much as it did the cat, but he didn't care. He had faced off with a powerful predator in its element, and he had won.

"I didn't have a gun, you beautiful animal." He crowed repeatedly and feebly danced a makeshift jig. After several turns, he sank to his knees, winded and in pain. With effort, he propped himself against the shrub oak, where he contemplated his victory. Despite his conquest, he realized that the world hadn't changed. The moon and stars still hung in the heavens. The stream continued to flow downhill. Time went on. The path to Triple Divide lay ahead, waiting for him.

He pushed his rucksack against a rock, stretched out, and rested his head. His eyes closed and his body relaxed. He knew the cougar wouldn't return. Easier prey existed out there in the darkness.

Alex felt himself sinking into sleep. He would sleep tonight and walk in the daylight tomorrow. As he drifted off, he knew he'd make it to the summit of Triple Divide Peak. Within minutes, he was sound asleep.

CHAPTER THIRTY-THREE

It was past midnight when Brian remembered his promise to Teresa.

By that time, Brian and his father had trekked to the Pass, selected a secluded spot off the trail, set up camp, and reconned the area. Triple Divide Peak loomed over their heads and blocked their view of the moon. Frost had settled on the ground. The stiff wind howled through the Pass, forcing them to raise their voices as they talked.

"Do you think I should call Alex's mom?" Brian asked his father, who was stowing away the last of their provisions to keep them safe from nocturnal intruders. "It's late, but I told her I'd call."

Bill looked at his watch. "12:17? Not too late. I think you should call. Otherwise, she'll worry. And who knows? Maybe she's heard something from the rangers."

Brian extracted the satellite phone from his pack and made the call.

A frantic voice answered. "Hello?"

"It's Brian McEnroe."

"Thank God."

"I'm sorry I called so late."

"No, it's all right."

"Are you sure?"

"I've been waiting for your call. I tried to reach you."

"Sorry, Mrs. Vilanova. I turned our handset off to preserve the battery. We have no way to charge it if it gets drained, and

I didn't bring a spare."

"Where are you?"

He paused. His tendency to keep tactics close to his chest had kicked in. But then he remembered he had given her his word.

"We're close to the eastern approach to the summit of Triple Divide. We'll camp here tonight in the Pass. At dawn, we'll make our ascent of the peak."

"And do you think my son might already be on the summit?"

"It's possible, but my father thinks he's probably still on his way. We will make sure, though. Any word from the rangers?"

"I spoke to the ranger captain at half-past seven. He believes Alex is near the Going to the Sun Road near the St. Mary's area. They have dog teams, mounted rangers, volunteers, and a helicopter, all looking for him."

The news surprised Brian. St. Mary's was a long way from Triple Divide. "Did they spot him?"

"No, and the captain said 'We'll find him' so many times I figured he has no idea where Alex is."

"Glacier has sixteen hundred square miles of wilderness in which to hide, Mrs. Vilanova. Finding someone in so large an area is tough, even for a seasoned search party."

"But you'll find him, won't you?"

Brian paused before answering. He believed Alex was nearby. Given where Alex went off the trail, his best route to Triple Divide Peak was via the eastern approach. To take that route, he had to come through this area where Brian and his father had set up camp. Tonight, Brian would take turns with his father, keeping watch for Alex. At sunrise, if they had not met up with him, they'd hike to the summit to make sure he had not gotten ahead of them. If they had no luck on the mountain, they would head back down the same way and search for his tracks.

"We're bound to meet up with him tomorrow or the next day," said Brian.

"Thank God."

"Well, I guess that's all."

"Someone else called."

"Who?"

Teresa made a trilling noise with her lips. "Let's see. I wrote his name and number down somewhere."

Brian heard her rummaging through what he assumed was her bag. He overheard her cursing and the clanking of metal objects thrown down on what sounded like a glass table. His patience wore thin as she muttered a string of curse words. Finally, she spoke. "I found it. His name is Captain Nicholas Sowinski. Do you know him?"

"I never heard his name before. Did he say where he was from and what he wanted?"

"No, he just said he was from the Army and wanted to speak to Alex. When I told him what was happening — don't worry, I didn't tell him anything you told me — he said he would send someone to meet with me tomorrow . . . I mean today, no later than four."

"What was the number he gave you?" He motioned to his father to prepare to write.

"703-806-0416."

Brian repeated the number slowly so that Bill could jot it down. It surprised him it wasn't a Fayetteville area number. If his memory served him, the 703 exchange was a Virginia number.

Who in Virginia would call? That state maintains dozens

of military installations, but Brian couldn't imagine an officer in one of them being interested in a lowly sergeant missing in Glacier Park. He'd call Captain Sowinski tomorrow and see what he could find out.

"Do you think it's something important?" Teresa asked, her words racing ahead of her.

"I don't know. That the Army is sending someone to talk to you tells me they *think* it's important."

"Jesus, this whole thing is a nightmare."

"Don't worry. It's probably nothing."

"You know I hate the word 'probably.' Whenever my ex-husband wanted to get his pecker into another woman, he'd say, 'I'll be home for dinner, probably.'"

From her slurred speech, Brian guessed Teresa was drunk. "Mrs. Vilanova, there's not much more we can do tonight. Why don't you get some sleep?"

"Ok, I'll call you tomorrow."

"No, I'll call you late afternoon," he said with an edge in his voice. "It will make things easier."

Teresa didn't answer right away, and Brian wondered if he had ticked her off. Every time he came back from overseas, he noticed how civilians reacted to something he said or how he said it. In a war zone, men and women learned to talk with each other in a direct, no-frills way. When they returned to the States, they found it awkward to communicate with non-military people. It was as if soldiers and civilians spoke different languages. And the soldier always bore the burden of adapting. For Brian, it meant he had to exercise vigilance all the time. What words should he use with Kate and his family to avoid a misunderstanding? What does he say when a driver cuts him off, or a store clerk makes a joke about his uniform? How might the stranger in the local bar interpret his tone of voice?

The silence on the other end of the line was disconcerting.

"Mrs. Vilanova?

"I'm here."

"Are you OK? Remember to call me."

She hung up.

When Brian lowered the phone, his father said, "You look troubled. What is it?"

"I'm not sure. An officer tried to reach Alex. When he heard about Alex in Glacier, he told Mrs. Vilanova that he'd send someone to talk to her."

Abruptly, he stopped talking and dialed the Virginia number. "Let me try something."

The phone on the other end rang three times, and an automated voice broke in. "You have reached the headquarters of the United States Army Criminal Investigation Command. We are currently unavailable. If you want to leave a message, please wait for the beep, and we will return your call as soon as possible."

Brian ended the call and pondered this latest development. The CID was the agency that investigated violations of civilian and military law within the U.S. Army. Their agents operated in the United States and around the world.

Brian turned to his father. "Bad news. The number you wrote is for the CID."

Puzzled, Bill shook his head. "Would they get into a case involving a missing soldier in Glacier?"

"It seems unlikely. Glacier is federal property, but why the interest in a lost soldier? It's got me worried."

Bill nodded and stood up. "I hope my hunch about Alex heading for Triple Divide Peak isn't just an old man's foolish notion."

Brian nudged his father towards the tent. "Get some sleep."

Turning halfway around, Bill said, "Are you coming?"

"You go ahead. I'll be right there."

Bill retired to the tent, and Brian retreated to a spot where he could get a better view of the Pass. The night made visibility minimal, but he stared into the darkness, anyway. Gradually, he discerned the unmistakable sweep of sleeping giants lying on their sides. Mountains had always made him feel small yet part of something big. He guessed Alex felt the same way. Otherwise, why was he here? This sacred place didn't need stained glass windows, marble columns, or The Stations of the Cross. The sky was its dome. The mountains were its walls. This was a place of deliverance.

"I'm going to find you, Alex. I promise."

CHAPTER THIRTY-FOUR

The next morning, Jenner worried that another hunter might have beaten him to Alex.

Since dawn, he had followed Alex's tracks until he came to a place where they intermingled with the prints of a giant cat. The tracks bore the unmistakable signs of a mountain lion. On each paw, there were four toes and three distinct lobes, and the hind pads stepped into the imprints left by the front paws. Based on the breadth and depth of the prints, Jenner estimated the animal was over eight feet long and weighed about two hundred pounds. The cougar's tracks were as fresh as Alex's, a sign the cat had been close to overtaking him. If the mountain lion had attacked from the rear, as they usually do, his friend was already dead.

Without making a sound, Jenner took out his semi-automatic pistol. The goat path took a sharp turn to the right about twenty yards ahead, so he prepared to fire once he turned the corner. Jenner's heart pumped fast, and his face flushed as he advanced. His breathing grew choppy and rapid. A bead of sweat ran down his forehead and into his eye. If the cat lurked just around the bend, Jenner would only have a second or two, if that, to get off a shot.

As he made the turn, he held the 9mm in front of him, ready to fire. But the path ahead was empty. He swiveled around to check his rear, but the path was clear. Maybe he was wrong about how close the big cat came to Alex. Jenner bent down and noticed how the cat's tracks proceeded towards him, then veered off the path and up the steep slope. Alex's tracks continued up the path in the opposite direction.

Jenner scratched his head and tried to make sense of the signs. Then the truth dawned on him. The mountain lion had run away from Alex. The tracks did not lie.

Given how big the cat was, it must have been a mature, experienced killer and not scared off easily. "I give you credit, Hammer. I don't know how you did it, but you get the Shackleton award from me."

He holstered his Beretta. "When I find your sorry ass alive, I'll give the award to you personally."

Within five minutes, Jenner had scouted the area and found the place where Alex had waited for the mountain lion. From a perch so high, Jenner imagined Alex could easily keep his eye on the big cat while making his body look bigger and more threatening than it really was.

He took off his cap and smacked it against his thigh. "Great fucking job holding the high ground, bro'."

Jenner swigged water from his canteen. The water tasted sweet in his mouth. He swirled the last mouthful, raised his chin skyward, and spat the clear liquid out like a stone cherub in a garden fountain. The stream fell on the dry earth in front of the shrub oak, darkening the ground.

He withdrew the binoculars from his pack and sat cross-legged, scanning the valley below and the ridge above. Below him, Hudson Bay Creek meandered through the valley like a silvery snake. On either side of him, high snow-covered peaks towered, blinding in the sun. To his left, he saw a herd of Rocky Mountain elk — a bull and twenty cows and calves — traversing the slope on the other side of the valley. Above him, a V-shaped flock of black-billed trumpeter swans crossed the blue cloudless sky, piercing the silence with their hollow nasal honking. But he saw no signs of Alex.

Jenner dropped the binoculars to his waist, where they dangled on a leather strap. He imagined an injured Alex, pumped up after confronting the cougar and focused like a laser gun on some target only he knew. Though Jenner couldn't see Alex, Jenner knew his friend was out there in the clash of rock and dirt. He squeezed his eyes shut and sniffed, half-wishing he could detect Alex's scent, but recognizing only his own body odor and the ever-present whiff of pine. Frustrated, he leaned back on his elbows and felt the hard ground beneath him.

Jenner had begun his endgame. His quarry was close. It was only a matter of time. He'd find Alex, then make sure that Hammer wouldn't tell anyone what he knew.

CHAPTER THIRTY-FIVE

As Bill prepared to make breakfast, he heard a rustling sound emanating from his tent. He tip-toed to its entrance, where he peeled back the inner flap and peeked inside. He saw his weathered leather boots trembling in the corner. Two furry rumps filled the openings like rolled-up wool socks.

"Marmots!" Bill wailed, then snatched one boot. Two startled rodents let out a shrill whistle, shot out of the boots, and scrambled through a hole they had chewed in the tent. Bill lunged for them, fell into the tent, and rolled over.

Brian peeked through the opening and covered his mouth to suppress a laugh. "Are you OK?"

His father pushed up on his elbows and grinned. "Only my pride hurts."

Bill crawled out of the tent with his boots in hand, and Brian helped him to his feet. Bill turned his boots over so Brian could see their shredded inner linings. "The little devils gnawed on them pretty good."

"Marmots like leather?"

"Not leather. Sweat. They love the salt in sweat. A similar thing happened to me in the Canadian Rockies a long time ago. A mule deer snatched one of my boots and I never saw it again. You would've thought I'd learned my lesson, but I guess the only thing worse than a fool is an old fool."

Brian took over the duties of making breakfast while his father traded his sandals for the marmot-damaged footwear. Brian had no time for his father's silliness. He came here to find

Alex, not to mess around with rodents. He couldn't let anything divert him from that one overriding goal. As he scrambled the eggs, he peered down the Red Eagle Valley, which was a palette of greens, reds, yellows, and a dab of orange. At the far end, Split Mountain dominated like a medieval fortress. In between, smaller peaks bordered each side, their slopes emblazoned with red mudstone.

"What do you see?" Bill asked, taking the pan from his son.

"I don't see Alex, if that's what you mean."

Bill ladled the eggs onto their plates. "I hoped we'd get lucky last night."

Brian took his plate and sat. "Lucky? Not yet. But today's the day. Let's eat breakfast."

Bill sat next to him. "We have eggs, dried fruit, and cowboy coffee."

"Sounds good, and probably tastes a lot better than leather boots."

Bill groaned at the joke and poured his son a cup of coffee.

As they ate breakfast, Brian lifted his head to view Triple Divide Peak. From this angle, the wedge-shaped peak rose hundreds of feet straight up and looked like the massive prow of a battleship. It cast a shadow over him, and he stood still, taking its measure. He'd scaled much higher mountains in the Hindu Kush, but he knew every mountain possessed its secrets and dangers.

Then he heard it.

"Hear that, Dad?"

Bill lifted his head. "Hear what?"

Brian turned to face his father. "That high-pitched sound. I heard it last night, too."

"I was too tired to hear anything last night. Now, I just hear my bones creaking."

"So, you hear nothing?"

Bill shook his head. "My hearing's not so good anymore. Maybe you hear the song of the sirens?"

"The what?"

"Ah, you don't remember. Sirens, the beautiful women who lured sailors and warriors to their death with their songs. When you were little, I took you sailing on a pulling boat and told you to listen for them. Do you remember me doing that?"

Brian scrunched his face. "Not really."

Bill's face reflected disappointment. "You were about ten. We watched a TV mini-series based on *The Odyssey*, and when the sirens sang, you ran out of the room."

Brian chuckled. "I was brave, even then."

"The sirens were scary. Odysseus plugged his men's ears, then lashed himself to his ship's mast to protect himself and his crew from their singing."

Brian listened for the sound, but it was gone. He heard the same sound in the Hindu Kush mountains. The Sirens' songs. The voices of the wind. Whatever they were, they stuck in his head when he returned home. He inserted the Hindu Kush mountains into conversations with people who knew nothing about them or cared to learn. They would listen to him drone on about the beauty of the glacier-fed lakes and the jasmine-like fragrance from ancient wild olive trees in bloom. He'd say the air is not as cold here as in the Kush, the sky is not as clear, and the colors are not as bright. People would look at him as if he came from the moon.

Brian pushed thoughts of the Kush away. "Is the coffee still hot?"

Bill poured more coffee into their cups. Brian took a sip. but

Bill didn't drink his. Instead, he held the cup between his hands to warm them. "I think I know what you mean about hearing sounds, but, for my buddies and me, it was the jungle, not the mountains, that left its mark. When I came back from 'Nam, the color green triggered all kinds of flashbacks. I'd pass a park or a woman in a green dress, and I'd suddenly smell the jungle all around me. It was mind-blowing."

Brian eyed his father, then put his cup down. "You never told me about your time in Vietnam."

His father looked down and didn't answer. Brian remembered when he was a little kid and hid behind the sofa one night while his father and his Army friends shared their stories. The men recounted funny anecdotes of befuddled officers or pranks they played on one another, but none of them shared their stories of battle. The kind he wanted to hear. Like the stories he saw in movies and TV shows. Later, when he was a freshman in high school, he asked his father to share one of his "real war stories" but his father changed the subject. When Brian persisted, his father grew impatient and said, "The war's just history now. If you want to know about it, ask your history teacher."

After that, Brian stopped asking.

Bill raised his head and eyed Brian. Finally, he lifted his cup to his lips and took a sip. "No, I guess I didn't talk about it much. I guess I figured you wouldn't be interested."

"Not interested? You can't be serious. I must have asked you a dozen times when I was a kid, but you wouldn't tell me. You said, 'Ask your history teacher.' Remember?"

"I did? I don't recall. I suppose I wanted to get on with my life. The entire country wanted to forget the war, but couldn't. When I came back, I felt like I was drowning, and the harder I struggled, the deeper I sank. Even now — this thing with Alex

— it's like the woman in green all over again."

Brian put down his cup and rose. "Forget it, Dad."

Bill motioned for Brian to sit down. "Wait a minute. I want to tell you. It's something we have in common. We know what it's like to go to war."

Brian sat down across from his father and waited, expecting his dad to disappoint him again.

Bill cleared his throat and took a second sip of his coffee before speaking. "I was only twenty when I went to 'Nam as part of the Fifth Special Forces. Most of the other Green Berets were older than me, all harder than nails, all Clint Eastwood-type guys. But by 1970, the Snake Eaters were so hard up they took young pups like me. They made me a second lieutenant and stationed me at Thanh Tri, a hamlet near the Cambodian border. I was on a mobile strike team ambushing NVA and Viet Cong troops infiltrating the area. I did what I'd come to Nam to do. Kill the enemy. Every night my team set up shop in the jungle. For hours we'd wait; then we'd see shadows, or maybe just hear a rustle, but we knew it was them. They wore all-black, and until they came very close, we'd only see their eyes. They looked like ghosts. The first time I saw those eyes moving toward me, they spooked me. I was sure the Cong could smell the stink of my fear, but they didn't. They walked right into our crossfire."

Bill paused and looked deep into his son's eyes. "Have I lost you?"

"No, I was just thinking of nights in the Kush . . . the ghosts. Never mind. Go on."

"Well, I did that for about a month when my captain called me in. He had this pencil-thin mustache and liked to call me Boy Wonder. I was just back from a night in the jungle, and all I wanted to do was get some sleep. What did I do wrong now? I said to myself. In my head, I'm listing all the things I could have screwed up. But instead of reaming me out, he says, 'We've been watching you, Boy Wonder, and we think you have what it takes for a special mission.'"

"Of course, I loved the flattery. I should have asked, 'What suicidal mission do you have in mind for me?' But I was full of myself back then, that's for sure. So, I didn't ask."

"You volunteered?"

"Damn right, I volunteered. I later find out I'm part of a top-secret mission called Project Gamma, conducting covert operations in Cambodia."

"A neutral country at the time?"

"That's right. Nixon thought Cambodia's Prince Sihanouk did diddly squat to keep the North Vietnamese from using his border areas to transport troops and supplies. They tasked me with recruiting native agents from Cambodian refugees in Vietnam and the Khmer Serei tribe in Cambodia. My superiors wanted to use them to take out government officials who they deemed too pro-NVA."

"Take out? You mean assassinate?"

Bill folded his arms across his chest and looked away. His tongue rolled inside his cheek as if searching for words to say. "The command called the operation Project Cherry, a sweet name for a horrendous idea. I told myself that the other side played dirty, so we had to. But when both sides commit immoral acts, there's not much difference between us. Nietzsche said, 'He who fights with monsters might take care lest he thereby becomes a monster.'"

Brian studied his father's visage as he stopped talking and looked down. The memories showed on his father's face, and

Brian felt uncomfortable looking at his expression. "In war, there are no clear-cut choices."

His father looked up and shook his head. "Maybe, but what I did helped nobody, least of all the Cambodians. Unlike politicians, I knew it was wrong. I transferred out of the unit as soon as I could. A month later, an American-backed military junta overthrew Prince Sihanouk. Then the Marxist Khmer Rouge drove out the junta. The Rouge wiped out two million people. It was madness. Zealots shot men and women for owning a book, wearing glasses, and even laughing. A Khmer Rouge slogan was 'to spare you is no profit; to destroy you is no loss.'"

Bill paused and kicked aside a spider climbing over his boot. "When we left, all my Cambodian recruits and their families had to fend for themselves. I doubt many survived. I fought like hell from the States to broker a deal to expatriate my most loyal man, Heng Pok, his wife, and his three children. But a US diplomat found out about it and killed the deal. He later told me he needed the space on the plane for a junta member."

"And Heng Pok?"

"Mutual friends wrote to me that Heng and his family fled into the jungle. No one knows if they survived. Sometimes I think about Heng and my time over there, but mostly I try to forget."

Bill stood up and brushed off his pants. "So that's my war story. You want some more coffee?"

"No, thanks."

"Then I guess we should be going."

"Yeah."

Bill turned away.

"Dad."

Bill turned back and looked at his son.

Brian stepped forward and embraced his father. He couldn't remember the last time he hugged his father or his father hugged him. It was as if there were a thin wall keeping them apart. They were men of different times and experiences, soldiers bent in different places, father and son trapped in restraints of their own making. His father felt stiff in his arms, eager to pull away. But Brian held on, unwilling to let go.

***

The two men broke camp, hid all their extra gear, and wiped away any traces of their presence. If Alex stumbled upon this spot, he would find nothing to concern him. He would walk by, suspecting nothing.

Brian checked the site one more time before he picked up his pack. "I think you should lead, Dad. I'll bring up the rear and cover our tracks as we go."

"Sure thing. It's not a long climb."

"Then let's get started."

"Wait." Bill extracted his notebook from his pocket. "Before we set out, I'd like to read a poem I thought about when you talked about the mountains. It's one I often use before a mountain expedition. May I?"

Brian saw the importance of the moment on his father's face. "Sure, fire away. I'm sorry I never agreed to go on an Outward Bound trip with you."

"It's okay. This journey is our expedition. Anyway, this poem is called 'Courage,' by Amelia Earhart."

> *Courage is the price that*
> *Life exacts for granting peace.*
> *The soul that knows it not*

Knows no release from little things:
Knows not the livid loneliness of fear,
Nor mountain heights
Where bitter joy can hear the sound of wings.

Bill looked up at Brian. "Maybe the sounds you heard before weren't songs. Maybe they were the sounds of wings."

Brian tapped Bill's upper arm with the side of his fist.

Bill closed his notebook and returned it to his pocket. "Ready for the mountain?"

"Ready."

"OK, let's do this."

"Lead on, old man."

CHAPTER THIRTY-SIX

Funny how the mind works, Alex thought. Surviving the cougar and getting a few hours of sleep had kick-started his internal engine. All morning he trekked towards Triple Divide with a renewed spirit, free of the corrosive acid of helplessness. He didn't feel hungry or cold, and the pain in his side had subsided. Even his evasive strategies — zigzagging, doubling back, jumping from rock to rock, masking his scent — felt more like play than stealth.

All morning he rambled on the high ridgeline where bare rock made him harder to track. But he grew thirsty, so he left the ridgeline and headed toward the stream slicing through the valley. As he descended, he hid under a canopy of aspen skirting an avalanche chute to his right. The chute was long and resembled a giant playground slide stuck between two mountains. For most of its length, the avalanche chute was barren, the aftermath of years of sliding snow and debris scraping trees and saplings from their roots and flinging them into a massive heap at the bottom.

But near the bottom of the chute, above the pile, low-lying mountain cranberry shrubs clung to the powdery surface. The creeping woody stems bore many slender shoots laden with cranberries so red that the middle of the chute appeared to be on fire. Despite the lure of the tantalizing berries, Alex stayed far away from the chute. He knew that crossing an avalanche chute always posed danger. Even in warmer seasons, a sudden break at the top of a snowfield might hurtle tons of snow and rock down on unsuspecting hikers in tee shirts and shorts. Alex harbored no desire to hear a sudden roar and look up at a slab of snow and ice racing toward him at two hundred miles per hour.

After he descended to the valley floor, Alex scanned the sky and surrounding ridgelines for evidence of human activity. Convinced he was safe, he plowed through the tall grass to the banks of the stream. There, Alex filled his canteen and threw in half an Aquatab to purify the water. Caution admonished him to keep moving, but he dismissed the voice in his head and stretched out on a rock to relax. He hummed a tune, then tried to remember where he heard it; finally recognizing it as the silly car insurance jingle he heard on TV the night he'd stayed in the cheap motel.

What was it with me and these commercials? he wondered.

He squeezed his eyes closed and tried to think of another song to drown out the ditty. By default, he dredged up "Little Sister," the Doc Pomus and Mort Shuman heartbreak tune that made people want to dance, especially when sung by the likes of Ry Cooder. Maybe it's why his mother sang it to him so often during those hard times with his father. He could hear his mother singing with him now, her voice melodic, vibrant, and high; his smoky, loud, and deep, their sadness and joy pouring out with a sweetness he could taste.

Suddenly, he stopped singing. Someone will hear, he thought. Sound carries far in the mountains. No sense making it easy for his pursuers to find him.

He stood up and peered down the valley. He came to Glacier to find redemption, but it had eluded him up to this point. Would he find it on Triple Divide? If not, he'd fling himself off the highest point.

But why should Aarmaan and Hector and the rest of the

dead forgive him? And why here in Glacier? Before he went to the motel in Fayetteville, he had wandered into a local church to find a priest to talk to, but the small church was empty and dark. The statues of saints looked down on him from their stone pedestals. He sat in the last pew for almost an hour and waited for a sign that God was present. But he saw and heard nothing. He left the way he came.

Alex jumped off the rock. "Get moving, Hammer. You need to make Triple Divide by nightfall."

As he was about to move, he glimpsed a flash of light. The sun's reflection on binocular lenses causes that kind of flash, he thought. Trackers must be on the ridge. They spotted him, for sure. The best tactic now was to pretend he didn't see them. He lifted his canteen to his lips and drank as if he hadn't a care in the world. The water went down easily, but he couldn't savor it. His mind locked into escape mode. How many searchers loomed above him? Were they on their way down the slope? Should he run or hide? Did they have dogs with them?

Until a few minutes ago, he believed he could avoid capture even if the searchers had dogs. He only needed enough time to reach Triple Divide, but his injury had slowed him down.

He scanned his surroundings out of the corners of his eyes. He could make a run for it and race upstream or backtrack and try to get behind them. The search party would expect him to run, so, if he doubled back on them instead, he might buy some time. He noticed how the stream went into a little bend no one could observe from the ridgeline. If he reached that spot, he could use the debris pile at the bottom of the chute to conceal his movements as he doubled back on his pursuers. The search party would likely head upstream and he could escape in a different direction.

In the Hindu Kush, his Delta squad members had often employed doubling-back tactics to outwit enemy fighters. If anyone spotted a Taliban or ISIS-K scout following the team, one man would peel off, circle the enemy, and lay in ambush. Most of the time, Brian picked Alex to backtrack and come up behind the unsuspecting fighter. He'd close the gap between him and the scout, stab him in the kidney to put him in shock, slit his throat, and guide him to the ground. Afterward, he'd catch up with the team.

With doubling-back in mind, Alex resisted the impulse to turn around and look behind him. He trudged upstream until he passed the bend. Hidden by a steep enbankment, he headed back downstream. After several minutes, he reached the debris pile at the foot of the avalanche chute and peered over the pile of rocks. He figured the members of the search party must still be on the path leading to the valley floor. If he hurried, he could get downstream from them and hide. As quietly as he could, he scrambled across the debris pile.

When he arrived at the intersection where the ridge trail met the tall grass, he sprinkled cayenne pepper on the ground. Chili pepper wouldn't stop dogs for long, but it might confuse them for a few minutes, long enough for their handlers to get frustrated and push them upstream. If the dogs picked up his fresh scent and followed it, the search party would find him.

After Alex stored his can of pepper, he found a fallen tree about fifty yards north of the intersection. From behind the dead tree, he waited for the search party. He hoped his pursuers would head the wrong way. His ruse was a gamble, but he had no better hand to play.

Several minutes later, Alex heard someone rushing down the trail to the valley floor. As the sound grew louder, he realized the noise wasn't coming from a search party but from a single tracker. Alex peered from the dark scrim of the dead tree's branches to catch the first glimpse of his pursuer. When Jenner appeared a few seconds later, Alex felt the impulse to leap to his feet and call out to him, then stopped himself.

Jenner knelt at the intersection and scooped up a handful of dirt to inspect it.

Alex slid lower behind the trunk of the tree. The sight of Jenner puzzled him. How did Jenner know he was missing in Glacier? Brian must have called Jenner after reading the letter. It was the only thing that made sense. It was a mistake asking Petra to mail that letter. Even so, how did Jenner get to Glacier so quickly? And why was he here? Did Jenner want to save him or did he have some other motive, like making sure no one learns the truth about the Afghan soldier? It didn't matter. No one—not even Jenner— would prevent him from finishing his quest.

He heard Jenner moving toward him. He steeled himself, but a loud noise startled him. It was a sneeze, then another, one more violent than the other.

Jenner had sniffed the cayenne pepper.

"Ah, shit," Jenner yelled in frustration, then sneezed again. "Damn you, Hammer."

The next sound Alex heard was of Jenner charging downstream.

CHAPTER THIRTY-SEVEN

When Jenner disappeared out of sight, Alex scrambled up the slope. As he crested the ridgeline, he saw Triple Divide Peak in front of him to the south. Two routes led there. One was long and easily hiked, the other shorter but dangerous. If he took the first option, Jenner would certainly overtake him once he realized Alex had doubled-back on him. The second route involved a traverse across the snowfield at the top of the avalanche chute. Jenner wouldn't expect him to attempt such a suicidal stunt. And if Jenner did, he'd not take such a risk himself. To Alex's way of thinking, neither option was optimal. Alex remembered how Odysseus found himself caught between Scylla and Charybdis and had to choose between the two. Now, he stood at a similar crossroad.

Quickly, Alex untied the cloth covering his boots. He took a deep breath and plunged into the snowfield, where he encountered an impassable patch of ice. To circumvent the ice, he needed to slide down the slope to a freshly fallen flap of snow, then cross under an icy overhang. With slow and careful movements, Alex leaned back in the snow until he was lying flat on the surface. He pushed off with his elbows and tobogganed down to the snow flap and sank into the ice-blue snow. He righted himself and inched his way under the overhang, aware that any slip might trigger an avalanche that would hurtle him down the incline and bury him at the bottom.

When he was beyond the ice, Alex searched for the best way to cross the rest of the snowfield. The glistening surface was slick. Crackling sounds rumbled from below. Deep cracks crisscrossed the slope.

He had to move. There was no other way to find out if the hard-packed snow would hold. As he stepped forward, he heard more crackling sounds. Each step was a question: Would it hold? Would it break? Every inch brought him closer to oblivion or salvation. Step. *Crack.* Step. *Crack.* A massive chunk of snow broke loose below him, sending a wall of snow and ice hurtling down the slope. The silence-splitting roar shook him, and he felt the ground tremble below his feet. Without thinking, he lay flat, pressing his body against the crust of ice, and held on.

Alex didn't know how long he lay there until the crackling noises subsided and his heart stilled. He thought of giving up and just lying there until the search party or Jenner or a scavenging animal found him. He was tired and numb from the cold. He had traveled so far. Maybe as far as he could. Not every traveler completes the journey. How many souls never even begin the quest? Or get far? Or die before they finish? Why did he feel it was his journey to make? It would be so easy to give up here.

Alex groaned, pushed himself up, and brushed the snow off his jacket. Sweat had soaked his inner garments, which clung to him like wet rags. He stared down at the mass of snow and debris at the bottom of the chute. He inhaled a great swallow of air, imprisoned it in his lungs until he couldn't hold it any longer, and exhaled slowly.

Then he moved forward.

The next hundred feet unfolded smoothly. But at the end of the chute, another slick patch of ice challenged him. This one was smaller than the first, but it adhered to the rocks like a giant claw. To climb above or below the ice was impossible without equipment. Alex had no choice but to cross this section relying on a few exposed rocks for support. He took off his gloves and stowed them in his pockets. With his left hand, he grasped the first rock and stretched his left leg to a second one, just beyond the first. But, as he placed his full weight on the second rock, it gave way and sent him into free fall. He flailed wildly and cried out. A sharp pain exploded in his armpits and across his shoulders. His back smashed into a hard surface and his body jerked up and down like a string toy.

Alex stared down the chute to the debris field below. He peered upward. The netting on the back of his rucksack had snagged on a rock crag and stopped his fall. If he had lost his footing a few inches to his left or right, he would have missed the rock snag and plummeted to the bottom. He noticed the cords on the netting stretched to a breaking point. Quickly, he wrestled out of his pack, freed it from the rock, and clambered to firm ground on the other side. He stopped to catch his breath and peered down.

The bottom was a long way down.

That was close, he thought.

Aside from a scrape on his face and bruised armpits, his body bore no additional damage. Fate had spared him again. Maybe God watched over him.

Then Alex realized he had lost his canteen. He shook his head at the irony. "I won't die from a fall, just a lack of water."

Alex brushed himself off. The traverse of the chute had saved him at least an hour and gave him a good head start on Jenner. As daring as Jenner was, he wouldn't cross the chute to catch him. But Jenner wouldn't quit. He'd circumvent the chute and follow the trail to the other side. Alex shielded his eyes from the sun and peered downstream. No signs of Jenner.

But he was coming. It was only a matter of time before they would be together again.

Alex waved to Jenner as if he were in view.

"You'll find me on the summit of Triple Divide, my friend."

CHAPTER THIRTY-EIGHT

After trudging up a rocky path, Brian and Bill arrived at an enormous, glacier-carved bowl called a cirque. At one end of the formation, a six-hundred-foot vertical cliff loomed over them like the wall of a fortress.

"It's the shortest route," Bill said, looking at his trail map. "We can save some time. I'm game to climb it if you are."

Brian shielded his eyes from the sun and shook his head. "Too dangerous. We'll take the route that contours around, then climb the ridgeline."

"Your call."

They hiked for two hours until they reached the ridge, where the men took a break to get their bearings. Bill knelt on one knee and scratched what resembled a three-pointed star in the dirt. "You see this? Think of Triple Divide Peak as a starfish. If you look at the mountain from the sky in satellite photos, that's what you see: three distinct ridges joined at the summit, like a a giant three-armed starfish resting in the middle of the Continental Divide."

He made an X in the dirt. "We're here on this eastern ridge."

Brian glanced at the starfish, but his mind was elsewhere. His father's knowledge of the terrain was helpful, but the fear that his father might run into Alex alone nagged at him. In Alex's state of mind, he was unpredictable, and perhaps dangerous. He was skilled in martial arts and possibly armed. If his father got in his way, what would Hammer do?

"Let's go," Brian said, then took the lead. In the distance, he saw what looked like a summit, but his father had warned him at the start of their climb that Triple Divide presented two false summits, so he didn't quicken his pace. There was still a long way to go.

To the west, they spotted mountain goats crossing a high meadow splattered with white patches. To the east, a permanent snowfield survived in the shadow of Razor Edge Mountain. A thin coat of frost crusted many of the boulders along the way. The higher they went, the colder it became. Brian worried that, if Alex reached Triple Divide's summit, he'd face real danger. Without fire or heavy Alpine clothing, Alex might freeze to death.

Brian zippered his outer jacket. "Bundle up, Dad. We're not stopping till we reach the top."

The men continued their climb at a quicker pace, hardly noticing how the path narrowed before them. When they reached the long rise of the ridge leading to the true summit, Bill tapped Brian on the shoulder rather than make a sound. He pointed to the treeless summit. Anyone up there would see them approaching.

Brian broke into a half-run, leaving Bill far behind. As he approached the top, he stowed his hat to make sure Alex had no trouble recognizing him. After reaching the treeless summit, he dropped his pack and came to a halt next to the summit cairn, a pile of rocks marking the highest point. He stood all alone on top of Triple Divide Peak.

He spied all three approaches but saw only his father on the path below.

When Bill reached the summit, he spotted his son walking in an ever-increasing circle outward from the cairn. Bill threw down his pack in disgust.

Brian strode over to his father. "No sign of Alex. Or anyone else. Not for some time."

"He hasn't been here yet," Bill said, with more hope than expectation.

Brian nodded. "That's right. Yet. Let's hope it's soon. We need to decide whether we wait for him here or go back down."

"I say we go back. Up here, we're too exposed. There's no place to hide from either Alex or the wind, which is going to get pretty strong in the next few hours. Down below, at least, we can find a sheltered place to hunker down and wait for him to show up."

Brian pointed at another ridge intersecting with the summit from the northwest. "Couldn't he come from that direction?"

Bill scratched his head. "It's not likely. He doesn't expect anyone knows his destination, so why would he hike extra days to take a different approach?"

"Let's go down then. We'll find a place to hide near the Pass. I'll call the CID officer and find out why the agency wants to talk with Alex. If there's still some light left afterwards, I'll scout around the Pass to see if I can pick up his tracks."

"Sounds good," Bill said and extended his hand palm up. "Give me your water."

"My water?"

"Yes."

Brian removed the insulated water bottle hanging upside down on his pack and handed it to his father.

Bill uncapped the bottle and explained, "We can't leave here without adding water to the three oceans. Only two other places in the world can claim they're the source of three oceans. One is in Jasper, and the other is in Siberia. I think that's why Alex chose this place. It has special meaning."

Bill pointed in different directions as he continued speaking. "Look over there at the stream below. Water here will feed into the Flathead River and later into the Columbia emptying into the Pacific Ocean. And to the north, that smaller stream feeds into St. Mary's Lake and flows downstream, via the Nelson River Basin, into Hudson Bay and the Arctic Ocean. Back the way we came, you can see Atlantic Creek, which flows into Medicine Grizzly Lake, out into Cut Bank Creek, and after thousands of miles, into the Gulf of Mexico and the Atlantic Ocean at New Orleans via the mighty Mississippi."

"Dad, I don't think we should waste time or water."

Bill held out the open bottle. "How can it hurt? Who knows, maybe if the sirens are watching, they'll see you doing this and help us." He paused. "For Alex?"

Brian shook his head in frustration, but took the bottle anyway and advanced to the cairn. "For Alex," he shouted, and ceremoniously poured a trickle of water onto the pile of rocks. Then he offered the canteen to his father. "Your turn."

Bill shook his head. "I've done it before. Years ago. The rest of the water will be better off going down our throats. And Alex's, when we find him."

Brian peered down at the stunning blue-green lake below them on the other side of the Pass. "Is that the lake we passed last night?"

"That's it, Medicine Grizzly Lake, named after a Flathead chief. Legend has it the chief was slain by a Blackfeet war party but came back to life as a huge grizzly wreaking revenge on the braves who killed him. It's an awfully pretty lake for a vengeful warrior, don't you think?"

Brian nodded and smiled at his father's remark. Here in Glacier, he saw a side of his father he never knew. Perhaps his father hid it all these years, or maybe Brian had turned a blind eye to it. Maybe fathers and sons were mysteries to each other. He and his father were very much alike. Both kept their secrets close to their chest. Both lost men they loved. And both carried memories of friends left behind.

"I think we should go," Brian said.

Without speaking, they began their descent off the eastern ridge. It would be quicker than the ascent, but trickier. They could easily lose their balance on the crusty rock surface. Bill found the loose footing difficult, and Brian twice caught him before he fell. As they neared the bottom, Bill tottered and reached out to brace his hand against a large boulder. As he did, something dropped from the sky and splattered on the top of the stone.

Bill recoiled and pointed at a splash of red and gore. "You see that?"

Drawing closer, Brian stared at the split-open carcass, still moist with blood. "What is it?"

Bill bent down close to inspect. "I'm not sure, but it may be one of our marmots."

"Jesus," Brian said in disgust. "What did this?"

He peered skyward to see a golden eagle soaring above them, an eagle much like the one he and his men saw before their last mission. "There it is."

Bill shielded his eyes and watched as the eagle circled above. "I'd say we've caught a killer in the act."

CHAPTER THIRTY-NINE

Jenner seethed when he discovered his mistake. He hated that Alex had eluded him. It was a blow to his pride, causing the same frustration he felt when a young player in a game of one-on-one basketball managed to beat him. Alex was good, but not that good. Jenner cursed himself for underestimating his quarry.

He wouldn't do it again.

Jenner circled the avalanche chute and picked up Alex's trail on the other side. The fresh tracks yielded key information. He had lost almost an hour in his pursuit. And Alex's stride had lengthened again, showing that the pain of his injury had diminished. Most telling, his brother-in-arms no longer covered his tracks.

His destination must be near.

Jenner kicked the dirt and obliterated the tracks. "Your only advantage now, Hammer, is you know where you want to go."

Jenner stared south. Triple Divide Peak stood as the closest pinnacle. It had three approaches, any of which might provide an escape route. If he were Alex, he would go there if pursued. But he was not his troubled and unpredictable friend.

Jenner prided himself on being predictable. In the fog of war, his fellow soldiers could count on him to perform with skill and courage. When other men failed amid the bedlam and enemy fire, he proved a constant. When self-doubt and recrimination ambushed other men's thoughts, he never wavered from what he needed to do.

In the mundane world back home, his take on life stood in stark contrast to those of other men. They strove for financial success, a family, a secure retirement, and a long life. But Jenner only lived for the certainty and immediacy of today. He didn't measure his life in the slow burn of years, only the fiery combustion of fully lived moments. He wanted to be young Icarus with wings of feathers and wax whose life ended in flames. Growing old like his grandfather, spent and infirm, frightened him more than bullets.

Be careful, Jenner thought, patting the bulge under his coat. He wouldn't use his weapon unless he had no other choice. He came here to save Alex's life, not end it. But he valued his own life above all others. Hector had always half-joked with Jenner about what he called his death wish, but Hector had mistaken Jenner's risk-taking for something dark. Treading as close as he dared to the hard-to-see borders between life and death was life-affirming, not death-seeking. He embraced life as often as he could wherever and whenever it showed its pretty face.

Jenner reached into his breast pocket and withdrew a string of amber beads. As he held them in his hand, he felt the smooth surface of the beads against his palm. He rubbed the tiny orbs between his index finger and his thumb and thought about Alex. He had noticed his friend unraveling long before the night raid in the village. For months, Jenner had watched him grow much too close to the interpreter, visiting his home, and befriending the man's wife and children. Alex always seemed to have a new story to tell about his Afghan friend. It was as if Alex had fallen in love with the man and his culture.

Jenner had seen it happen to others: aid workers, soldiers, journalists, and people who should have known better. They became bleeding hearts and sympathizers. You could spot them in the markets or urban alleyways: American women and men trying to master the local language, women wearing headscarves, and men donning pakuls. Some even converted to Islam, trying to become more native than the natives. Soldiers called it "going country."

Jenner had warned Alex but to no avail. His friend laughed at him and called him a closet racist. He even suggested Jenner should join him the next time Aarmaan invited him home for dinner. At Alex's request, Aarmaan had reached out to Jenner, but the interpreter did not fool him. He didn't believe for one moment that the Afghan ex-professor was genuine. The interpreter was born in the United States, but he lived and worked and raised a family in Afghanistan. Jenner suspected the interpreter just wanted access to American goodies from the PX.

When Aarmaan had invited Jenner to his home for dinner, Jenner said, "I'd rather spend my night in the brig."

Jenner remembered the shock on Alex's face, but Alex should have expected it.

Jenner opened his palm and admired the translucent, yellow-orange beads. Composed of tree resin that solidified millions of years ago, the beads were remnants of the Dinosaur Age. Jenner loved to rub them between his fingers whenever he was deep in thought. Jenner felt God's touch in these thirty-three beads, strung together with silken thread and adorned with a silver tassel.

A chaplain told him the word "bead" came from the Old English word for prayer, and Jenner felt something devotional in these pieces of amber. It didn't matter that he had pulled the string of beads from the hand of the young Afghan soldier, lying unconscious at his feet, the night he came back from the snatch mission. Nor did he concern himself with the fact that whoever fashioned these beads intended them to be prayer beads for a believer of Islam. To Jenner, these bits of resin gave him a sense of serenity.

Jenner looked at Triple Divide Peak and fingered his beads. Alex was close, and Jenner needed to catch him before Brian did.

CHAPTER FORTY

When he returned to camp, Brian phoned the Army Criminal Investigation Command. It took him ten minutes to get past the duty officer and the department secretary before Captain Benjamin Sowinski picked up the call.

"Sowinski speaking." The hard-edged voice bore a Minnesota accent.

"Sir, my name is First Sergeant Brian McEnroe. I'm Sergeant Alejandro Vilanova's team leader."

"Yes? What can I do for you, first sergeant?"

"I spoke to Mrs. Vilanova. She said you called her yesterday regarding her son. She's concerned, as am I. Sergeant Vilanova is on my team."

"And?"

"I'm responsible for every member of my team."

"First Sergeant, I still haven't heard the purpose of your call, and I'm very busy."

Acid seeped through the captain's tone. Brian visualized Sowinski beaming with delight at the prospect of toying with him. Most officers were stand-up guys, but Brian knew a few who used rank like a blunt weapon.

"I want to find out if Sergeant Vilanova is in trouble."

Sowinski made no reply.

Brian gritted his teeth. He imagined the captain leaning back in his chair with a smug smile on his face. Perhaps the captain had a bad day. Maybe he had too much to drink the night before. Or maybe he quarreled with his wife. Brian didn't give a damn. Sowinski had stuck the knife in and twisted it.

"Sir?"

"I won't go into the reasons for my call to Mrs. Vilanova, First Sergeant."

Sowinski pronounced Sergeant as if the word oozed. "It's part of an ongoing investigation."

"If it impacts my team, I am on a need-to-know basis."

"That's not how I see it from here."

The CID officer irritated him, but Brian answered calmly. "Sir, I respectfully repeat. As Sergeant Vilanova's team leader, I have a duty to inform myself of anything impacting his ability to serve."

"You're repeating yourself, soldier."

"With all due respect, sir, I need to know if my man is in any trouble, and, if he is, what kind of trouble it is."

"I can't tell you that," Sowinski said, pronouncing each word with slow precision. "Those are the regulations, First Sergeant."

Regulations? The military ran on regulations as much as it did on diesel fuel. Brian thought it ironic Sowinski would remind him of that. After all, Jenner often accused Brian of being a "by-the-book" leader and citing regulations to keep him in line. Now, Sowinski was doing the same thing to him. And Brian didn't like it.

"Regulations? Sir, right now my man might freeze to death in Glacier National Park. What are regulations when a man's life is at stake?"

Brian counted as he waited for an answer. He couldn't be sure if the officer was considering his question or playing with him.

"First Sergeant McEnroe, where was Vilanova's whereabouts the night after you lost two men in a raid?"

Sowinski surprised Brian with the question. After stonewalling Brian, the pompous bastard wanted information from him. The man had gall. But Brian played along to find out more about the investigation.

"He was in his quarters, sir."

"All night?"

"He may have gone out for a time with another member of the team."

"A Sergeant Chapman?"

"That's right."

"Are you sure?"

Brian rewound the events of the day in his head: the flight back, the unit and team meetings, the session with the psychologist, and the dinner with his commanding officer. Brian had ordered Jenner to take care of Alex, but he never saw either of them until the next morning. He couldn't be sure what either did after he had left them.

"No, sir, I'm not sure."

"Did you see Sergeant Vilanova at all that evening?"

"No."

"Thank you, First Sergeant. You've been most helpful. We may order you back to Fort Bragg for an interview. We'll be in touch."

"Wait a minute, sir. What's this all about? Why is the CID investigating Sergeant Vilanova?"

The phone on the other end clicked down.

CHAPTER FORTY-ONE

Teresa kept her cell phone on night and day. It was the only tie she had to the people who were searching for her son. She kept it charged, wishing she had purchased an expensive one having better reception. She had almost finished her beer when the phone rang. Before she answered, she pulled the tab to open a full can.

The brew was potent, and the buzz calmed her nerves. "Oh, Brian, I'm glad you called. I haven't heard from the rangers."

"Your signal is weak. Can you hear me?"

"Sort of."

"I'll talk fast. Is that Army officer still coming to interview you?"

"Yes, in fact, he called about ten minutes ago. His plane arrived early, and he asked if he could come sooner."

"What did you tell him?"

"What was I supposed to tell him? I said, 'Yes, of course.' Did I do something wrong?"

"No, but you must get out of there before he comes. You don't want to answer any of his questions without talking to a lawyer first."

"Now you're scaring me. What do you know that I don't?"

Brian explained that he had called the number she gave him. Captain Sowinski was with the CID, the Army's Criminal Investigation Department.

As Brian recounted the conversation, Teresa grew more fearful. She knew Alex had nothing to do with any criminal activity, but her history with law enforcement officials made her suspicious of their motives and tactics. She understood the rules and how they worked. Ordinary people — folks without money or power — played in a different league than those above them. In her life, the game was always rigged against her.

"This is terrible. What are we going to do?"

"Don't worry. We'll find Alex and straighten this out, but you need to get out of your apartment. You don't want to answer questions about the letter, or why Alex walked off into the wilderness, or anything else he said to you. You need to talk to a lawyer. We don't know how much the CID already knows. So go now, please."

"I'm going. I'll call you. Bye." Teresa ended the call, guzzled her beer, then tossed her phone into her satchel. She shut the window, threw on her jacket, fished out her keys, and left the apartment. After locking the door, she raced down the stairs, but halted when she reached the street. Frantically, she searched through her purse, then ran back up the stairs. She unlocked her door and flung it open.

She surveyed the room. "Where the hell did I leave my cigarettes?"

Muttering to herself, she searched the space.

"There they are," she gasped and dashed to the small table by the window to retrieve her pack.

"Damn it," she said and withdrew a cigarette. After lighting it, she took a long drag and exhaled a cloud of smoke. She watched it dissipate, then threw the pack of cigarettes into her bag.

A voice startled her.

"Mrs. Vilanova?"

Teresa swiveled to discover Petra facing her in the doorway. "Oh, it's you. What are you doing here?"

Petra tip-toed into the apartment. "I'm sorry to bother you, but I wonder if there's news about Alex?"

Teresa's voice broke. "No, he . . . he's still missing."

Her hand shook as she took another drag of her cigarette, trying to hold back a sob.

Petra hesitated, then rushed to Teresa's side and placed her hand on the smaller woman's arm.

"I don't know what to do," Teresa said in a halting voice. "I'm afraid he's dead."

Petra rubbed Teresa's shoulder. "He's not. They'll find him."

"He's all I have."

They jumped at the sound of three loud knocks on the open door.

A tall woman in a dark suit stood just inside the apartment. "I didn't mean to startle you."

The woman's voice was smoky and strong, with the barest hint of Mississippi backwaters.

"Are you Teresa Vilanova?" the woman asked, pointing her index finger at Teresa.

Teresa spread her legs apart and crossed her arms. "I am. And who are you?"

The woman took a step closer and held up an identification card. "I'm Special Agent Pinckney from the U.S. Army Criminal Investigation Command. I spoke to you earlier on the phone."

Taken aback, Teresa didn't know what to say. She thought the agent she spoke to was a man. The agent's voice was deep and husky, and she assumed the agent was male. In the picture she had created in her mind, the agent was a no-nonsense guy with a crisp uniform, polished shoes, and white skin.

But Special Agent Pinckney — Adrienne Pinckney as it said on her ID card — had dark-cocoa skin, a close-cropped afro, large brown eyes framed by tortoise-shell glasses, ruby lips, and an athletic body partly hidden by a tailored navy-blue suit, a white silk blouse, and an unbuttoned lamb's wool coat.

"Oh, you have a lovely view of the mountains from your window," Pinckney said, leaning around Teresa and moving further into the apartment. "I live in Fort Carson, Colorado, but I only see a warehouse when I look out my window. I bet you sit here every day at this table and watch the sunset, don't you?"

Teresa took the last puff of her cigarette and ground it out in an ashtray. "I do, but my friend and I are busy."

Pinckney reached her hand out to Petra. "Oh, excuse me, I should have introduced myself. My name is Adrienne Pinckney. And you are?"

Petra shook hands. "Petra."

"Petra what?"

"Engel. Petra Engel."

"Are you a friend of Sergeant Vilanova?"

"Yes, I met him in Glacier National Park."

Teresa came between them. "Agent Pinckney, I'm sorry, but we can't talk."

Pinckney interrupted her. "Can I have one of your cigarettes? I'm dying for a smoke."

Teresa fumbled for her pack. "Listen, Petra and I need to leave. I can do the interview some other time."

"I've come a long way," Pinckney said as she pulled a cigarette from Teresa's outstretched pack.

"I know. I'm sorry but —"

"A match?"

"What?"

"Do you have a match?"

Teresa struck a match and lit Pinckney's cigarette. The agent took a drag and blew the smoke out of the side of her mouth. "This is my only vice, but nowadays it's harder to indulge, isn't it? Working for the government is the worst. Every place is a no-smoking zone. You know what I mean?"

Before Teresa could answer, the agent continued. "Mrs. Vilanova, the CID is investigating an alleged assault on an Afghan soldier. The investigation is in its preliminary stage. We've brought no charges. The CID made no apprehensions, or arrests, as you might call them. We're just gathering information to determine if someone committed a crime, and, if so, what to charge that individual with. As part of our procedures, we interview lots of people. When the rangers find your son, I intend to interview him. But, in the meantime, I'd like to ask you and Ms. Engel some questions."

"Alex would never commit a crime."

"Mrs. Vilanova, as I said before, at this stage we only have an alleged crime and no designated suspects. Because this is an ongoing investigation, I cannot give you any details. However, if someone isn't involved in a crime, we should learn that as soon as possible so we can rule out that person."

Teresa bit her lip. The woman made sense, she thought. Alejandro would answer her questions because he had nothing to hide. She remembered her son speaking up and telling the truth, even when his father would beat him for doing so.

"I'll try to answer your questions."

Pinckney turned to Petra. "And how about you, Ms. Engel?"

"I guess so."

"Good." The agent removed her coat and scanned the small apartment. "Ms. Engel, could you wait outside in the hall while I interview Mrs. Vilanova?"

Teresa moved in front of Petra. "No, she's not leaving. Either you interview us together or you can forget about it."

Pinckney put her coat over a chair and spoke in a low, soothing voice. "Don't worry. It's standard procedure to do an interview one on one."

"Not in my house, it isn't." Teresa looked at Petra and helped her take off her jacket. "She stays with me. Otherwise, you can go."

Pinckney's face reflected the debate going on behind it. Finally, she bit her lower lip, pulled out a pen, and clicked it. "We'll do it your way."

The agent directed Petra and Teresa over to the couch and pulled up a chair perpendicular to them. "All right, let me just go over a few things before we begin. While you're speaking, I'll take notes so I can remember everything you say. If you don't understand a question, let me know, and I'll rephrase it. I have no knowledge of what Alex said or did here in Montana, so I encourage you to tell me everything you remember, even if it seems insignificant. Even if you think I know something, or should know it, please tell me anyway. On the other hand, don't make up a response because you can't remember something. Just say, 'I don't remember.' Feel free to correct me if I say something wrong, and if I ask the same question more than once, don't think your first response was wrong. Is that understood?"

Teresa and Petra nodded.

"Any questions?"

The two women looked at each other, then at Pinckney.

"No," they answered.

"Good . . . Now, Mrs. Vilanova, tell me everything you can remember since your son came home."

Teresa recounted the last several days: Alex's surprise homecoming, their conversations before he left to go camping in Glacier, what he did while he was in her apartment, what he took with him when he left, and her conversations with Petra, Leo, and the Park Rangers. What she left out was the letter Alex sent to Brian and her conversations with Jenner, Brian, and Bill.

Petra must have noticed because when Pickney asked her the same question, she told her story without mentioning the letter or her conversation outside Buster's with Jenner.

Throughout the first part of the interviews, Pinckney listened and said little other than an occasional "go on" or "tell me more." Most of the time, she just nodded. But when both women had exhausted their memories, Pinckney raked through her notebook and spent another hour asking Teresa and Petra to clarify or expand their answers.

In the end, the investigator closed her notebook. She stood and thanked both women for their time. But as she put on her coat, she pursed her lips. "Just one thing bothers me, Mrs. Vilanova. You didn't mention Brian McEnroe, your son's team sergeant. Just before I came here, he called one of my colleagues in Virginia, a Captain Sowinski. First Sergeant McEnroe said you told him about our investigation. Oddly, his name didn't come up during our interview. Is there anything else you forgot to tell me?"

Teresa felt guilty. She wanted to keep Brian out of all this. "I don't know what you're talking about."

"I think you do. Would you like to tell me about your conversations with First Sergeant McEnroe?"

Teresa rose to her feet and circled the coffee table to escort Pickney out. "I don't know what you're talking about."

Pinckney clicked her ballpoint pen and dropped it in her bag. "Are you sure?"

Teresa's mouth was dry, which made it hard for her to speak. "I never spoke to Sergeant McEnroe."

Pinckney smirked. "Then I guess you don't know he's in Glacier searching for your son."

"I don't."

"No?"

"No. And I want you to leave."

Pinckney lifted her bag and moved toward the open door. "Thanks for the cigarette. I'll be in touch."

She didn't look back as the door slammed shut behind her.

CHAPTER FORTY-TWO

Afternoon storm clouds shadowed the bluff where Bill and Brian stood overlooking the Red Eagle Valley. Scattered patches of sunshine shone through gaps in the clouds and lit the valley below like spotlights illuminating a dark stage. The two men huddled close to each other, arms folded across their chests, hopping foot to foot to generate heat. Tiny clouds wafted out of their mouths as their warm breath clashed with the chilly mountain air.

"I think we're in for a snowstorm," Bill said. "I feel it in my bones."

Both men knew that a mountain storm carried death in its wake. At this time of year, a storm often brought sudden blizzards. Howling winds could sweep snow off the mountains and into the air like spray off a crashing surf. Snow could bury both flora and fauna so quickly even experienced guides lost their way.

"I think we need to move most of our stuff into the tent, then make sure we erect a windbreak," Bill said.

Without saying a word, Brian picked up the cooking equipment and walked into the tent. When he reemerged empty-handed, Bill confronted him as he picked up a lantern.

"Wait."

Brian shrugged. "You said we should — "

"Oh, suddenly you're listening to what I say? You've not said a word since Teresa called you. I've waited for a reasonable time for you to tell me. Something is troubling you. What is it?"

Brian did not respond.

Bill fixed his eyes on his son's. "Look at me. Alex's mom told you something that's bothering you. I can tell. Let's get it out and talk it through before we lose more daylight and a snowstorm hits."

Brian knew his father was right. They had to prepare for a potential blizzard. But he also had to find Alex before a snow squall blanketed his trail, or in a worst-case scenario, his unprotected body.

"Teresa spoke to the CID. She told the investigator almost everything."

"Almost?"

"She kept silent about us. But the agent somehow knew we were in Glacier."

"Hawkins?"

"Maybe."

"Anything else?"

Brian told his father the rest of the story. The agent had mentioned that the CID was investigating an assault on an Afghan soldier at Bagram. He relayed how he had heard rumors about the assault before the team flew back home. The guy was in a coma for a while. Witnesses had seen him earlier with an American GI. The Afghan government was outraged about the case. The Army brass freaked out and wanted answers.

"I did not know Alex might be involved."

Worry crossed Bill's face. "You don't think —"

"Stop there. I know Alex. We're brothers."

"But anyone can lose it."

"I know my men. I know what they can and cannot do. Alex is the peacemaker on our team. Trust me, he would never attack an Afghan soldier."

Brian paused and shook his head. "Listen to me. I sound like his lawyer. The truth is, I'm worried. Alex isn't acting normally. I assumed his grief over the deaths of Aarmaan and Hector brought him here, but who knows? Maybe it's this other thing. That's why you must stand down when I tell you to. I can't shake this feeling that if you got in his way, he might hurt you."

Bill's face fell. "Don't worry about me."

"Let's not argue about this now. There's no time. I want to scout out the area north of here before it snows. He's out there somewhere close by. I know it."

"I'll come with you."

Brian stopped him from moving forward by straight-arming his shoulder. "I want you to stay here and prepare for the storm."

"Fair enough," Bill said, but as Brian turned from him, he added, "And what do you want me to do if I see him?"

Brian turned back and gave his father a puzzled look. "Wait here."

He disappeared into the tent, then emerged with their two satellite phones. One of them he handed to Bill.

"Use this to call me if you see him. Don't try to stop him yourself."

"You're not making any sense. We didn't come all this way to let him go."

"All the same, I want you to just back off if you see him."

Brian didn't want to get into a debate. But his father wasn't one of his soldiers. He couldn't issue an order, then expect his father to obey. All his life he had deferred to his father, but now circumstances had shifted. He didn't have the luxury of playing the dutiful son.

"Brian . . ."

"Don't argue, please. Let him go, you hear me?"

Bill looked miffed. "Hey, I've worked with troubled vets for years. Many jumped down my throat for imagined offenses. But I know how to defuse a tense situation."

Brian grew exasperated. "Listen to me."

"I am, but you're treating me like some kid you need to look after. Till now, I've kept my mouth shut. But you're off mission now."

Brian knew his father was right. If Jenner had joined him instead of his father, he'd expect him to prevent Alex from reaching Triple Divide, no matter what. They'd find Alex and bring him home with no excuses.

But this was not Jenner. This was his father.

"The mission has changed," Brian said.

Bill's eyes widened with surprise. "But if he gets by, there's nothing to stop him from getting to the top of Triple Divide and ending his life. Remember what he said in the letter?"

"I know, but I don't intend to let him slip by me."

"And if he does?"

"It's up to Fate."

Bill's face reddened. "Fate? What are you talking about? We trudged out here to rescue your friend, and now you're willing to let him die? I don't understand."

Brian turned to walk away, but Bill spun him around. "Don't walk away from me without answering. You face me. Tell me why I should let him go."

Brian tried to pull away, but Bill held onto his arm.

"Tell me. Why should I let him go?"

Brian pushed his father's hand away. "Back off, Dad."

"I'm not backing off until you level with me."

Brian stomped away, but Bill grabbed his arm again.

Infuriated, Brian spun around and shook Bill's shoulders.

"Don't you get it? If Alex hurt you, I'd blame myself."

Bill pushed Brian's hands from his shoulders.

"And if Alex dies, and we could have stopped him? You wouldn't regret your decision?"

"You're here because of me."

"It's not so simple. Of course, I want to help you. I'm your father. But that's only part of it. I told you about Heng Pok. I never told anyone the complete story before."

"Why tell me then?"

"Because you came here to save your friend. I'm proud of you for that. But helping you digs up my past too. Don't you see?"

Bill looked away, then looked back. "Coming here reminds me I left my friend behind. When I returned home, I tried to put Heng Pok out of my head. But for the longest time, I couldn't get through the night without dreaming of him. It got so bad — the rages, the nightmares, the fear I'd hurt your mother in my sleep, her finally leaving me."

"Mom left you? I don't believe it."

"It's true. She went to live with your grandmother."

"What did you do?"

"Nothing," Bill said, looking to the side. "I was too ashamed. I thought no one could help me."

"But you must have gotten help."

Bill stiffened and looked as if all he wanted to do was to be somewhere else. He took off his cap and rolled it with his fingers, then placed it on his head and tilted the visor so it shielded his eyes. When he spoke, he stared at the ground. "Our priest convinced your mother to commit me. I was in a locked psychiatric ward in a VA hospital for three months."

"You in a psych unit? I don't believe it. You were Superman."

Bill scoffed and raised his eyes to Brian's. "In life, there are no superheroes, only people."

Only people? Brian thought. He remembered a little girl, her parents lying next to her like rag dolls, their house reduced to rubble, villagers outside wailing and shouting, the girl staring at him with hate, her teeth bared, her hands clutching her dead baby brother, not a bruise or cut showing on her. In war, there are only people.

Brian squeezed his father's shoulder and saw the old man's eyes water. "I'm glad you got the help you needed."

"So am I. Even though I fought it tooth and nail at first."

"And what happened after the hospital?"

"I convinced your mother to come back to me. She said I had to join a PTSD group, and I did. Not long after that, I accepted a discharge from the Army because my chances for promotion hovered around zero. I floundered for a while. Luckily, Outward Bound rescued me with a job offer and an opportunity to help vets. Vets just like Alex."

Bill paused. "So, I have my reasons for being here."

Thunder sounded in the distance. Bill added, "It's coming,"

Brian's mouth tightened. I can't let you put yourself in danger with Alex."

Bill put both hands on his son's shoulders. "If I see him, I'll not rush into anything. I'll judge the situation. If I think I can do some good, I'll go for it. Do you trust me?"

"I'd like to."

"You can."

"But what if he has a gun?"

"If I see any weapon, he won't see me."

"Promise?"

Bill chuckled and held up his right hand using the Eagle Scout three-fingered salute.

"Of course, I promise. Do you think I'm crazy?"

Brian grinned.

"I do."

Bill patted his son's cheek. "Well, it runs in the family."

CHAPTER FORTY-THREE

As he left the campsite, Brian broke into a fast walk, then into a brisk run. He felt liberated; able to move at his own pace.

When he entered the Pass, he surveyed the landscape for an observation outpost. The ideal lookout would provide a sweeping view of both the valley and the bordering heights. He spied a well-used animal trail on the western ridge and followed it to a spot just below a large rock slab offering excellent sightlines to the valley floor. He hoisted himself onto the rock and inspected it. The slab projected from the mountain in a way that made it possible for him to see below while remaining undetectable from above.

Brian hunkered down. He noticed small bones striped with sinew, still reeking of rot, and deduced he wasn't the first to use this spot. With his binoculars, Brian scoped the terrain from north to south. The storm clouds were moving in, and afternoon shadows flowed down the western slope like cascades of lava.

He spotted movement, but nothing that looked human. A female wolverine, foraging near the creek, captured his attention. She had found a half-eaten moose carcass and stood guard while her three young offspring fed on the scraps. About the size of a dog, she looked fierce with her muscular shoulders, sharp claws, and face rimmed with thick fur streaked like war paint. Her neck and head thrust out aggressively while her kits tore at the meat and bloodied their tiny bear-like faces.

Though wolves had probably killed the moose, this "skunk bear" marked the carcass as her own. Other predators were well-advised to surrender any claims.

On his second scan of the valley, Brian spotted a dark figure moving through the tall grass on the east side of the creek, but the shape disappeared. Just a shadow, he figured, then reminded himself how easy it was in the mountains to see something that wasn't there.

He sighed, dropped to his knees, and withdrew from his breast pocket a waterproof trail map of Glacier-Waterton Lakes National Park. He spread the map on the rock slab and placed one index finger on the point where Alex left the trail and another finger on the marking for Triple Divide Peak.

Then Brian imagined himself walking in Alex's shoes.

So, I leave the trail here and head south. To avoid a search party, I stay off the trails. Maybe I try to follow goat paths, maybe I trail blaze. It's too dangerous to travel at night without equipment, so I travel by day and seek cover when I hear aircraft. I cross trails only when necessary. I hike through Jefferson's Pass, skirt the Waterton Valley Trail, and make my way through the Kootenai and Piegan Passes. This next stretch from Going to the Sun Road to St. Mary's Lake poses a major problem. Too many rangers there and not much cover. How do I get by?

Brian figured Alex must have found a way. Otherwise, the rangers at St. Mary's Lake would have reported a sighting to Alex's mother. Unless he was dead and didn't make it that far.

Brian dismissed the idea as soon as it crossed his mind.

OK. Let's say I got through there. So where am I now? Somewhere in this valley or on the ridge. I'm close. I'm tired and cold, but I want to make Triple Divide Peak by nightfall.

Brian looked at the mountains surrounding him. "Where are you, Hammer? Show yourself."

Brian pushed aside the map and sat on his haunches, pondering what to do next. He could wait here until dusk and see if his brother-in-arms showed up. Or he could hike down to the valley to search through the tall grass. Or he could give up and return to camp. After going over his options, Brian decided to remain at his outpost for another thirty minutes, then return to camp. When he got back, he and his father could decide how to share the night watch.

He pointed his binoculars toward the place where he had last seen the shadow in the grass. He hoped to see a glimpse of clothing in a sea of yellowed green.

Nothing appeared out of the ordinary.

For the next fifteen minutes, Brian scoured every nook and crevice with his binoculars. Alex was nearby. Brian was sure of it. Still, he saw no trace of him. He crawled farther onto the rock and listened. He heard nothing unusual and inched his way back.

Suddenly, a noise, like that of splattering rain, sounded from above. A sprinkling of pebbles bounced over the side of the outpost and landed on the goat path below. Someone or something had disturbed the loose surface of the slope above. Brian peeked out as a few more pebbles rolled down and came to a rest near the opening of his hiding place. He heard someone grunt from above. Must be Alex, Brian thought. He rose into a crouching position and pressed himself against the far wall. At that moment, he saw a leather boot appear on his left side. The toe of the boot dug into the ground to slow its owner's downward movement.

Brian made a snap decision. Afraid that Alex would run

away or reach for a weapon, Brian grabbed the lead leg from behind the knee and yanked it swiftly toward his chest. A twisting body somersaulted in the air and landed chest first on the ground.

"Alex," Brian said with alarm.

But, as he did, the figure launched off the ground, spun in Brian's direction, and held up his hands to parry an attack.

It was Jenner.

His forehead bled from a gash over his right eye. For a moment, Jenner remained in his crouched position like an animal poised to spring. His eyes glared, his teeth clenched, and his hands curled into fists. He looked as if he wanted to kill. But then a beam of recognition crossed his face. The vicious stare disappeared and his fists unclenched. He exhaled and sucked in a deep, slow breath. He grinned as he wiped the blood from his eyes.

"Falcon, is this any way to greet a brother?"

Brian was still in a state of shock. "What the hell are you doing here?"

"Aren't you glad to see me?"

Dumbfounded, Brian walked to Jenner and retrieved his friend's fallen cap. "Here. Take this. I'm sorry. I thought you were Hammer. I thought . . . Jesus, let me put a compress on that cut."

"I'll do it!" Jenner said.

"Let me." Brian reached up to examine the wound, but Jenner brushed his hand aside.

"I said I'll do it."

Brian stepped back. "Okay."

Jenner withdrew a small field dressing kit and used it to administer to his wound as he spoke. "You sure picked a hull-down, piss-ass place for an ambush. From up there, I couldn't see anything but this mountain's backside. I haven't gotten bush-whacked like that since I was in grade school and the nuns caught me sneaking into the girls' bathroom. My face must look like I went twelve rounds with Mike Tyson."

"I'm sorry, man. I was just trying to knock you — I mean Alex — off his feet so he couldn't get away."

Jenner looked around. "No problem. I probably would have done the same thing."

He smirked. "But maybe with a little more finesse."

Brian ignored the barb. "Why didn't you answer your phone or return my messages?"

"I never got a message. My cell phone battery died in Kalispell. It wouldn't take a charge, so I left it behind."

Despite Jenner's sincere demeanor, Brian doubted his story.

"So why didn't you wait for me?"

"I thought you'd be too late to help."

"You were wrong."

"I can see that. I don't know how you did it. I've been tracking Hammer for days. He had a big head start on me, but I closed the distance. How did you get here ahead of me? Are you a Jedi Warrior?"

"I didn't track Alex. I've been waiting for him since last night at the base of Triple Divide Peak."

"Why there?

"It's where he's headed."

"How do you know?"

"He sent me the clue in his letter, the one you heard me read to his mom. Remember? Alex wrote he was going to die where the waters of three oceans begin. My father figured out the only place in Glacier fitting that description is the Peak."

"I wish I had noticed that detail. It would have saved me a lot of time."

"He also wrote that he dishonored his country after the raid in the village. Not during. After. That's the part that got to me."

Jenner fidgeted. "What do you think he meant?"

Brian hesitated before answering. When he first read the letter, he thought Alex had made a simple error, substituting one word for another. People make that kind of mistake every day. But when he learned about the CID investigation, he started questioning his assumptions. He also wondered what role Jenner played in the whole mess.

"What do you think it means, Icarus?"

"Me? How would I know?"

"You were with Alex the night after the raid, weren't you?"

"The whole sweet night. I never left his side. I told you that."

"So, did he do anything you are keeping from me? Something he should not have done?"

Jenner scoffed. "I wish there was something you could do at Bagram to feel sorry for. Other than eating the meatloaf. No, all we did was chill at the MWR, then walk back to quarters."

"And did you come across any Afghan soldiers?"

"Us? No. We saw no rag heads, friend, or foe. Why?"

"Just asking."

Jenner stepped closer. "Kiss my ass, Falcon. You never just ask. You want to know something. Now, unless you have something you want to say to me straight out, let's get moving. I came here to find Hammer, and you're wasting my time."

Brian looked hard into Jenner's eyes. What did his comrade know? Was he really with Alex that night, or was he covering for him? If Alex was in a fight with the Afghan soldier, did Jenner see it? Did he try to stop it or did he cheer him on? A thought wormed into his mind. Jenner, not Alex, was always the one most likely to cross the line. Jenner had something dark, wounded, and dangerous inside his heart. It was Jenner who treated Afghans like caked mud on his boots. Maybe it was Jenner who had bumped into the Afghan soldier that night. Maybe the CID wanted Alex not as a suspect but as a witness.

Whatever his suspicions, Brian could not detect any signs of deception in Jenner's mannerisms. The only way he could be sure of the truth was to find Alex. "Did you pick up his trail on the ridgeline?"

"I did, but I lost it. Hammer doesn't seem to trek in a straight line. That's why I came down. I saw the path and figured he was on it or in the grass below."

"I saw something in the grass."

"Maybe our boy."

"If so, he's ahead of us now and apt to meet head-on with my father."

Jenner's eyes opened wide. "Your father's here?"

"He's watching the approach to the peak."

Jenner shook his head from side to side. "I can't believe you brought your old man."

"My father knows Glacier."

"He might get hurt."

"He's not your concern. He's my responsibility."

Jenner puckered his lips and blew out his breath in a stream of white vapor. "OK, take it easy. Your father's your concern. My concern is Hammer. So, what do we do now?"

Brian pointed to Triple Divide. "Our camp is that way, through the Pass, near the eastern approach to the peak. Let's hightail it there. I want to make sure my dad is OK, then you and I will go after Alex. We'll catch him before he does something stupid. Roger?”

Jenner clutched Brian's hand and shoulder and bumped his shoulder with his own. “HUA! Heard, understood, and acknowledged.”

Brian smiled. The same old Jenner, he thought. “It's good to see you, Icarus.”

Jenner stepped back and made the “I Love You” sign with his hand. He winked and, mimicking Alex's East Texas accent, drawled, “That's enough sweet talk. Let's go find our brother.”

CHAPTER FORTY-FOUR

Bill lay prone on a horseshoe-shaped landing overlooking Triple Divide's eastern approach. After several minutes, he shifted his body to make himself more comfortable. The ground was hard and cold. His joints were stiff and aching. He was unaccustomed to lying on his stomach, and his gut grumbled a complaint about the three cups of cowboy coffee he had consumed earlier.

"Patience," Bill whispered. Saying the word, while breathing deeply, helped him enter a Zen-like state that opened his mind to his senses. He had mastered the skill late in life, after years of leading angry teens and wounded vets into the wilderness. He learned from experience that no one can alter the pace of tides or the currents of a river. Embracing this philosophy, he created a mindset utilizing patience like a sail to steer his way through life's treacherous shoals. Forbearance enabled him to navigate a ketch-rigged pulling boat through Penobscot Bay, sailing when the wind was up; rowing when it was down. More importantly, it served him whenever he waited for shattered souls to share their stories.

He wished he had used more patience in Vietnam and early in his marriage. But as a young man, he believed boldness was the only attribute meaning anything. That belief had caused much sorrow for himself and those he loved.

"Patience," he repeated and peered down the trail.

No trace of Alex.

He remembered the promise he made to his son. He would

let Alex pass if he saw a weapon. It would not surprise him if Alex did carry a gun or a knife. The vets he worked with often brought weapons to the vet center, thinking hey needed them. For many of them, their wars had not ended. In their heads, they still heard incoming rounds. Still saw flashes from muzzles. Still woke up afraid.

Where he worked, it was a strict rule that anyone who entered had to submit their weapons at the security desk. For some, it was very hard. But safe harbors are those that shield the vulnerable from the storm. Bill considered it a good sign of progress when his veterans felt safe enough to leave their weapons at home.

He glanced at the trail again.

Someone was walking his way.

CHAPTER FORTY-FIVE

When Alex turned the corner of the steep path, he spotted no one on the trail in front of him. That was good, he thought, but he was worried more about the man behind him than any person up ahead. Jenner was like a starving wolf smelling blood. Once locked in, he would never cease his hunt. Alex guessed only a half-hour separated the two men, at most. And the gap shrunk every minute he dallied.

Alex spurred himself onward. But the more he pushed his legs to speed up, the more they resisted. He swiped his brow with a checkered bandana and leaned forward. His breathing had grown ragged. His rucksack dragged on him like a dead weight. He toyed with the idea of dropping it off the trail, then dismissed the thought because he needed its contents when he summited Triple Divide Peak.

He told himself to press on.

He pictured the screaming face of Master Sergeant Buck Walsh, his lantern-jawed drill instructor during basic training.

What? Are you tired, Vilanova?

No, sir.

Then why were you slowing up? I say you're giving up.

No, sir.

Are you calling me a liar? Is that what you're doing?

No, sir.

I think that is what you're doing, you mealy mouth piece of Texas turd. You're calling me a liar.

No, sir.

You have enough breath to lie to my face, and you don't have enough to run hard?

I was running hard, sir.

By this time, Walsh was jumping up and down, shouting, his face crimson. Spittle and profanities sprayed from his mouth. His voice was deafening in Alex's ear.

You call that running hard, you miserable excuse for a soldier? I'm not your mommy, not your daddy. But I am your goddamn worst nightmare. I will destroy you if you do not move your ass. Do you hear me?

Yes, sir.

I can't hear you.

Yes, sir!

Then run like your worthless life depends on it. Now!

Alex's memory of his old DI suddenly injected a boost of adrenaline into his blood. His drill sergeant's dressing down came at the four-mile mark of a five-mile run when Alex was ahead of all the other recruits. He was winning the race. But, by the time Walsh finished reaming him out, eight other runners had passed him by, and he had to sprint the rest of the way to finish second. Walsh came over and sneered.

"You survived this time, Texas. We'll see about tomorrow."

Alex hated Walsh. He wanted to knock his DI down, spit in his eye, and smash that smug face into a pulp. Forget about the Army; forget about everything he worked for. No one was going to demean him like that again. Not ever. He had endured enough abuse as a boy. Now he was a man, and Walsh was going to find that out. Let him try that shit again.

But when Alex cooled off, he realized he had learned an important lesson from his drill instructor. During battle, it wasn't enough to be as good as, or better than, the next man.

To survive, you had to be better than you thought you could be. Walsh knew Alex could do better. It did not matter that Alex was running ahead of the pack. If he was pacing himself to encourage the rest of the squad, it was one thing. But he paced himself because he wanted to take the easy way out. Walsh insisted his raw recruit measure up. It would be a lesson that would stay with him through many tours of duty in battle zones around the world.

Alex picked up his pace again. His legs churned like a fullback running up the middle. His eyes did not stray from the path. He cared only about mounting that summit. There, he would honor his fallen brethren and decide whether to join them.

CHAPTER FORTY-SIX

Bill wondered if the distant figure laboring up the path was Alex. He was about the right size, and the man kept glancing back over his shoulder as if he expected someone was following him. The man wore a baseball cap in such a way it was impossible to see his face, but his dark, stringy hair fit the description. He looked preoccupied, and he leaned forward, his arms churning up and down like a man on a mission.

Bill grabbed his satellite phone.

Brian answered almost immediately.

Bill whispered. "It's me. I'm on the rock shelf just below our camp. There is a guy on the path heading this way. I can't see his face, but I think it's Alex."

"How far away is he?"

"I would say about two hundred yards. He can't see me. He's concentrating on getting up the path. I think he's hurt."

"Stay hidden. I'll be there as soon as I can."

"He's going to pass me unless I get down there."

"Don't go. I'll be there soon. OK?"

Bill ended the call without answering. No sense in belaboring what he and his son both knew. Bill could not let Alex pass by unimpeded. He had to save the soldier from hurting himself. Everything in Bill's life had prepared him for this moment. He rose to his feet and raced across the rock shelf to the far edge, where he slid on his backside down a gravelly, fifteen-foot-long slope. When he hit bottom, he turned and faced the large man running his way.

***

When Alex spotted the old man sliding down onto the path in front of him, he froze.

Who was he? he wondered. Part of a search party?

His eyes searched for an escape route, but Jenner lurked somewhere behind him, and the cliffs on either side of the path blocked a quick exit. Alex looked past the man. There were no signs of anyone else. But others could be hiding or on their way. Alex moved forward, keeping the man in focus as he tried to side-step around him. Before he could pass him by, the man took a step into his desired path and lifted his right arm at the elbow.

"Howdy," the man said. "Beautiful day for a hike."

Alex stopped and looked at him with suspicion.

"Where did you set out from?" the man asked with a smile.

Alex didn't reply.

"Well, judging by the way you came, I expect you took the Red Eagle Trail. Right?"

"Maybe."

"You live in St. Mary's?"

"No. I don't have time to —"

The old man interrupted, "I'm older than you, so I took a shorter route. I hiked from the Cut Bank campground."

Alex scoffed. "Cut Bank campground is closed."

"It is, but that's where I picked up the trail."

Alex scanned the old man's features. Something about the man's face gnawed at him. He could not pick it out. But his smile seemed genuine, and his eyes did not shift from side to side like a liar's might.

Alex brushed past the stranger.

"Wait a second," the old man said. "Are you going to the top of Triple Divide Peak?"

Alex whirled around. "Why do you want to know?"

The old man flinched in response to Alex's sharp tone. "Well, I hiked to the summit this morning, and I know it takes a while to get up there. You're a little late to start now. It's going to get dark soon."

"I'll take my chances."

"But I was up there this morning. It's dangerous to climb that ridgeline in the dark. It is a razor's edge up there. There's no cover, and the winds will freeze you to death or blow you off the side. Besides, a storm is coming in."

Alex was impatient. "As I said, I'll take my chances."

He walked off and didn't bother to turn around. He expected that he had rid himself of the old man until the man appeared alongside him, shuffling his feet sideways to face him.

"Hey, young fella, you don't want to go up there now. Why don't you come back to my camp? I'll build us a fire. You can get warm. I'll cook up some hot food. First thing tomorrow morning, you'll be on your way. How's that sound?"

Alex looked askance at the stranger who was struggling to keep up. "Are you alone?"

"I'm with my son. He's about your age. Right now, he is hiking. You and he would get along fine."

Alex wondered how many other "sons" he might discover if he accepted the old man's invitation. He was not about to find out. "Thanks, mister, but I don't think so."

Alex doubled his pace.

Again, the old man caught up. "Hey, can you hold up? I'm having a hard time keeping up. I'm not as young as you."

Exasperated, Alex turned on the old man. "Listen, I don't know what your game is, but you'd better go back to where you came from."

The man laughed and pointed his finger at Alex. "That's it. Now I know what I was thinking but couldn't put my finger on it. You're a soldier, right? The way you talk. The way you carry yourself. I'm a vet myself. What are you? Army? Navy? Marines? I was in the Army."

Alex's eyes turned into slits, and without answering, he charged ahead. He had wasted too much time. He would not stop again. It didn't matter if night fell, or a storm hit, or the ridgeline burst into flames. Even if the gates of hell opened in front of him, he would reach the summit tonight. In his mind, he heard Sergeant Walsh's gruff voice yelling at him. Run as if your worthless life depends on it.

Behind him, the old man called, "Alex."

Hearing his name shocked him. He pivoted to face the old man.

"Who are you?" Alex asked as he limped back to him. "Do you know me?"

The stranger stepped forward to meet him. "Don't you remember me? In Fayetteville, a few years ago. You looked different then. You had a buzz cut. And I guess I'm a little older now; maybe a lot greyer."

Alex stared at the stranger's face, trying to place him into the context of his life in Fayetteville. Was he someone from the base? A friend of a friend? A person he bumped into in town while getting his car serviced or his grocery shopping done? Someone, he said hello to or discussed the weather with? As much as he tried to remember, Alex had no clue as to the man's identity.

Then it came to him. The face had grown older and gaunt, the hair thinner and greyer. Alex felt like he was staring at his team leader's face, digitally morphed into a much older version. Alex felt like a character in a science fiction movie who suddenly meets his close friend after traveling forward in time. But this was no movie; the man in front of him was no actor. He remembered meeting Brian's family in front of a restaurant years ago.

"You're Brian's father. Right? I met you in Fayetteville."

"That's correct," he said. "Bill McEnroe. We met on the street years ago. You had just come back from playing basketball, remember?"

Alex's eyes darted up the slope. "Where's Brian?"

"He's in the Pass. He's on his way here. I called him."

Alex shook his head. "He shouldn't have come."

"He had to. I had to. We read your letter."

Alex's body deflated as if someone had punched him in the gut. "I just wanted him to know so he would understand. So he would be the one to break the news to my mom. But he shouldn't have come here, and he shouldn't have brought you."

"I wanted to help."

"You can't help. No one can."

"That's where you're wrong. Look, I can't say I know how you feel. But I know what it's like to come back home hurting and nothing you do can get the pain to stop. I've been there."

Alex turned away and looked up the trail.

"Don't go," Bill said, keeping his voice calm. "You won't find what you're looking for up there. Believe me."

Alex didn't answer, so Bill spoke more urgently: "Give yourself time, son. When I came home from Vietnam, I was in such a damn rush to get back to normal, to fit back in. You can't force it. It takes time to adapt to being home."

Alex pulled away. "I have to make th summit today."

"Bill placed his hand on Alex's shoulder. "We'll go together tomorrow, I promise. You, me, and Brian. What do you say?"

Alex's eyes hardened. "You need to go home."

Bill caught the look in Alex's eyes and knew he was going to lose him. His hand moved from the young man's shoulder to his arm.

Alex startled. "Let go of me."

Bill tugged on the young man's arm to prevent him from bolting.

Alex jerked back his arm and shoved Bill out of the way and marched past him. Bill lunged forward and wrapped his arms around Alex in a bear hug. Alex dropped his weight, rapped Bill's knuckles to open his hand, twisted Bill's arm, and threw him to the ground where he landed face down.

"Stay down! I don't want to hurt you."

Bill rose unsteadily and grabbed Alex's jacket.

Alex yelled in desperation and broke away, then stumbled and fell on his injured side. The pain hit him like a bayonet hitting bone. He turned over on his back and held his ribs. The old man's face loomed above him.

Without thinking, he grabbed the old man around the throat

CHAPTER FORTY-SEVEN

An insistent North wind buffeted Brian and Jenner as they abandoned the goat path for the trail leading to Triple Divide's eastern approach. As they ran, their lungs bellowed blasts of white vapor into the thinning air, and their arms and legs pumped in tandem as if responding to a military cadence. On the hard-pebbled surface of the trail, their boots scratched out a sound like that of a wire brush on a snare drum. They still had a quarter of a mile to go before they reached the camp.

Brian didn't want to think about what he might find there. His father had promised not to engage Alex if he presented a danger, but Brian's faith in his father's assurances lessened with every passing moment.

He motioned to Jenner. "Are you all right?"

Jenner didn't break stride as he emitted a deep-throated laugh. "No sweat. I just finished the Boston Marathon's Heartbreak Hill, and I'm coasting to the end."

Jenner picked up the pace and ran ahead.

Brian caught up.

Everything's a game to him, Brian thought. But this isn't a game.

He and Jenner rounded a curve that swung to the right around a gnarled whitebark pine clinging tenaciously to the slope. In front of them, the trail narrowed to a point where sky and earth merged. At the apex, a dark figure—no taller than an action figure at this distance—moved toward them.

Jenner grabbed his arm and pulled him to a stop, "Is that your old man up ahead?"

The figure half-walked, half-stumbled down the trail. His head was down.

"Can't tell if it's him" Brain said. He broke into a sprint and Jenner followed. They were about 250 yards away. As they raced closer, the man lifted his head.

Brian saw his father's face.

"Dad!" he screamed as loud as he could.

Perhaps in response, Bill picked up his speed for several seconds, then slowed to a shuffling walk. Like a sailor reaching shore, he raised his right arm and waved.

And then he fell.

Brian sprinted to his father and dropped to his knees. He cradled Bill's head and checked his vital signs. "Are you all right?"

Bill tried to sit up, but Brian prevented him from doing so. "Hold on. Just lie there."

"I tried to stop him," Bill said.

"Don't talk."

"He smashed the phone so I couldn't call you."

Jenner handed Brian his canteen.

Brian lifted his father to a sitting position and held the canteen as his father drank.

Jenner examined the back of Bill's head. "He has some swelling at the base of the skull. Either he fell or Alex hit him from behind."

His father pushed the canteen away with one hand, and with the other, pushed against Brian. "Enough talk. Let me up."

"Stay down." Brian pressed his forearm against Bill's chest. "You might have a concussion."

"I'm fine. I was just a little dizzy."

"Answer me. Where are you?"

Bill's face reddened. "I'm in the Holy Land."

"Dad!"

"I'm in Glacier National Park. My name is William McEnroe. Today is Tuesday. Now, let me up."

"But you're dizzy."

Bill sat up. "I was dizzy. Jesus, I have low blood pressure. I take pills. I get dizzy sometimes."

Jenner pointed a small penlight at Bill's eyes. "Look at the light, Mr. McEnroe."

He clicked the light off and stood. "His pupils constrict. Probably no concussion."

Bill snickered. "I told you. Now, get off me."

Brian helped his father to his feet. "You should take it easy for a while. We'll take you back to camp."

Bill shook his head. "Don't you understand? He's desperate. Once he reaches the summit, he's liable to do anything."

"Did he hit you?"

"He was just trying to get away. I tried to stop him. Thought I could. But I fell back and hit my head. When I got up, he was gone."

Brian turned to Jenner. "Take one of his arms."

The big man swooped in and propped up the older man on one side.

Bill's eyes grew large. "What the hell are you doing?"

"We're taking you back to camp," Brian said.

Bill squirmed in their grasp. "Are you crazy? You don't have time for this. Go after him."

Jenner let go of Bill's arm. "He's right, Falcon. No telling what Hammer will do. I tell you what. I'll go ahead. You look after your father."

Brian didn't know what to say. He didn't think his father had suffered a concussion, but he didn't want to take chances. He had seen too many soldiers with invisible wounds fall asleep and never wake up. Or walk around with addled minds, bereft of memories, raging to the heavens, terrified at their helplessness. Everyone showed concern and empathy for soldier's wounds and missing limbs but little for injuries no one could see. Until it was too late.

"I can't leave my father alone."

"Then you stay here. I'll catch Hammer before he reaches the summit."

"Go, then."

With a nod and a wave, Jenner strode away.

Bill broke free from his son's grasp. "Go with him."

Brian reached for his father's arm, but Bill stepped back before his son's hand took hold.

"I'm taking you back to camp," Brian said.

"Like hell you are. You're going up to that summit."

"Jenner can handle it."

"But you need to go. Don't you understand?"

Brian did understand. Alex was his responsibility. Soldiers have sacrificed their lives to honor their commitment to each other. Brian felt the same imperative at his core. His father felt it for Heng Pok. He felt it for Alex. It was as potent as love. If he didn't go up that mountain, he'd regret it his whole life.

Brian glanced at the trail to the peak, then turned to his father. "Are you sure?"

"Go."

Brian made a salute with an outstretched hand and ran to catch up to Jenner.

CHAPTER FORTY-EIGHT

Alex carried the dead as he climbed to the summit. As a soldier, he had to bear the burden. He brought them home from every unforgiving valley and desert hellhole where he had fought. The dead had no physical weight. Their heft massed in memories: blood seeping through cotton gauze, the sweet coppery smell of death, the rattle of a dying stranger. Alex accepted responsibility for keeping these memories alive. Friends told him to forget. Counselors warned of moral injury. Alex scoffed at the notion. But when he flew back home, the dead accompanied him.

Alex tried to shove his burden to the back of his mind and concentrate on the last section of his climb. When he had waved goodbye to Petra and walked off the trail, he had harbored little hope of making it this far. He had trekked at night over harsh terrain with minimal equipment and no firearm and persevered. The mountains, the weather, the cougar, and every pursuer were obstacles he had overcome. The completion of the journey he had begun at the motel in Fayetteville was just moments away.

As he crested the summit, Alex flung his arms wide to embrace the panorama. The mountains and valleys spread before him in the moon's ethereal glow. He had completed his odyssey, if not yet his quest. He felt exhilarated, then dejected. It was like watching a sunset in all its glory while anticipating the darkness that followed.

He imagined Hector teasing him: You think too much, my friend. Be like me. No thinking, ever.

Alex pictured his comrades-in-arms together again, like in the photo. Hector making a silly face in the middle. Jenner and Brian standing erect on the right, and he and Aarmaan smiling like schoolboys on the left.

Alive! All of them.

His mind played tricks on him, conjuring voices from thin air.

Hector, it's good to see you.

And you too, *mi amigo*. But I have to leave soon.

Leave? Where to?

Hector chuckled. Back to heaven. There are only Latinos up there. It looks like Miami.

Jenner tapped Hector on the back of the head. Mighty Mouse, you don't have wings.

Don't need any wings, Monster Man. I got charisma.

Brian leaned forward. Enough, Hector. Alex has things to do.

Hector gave him his put-upon look. Aw, I was helping him. He's thinking too much.

Jenner nudged him playfully. He's just doing his Odysseus thing again.

Alex smiled. Doing his Odysseus thing again? How many times had he heard that from his team? He remembered all those long nights in Bagram when Jenner regaled them with tales of King Odysseus, his ten years of war, then ten more years of trying to get back home. To Jenner, nothing mattered more than the journey. But Alex's interest had always fixated on what came after. Yes, the warrior king had regained his wife and kingdom. But Alex wanted to know about the hero's life in the ensuing years. How did Odysseus adjust to being back home in Ithaca? Did he live a full life? Did he grow old basking in the sun? Or did Odysseus grow restless and sail off on the open sea?

Alex sighed. His brain longed for answers, but none came. Only ghosts emerged in his mind. Somehow, he had summoned them.

Aarmaan stood before him with his right hand against his heart.

Aarmaan, why are you here?

I am waiting for you, my friend.

Why?

I want to help you finish what you came here to do.

A blast of cold air against Alex's neck broke his reverie. He trembled and hunched his shoulders and crossed his arms to protect himself. Enough daydreams, he thought, then spied the eastern approach to the mountain. There was no sign of Brian and Jenner, but he knew they weren't far behind. He had little time, and one last task remained.

He trudged to the stone cairn, marking the peak's highest point. Unknown travelers had constructed the pyramid-like structure of roundish stones the size of cannonballs cemented together by gravity. Each wall rose to an elevation of five feet. In the moonlight, two sides shone a ghostly gray while the third was out of his sight, though he imagined it cast in shadow. Alex stretched his hands out and leaned against the cairn.

"Forgive me," he murmured and pressed his forehead to the stones to say a prayer his mother taught him when he was a boy in Texas. "Eternal rest grant unto them, O Lord, and let perpetual light shine upon them. May the souls of the faithful departed, through the mercy of God, rest in peace. Amen."

Rest in peace. Alex did not know if God had heard him. But words needed saying. This was a fitting place to honor the dead and plead for their forgiveness. From here, water flowed into three oceans. Here, heaven touched land. Here, he could come to terms with his past. If he failed, he would end his life and join the fallen.

Alex knelt and opened the drawstring of his pack. He withdrew a leather-bound book with gold embossed letters: *The Holy Qur'an: An English Translation.* Aarmaan had given him the book during his first visit to the interpreter's home. Alex opened the Koran to one of its dog-eared pages and read: "And of His signs is this: thou seest the still earth, but when he sends down water thereupon, it stirs and swells. He who gives water life is surely the giver of life to the dead."

He closed the holy book and felt its weight in his hands. The gift of life? he wondered. If he consecrated this peak with water and then rain fell, cascading down the rocks into oceans, giving life elsewhere, would his friends' deaths mean something?

But he had no water. He had lost his canteen on the avalanche chute. Without hesitation, he removed his Yarborough knife from its sheath on his belt and cut a small slice in the palm of his left hand. As soon as blood flowed, he sprinkled the top of the cairn. This will have to do, he thought, and wrapped his hand with a blue bandana, pressing against the wound to stanch the bleeding.

In the distance, he heard what sounded like the Muslim call to prayer. He knew it was only his imagination playing tricks again. Still, he closed his eyes and listened to the evocative sound.

Aarmaan's voice rose from the melody. You must not give up, my friend.

Aarmaan, what more do I need to do?

No more, no less. The man who asks what he should do knows the answer. A wise man knows it is the question he must find.

But what is the question?

In two, there is none.

The words made no sense to Alex. In two, there is none. It sounded more like an answer than a question. But Alex knew Afghans often spoke privately in ways that Americans found strange. In their tea rooms and homes, Afghans spoke in poetry, in layers unfolding more layers, nesting inside of each other like Russian Matryoshka dolls. For a thousand years, tribesmen and women weaved news, history, and fantasy into elaborate stories resplendent with metaphors and mystery. The greatest storytellers memorized thousands of lines and enlivened their tales by drifting back and forth in time, exaggerating exploits, and confabulating stories when memory failed.

In two, there is none. Somehow, Alex had to find the question.

Alex opened his eyes when he felt something cold and wet fall on his upturned face. In the glow of moonlight, snowflakes swirled around him. He threw his head back and stuck out his tongue. As the snow melted, he realized just how parched he was. But the droplets didn't quench his thirst. He longed for his lost canteen.

With great care, he placed the Koran into his pack, then stood. He needed to find the perfect stone to place atop the summit cairn. It had to be as smooth and round and roughly the same size as the ones already in place. But it also had to be one he could carry to the cairn and lift to the top.

He skirted the summit and surrounding fringe. Thirty yards away from the memorial, he found the perfect rock. Slick with fallen snow, it lay in a bed of loose gravel. He didn't know if he had the strength to lift it and carry it to the cairn. But he was determined. He dug his hands under the stone and lifted, using his legs, until he stood with the rock cradled in the pit of his belly. Slightly hunched over, he hobbled halfway to the rock pyramid. Sharp pain in his side stopped him. He gritted his teeth. He staggered forward. Twice the stone almost slipped from his arms. Each time, he saved it, cradling it with his arms and chest.

When he reached the pyramid, Alex lowered the stone to the ground and stood up. He had re-injured his ribs. The pain twisted his guts into a knot. If he took a deep breath, he feared the spasms might be unbearable. But he needed one deep breath to power the stone to the top.

Forgive me, Aarmaan. I don't think I can do it.

Insha'Allah, Aarman said.

If God wills it, Alex replied.

Yes, my friend. It is so. It will always be so.

I have come so far. Too far to fail now.

You will not fail, my friend. I will help you.

Aarmaan?

His friend didn't answer. Alex wanted to ask him about his earlier riddle. He wanted to know what it meant. Alex hoped the meaning would come to him, but nothing stirred in him but doubt. Perhaps he was crazy, and the voices and this mission were nothing more than misfiring neurons. Maybe this entire journey was some strange hallucination.

But it wasn't an illusion. The icy wind chafed his face and his pants were wet. The collar of his shirt stiffened with a crust of ice. Hunger gnawed at his core. Pain throbbed in his side. The stone lay waiting at his feet.

Alex squatted and grabbed the stone with both hands. He grunted, took a deep breath, and grimaced as he hoisted the heavy rock up to his shoulders and pressed it overhead. Centering the stone, he let it fall into place. It rocked for a moment, then lay motionless as if it had always belonged there. Alex placed his right hand on the stone and let his left fall to his side. He waited for the pain to subside. Then, bowing his head, he spoke.

"I honor the lives lost on my watch. Your families waited for you to come home and cried when you did not. They will remember you. I honor everything you accomplished and mourn what you left undone. If there is a God, I hope you meet the one you know and pray to. May you find peace."

He made the sign of the cross and said, "Amen." His mission was over. He had completed his journey and his ceremony to honor the dead. Fate had protected him and given him the strength to lift the stone into place. When the snow melted, the water would flow down the cairn and the summit and stream toward three oceans.

He wondered if it was enough. He closed his eyes and sifted through his thoughts for an answer.

In two, there is none. What did Aarmaan mean by that?

"Aarmaan?" he called out.

There was no answer.

"Aarmaan, speak to me."

The only voice Alex heard was his own.

As he contemplated his next move, Alex's thirst returned worse than before. He felt light-headed and weak. His mouth was cottony. His throat hurt. He longed to scoop some snow and stuff it down his throat. But he knew that would cause hypothermia. Instead, Alex pulled a plastic Rite Aid bag from his pack. He spread it open to collect snow he could melt for clean drinking water. Like a giddy child in his first snowstorm, Alex closed his eyes and spun around, making increasingly larger circles with his steps. Round and round he went until he stumbled on a small rock and fell. Only then did he open his eyes. He had come within a foot of spiraling over the cliff.

"My god," he said, then rose to a sitting position.

He peeked into the plastic bag. Such a paltry amount, he thought. Still, he pressed the bag against his chest to melt the snow. When done, he lifted one end of the bag and drank its contents. No beer or wine had ever tasted as good.

Exhilarated, he held out the empty bag as if giving a toast. "Here's to you, Aarmaan. In two, there is none."

As he uttered the words, Alex hit upon the meaning of Aarmaan's riddle. In two, there is none. In life, everyone faces choices. Most require little thought. But the gods afflict some creatures with an awful dilemma — to choose between two actions when neither offers a good outcome. Isn't that what Aarmaan faced? On one hand, Aarmaan could kill American soldiers — his friends — and then die. Or he could do nothing and let the terrorists murder his wife and sons. The enemy had trapped Aarmaan in a Sophie's choice, a shell game that could only end in tragedy. By the time the interpreter had stumbled through the door of the hangar, he had made his choice. Alex and the others were just pieces on the chessboard. Alex could save neither Aarmaan or Hector.

Alex dropped the empty plastic bag. In this moment, what choices did he have? As he saw it, he could give himself up, return to Fort Bragg and subject his actions, and Jenner's, to CID scrutiny. Or he could fall on his spear on Triple Divide and end his life.

So, what do I do now, Aarmaan?

Find home, Aarmaan replied.

And then what?

Then choose your path.

Which path?

Aarmaan didn't answer.

Alex shook his head, then brushed snow off his chest, arms, and legs. He stood and stepped forward to peer over the edge of the precipice. Below, all he could see was darkness.

He imagined that hurdling off this cliff would be like plummeting off a high diving board for the first time — the leap off the edge, the thrill of flying into space, his legs churning as if running on air, the sudden rush, the realization of no-turning-back, the anticipation of a never-experienced landing, a final scream, then the unknown.

Alex dangled his foot over the brink.

CHAPTER FORTY-NINE

Brian and Jenner crested the summit of Triple Divide Peak as the snow flurry ended. A thin layer of frost covered the ground and hid any tracks Alex might have made. In the dim light from the moon, the men strained to see a shadow or an outline of their friend against the dark boulders strewn across the peak. They could have turned on their headlamps, but neither man thought it wise. The risk of frightening Alex away was too great. Better to get as close to him as possible before he spotted them.

Brian used a hand signal to ask Jenner if he saw anything.

Jenner answered in the negative, then indicated they should split up and search in two different directions.

No, Brian signaled and ordered Jenner to follow him with his finger pointing back and forth at each of them, then emphatically gesturing in one direction.

Jenner shook his head and whispered. "We should split up. It's dark and freezing. The sooner we find him, the better. If we separate, we cover twice the territory. Besides, Hammer might not spook if he sees just one of us."

"I don't think we —"

"Holler if you see him," Jenner said, then started in one direction while pointing Brian to take the opposite.

Brian almost called out to him, but, at the last moment, stopped himself. Instead, he remained silent as he watched him scuttle away. The big man moved like a cat, leaping across patches of ice, and scrambling over rocks. In a few moments, he was out of view.

Brian couldn't understand Jenner's stubbornness. Despite his maverick tendencies, Jenner grudgingly accepted his place as second on the team. That is, until he learned about Alex's letter. Since then, Icarus had turned rogue. Brian wanted to chase after Jenner and dress him down, but he decided finding Alex superseded anything else. A confrontation with Icarus could wait.

Brian strode to his left, where he came upon a steep drop-off. He peered over the edge of the cliff. The descent was straight down into a deep well of darkness. If anyone fell or jumped from this point, certain death waited below. Try as he might, Brian could not see what lay at the bottom. If the search of the summit came up empty, he'd come back here, climb down this cliff, and recover a body.

I'm going to find him, he thought. Alive!

Brian proceeded until he sighted the stone cairn at the summit's apex. At this distance, in this light, the landmark reminded Brian of a wedge-shaped grave marker he chanced upon in a cemetery outside Camden, Maine, where his father buried his mother. The marker memorialized a fourteen-year-old boy killed in action during the Civil War. Below a granite laurel leaf, the artist had carved an inscription in Latin: *Amor patriae ducit.*

Love of country leads me.

Brian didn't want this to be Alex's epitaph.

Brian scanned the area. He hoped to see Alex running toward him with his Cheshire-Cat smile and agile gait. If only he could rewind the clock back to the night of the mission. Back to when his friend and team were whole. Back to when he spotted Aarmaan reading the Koran.

The memory of that night came back to him. Something he saw in the interpreter's face must have bothered him because he asked the older man if he was afraid. The question seemed so banal, so off-mission, he surprised himself by asking it. Might as well have asked Aarmaan, "How do you like this weather?" for all the attention he paid to his answer. He couldn't even remember his answer. Wasn't even sure Aarmaan had answered. So locked on what his team had to do, he missed any telltale signs of trouble in his terp's behavior.

But Alex had noticed something.

Brian shuddered. He had told Alex to shut up.

Too late now to change things, he thought, and refocused on the cairn. The stone pyramid was big enough to hide behind. From this angle, he could see two sides, but the third side remained hidden from view. Maybe Alex was hiding there in the darkness.

Then a thought struck him. Maybe Alex was behind him.

He made a 180-degree turn and studied the approach he and Jenner had taken to the summit. In the Hindu Kush, Alex had mastered the art of circling back, getting behind unsuspecting mujahideen on their trail, then killing them.

If Alex had circled back, Brian thought, he was descending to the base of the mountain.

Right to where his father waited.

Brian's stomach churned.

He scanned the ridge again as best as he could in the moonlight. He saw no movement. Was it possible for anyone to descend so quickly? Alex had injured himself, but did that matter? His men had always surprised him with what they could do in the face of adversity. They possessed depths of resolve bordering on the superhuman. Because of them, he won medals. Because of them, he was alive.

He drew out his binoculars and scanned the trail below. He could see no one there, so he turned back to the cairn. To minimize the sound of his approach, he walked in a zig-zag motion, carefully placing his feet until he reached a point near the dark side of the cairn. He could make out the impression of something jutting from its surface. He observed no shiver or tremble, no plume of breath, no sudden jerk or gesture. There were no sounds or smells. No signs of life at all. But Brian knew better. It was Alex.

Brian's first instinct was to rush over to his friend, but a voice inside him commanded him to wait. He circled the stone landmark until he faced the dark side. Fifteen feet away, Alex sat as if in mourning with his knees locked in front, his elbows resting on his knees, and his hands holding his lowered head.

Brian called out to him. "Alex?"

His friend's head lifted and, and his eyes opened.

The grating edge in Alex's voice startled Brian. "Stop! Don't come any closer."

"It's me," Brian said as he took a step forward.

"Stay back. I mean it."

Brian crept nearer.

As if sprung by some unseen hand, Alex's body unfolded like a trap. He rose on his haunches, ready to pounce. His right hand held a large knife.

Brian extended his hands in front of him, palms out. "Easy. Easy. I'll stay right here."

Brian knelt on one knee, opened his arms, and waited for Alex to dictate what to do next. Let him feel he's in control, he thought. Get him to talk. Get him to put the knife down. Then hope Jenner uses his head when he shows up.

Alex's eyes darted left and right. "Where's Jenner?"

Brian gestured with his arm. "Back there, somewhere."

"What's he doing?"

"Looking for you."

"And your father?"

"He's at camp."

"Is he all right?"

"He'll be fine."

"I didn't want to hurt anyone."

"He knows that. Come, let's climb down together. You, me, and Jenner."

Alex didn't answer.

"Please, Hammer."

Silence.

"Talk to me. What's going on?"

Silence again.

Brian's mind shuffled through his options: Keep talking, hoping he could persuade Alex to surrender. Rush him and try to grab the knife before he could use it. Wait for Jenner, then create a diversion so Jenner could grab him.

No option seemed ideal. Perhaps he'd been too optimistic about his game plan. In his mind, the game was over when he found Alex. All the hard stuff came before. Once he found Alex, he felt certain his teammate would follow him out of Glacier. Hammer had always followed him.

He stared at Alex. "Put the knife down."

Alex only squeezed harder on the handle.

Brian felt the cold wetness of the snow seeping through his pants leg. "You're scaring me with that knife. Put it down, will you?"

Alex shivered and pulled the knife close to his chest. "I won't use it if you don't rush me."

"I'm scared you'll hurt yourself."

"What? You believe I want to hurt myself?"

"Do you?"

Alex raised the knife. He turned it over and pressed the back of his hand against his temple.

Then he laughed.

CHAPTER FIFTY

Jenner saw no trace of Alex. Either his comrade-in-arms had escaped Triple Divide, or he was on the other side of the summit. For a moment, he considered another possibility. His friend was dead and lying somewhere else in Glacier. The idea shook him to his core.

The stupid bastard, he thought. He's got a lot to live for. People who care whether he lives or dies. Women who love him. He's chucking that away. For what?

He pictured Petra in Kalispell waiting for news of Alex's rescue. No one ever longed for him like that.

For all his passion for Homer's *Odyssey*, he realized he had completely missed the essential truth in its pages. What drove Odysseus for ten years was not the gods, the giants, or the glory. It was the love of a woman. Sweet Penelope. The noble warrior needed her soft touch and kind words. Only she could heal his wounded soul.

Jenner snatched a twig from the ground, broke it in two, and threw it off the cliff. He thought of his grandfather. You taught me well, old man. Be strong. Be hard, like a rock, you said. A rock can't hurt. That's what you taught me. But look at you, alone in your cabin, waiting for death. And you locked your doors to keep me out.

Jenner closed his eyes, gripped his fingers behind his neck, and pushed his head as hard as he could until his neck hurt. Then he relaxed and opened his eyes.

Focus on the goddamn search, he said to himself.

Move.

He had to find Alex first, before Brian had a chance to ask him too many questions about the Afghan soldier.

Jenner imagined what his team leader would do if Alex told the truth. In Brian's world, there were no excuses and no exceptions. Every soldier had to live by the military code. That belief system was part of Brian's DNA. Without blinking, he'd turn Jenner and Alex over to the authorities.

Jenner couldn't let that happen.

Despite the poor visibility and traction, Jenner charged toward the other side of the summit. Suddenly, he spotted something moving in front of the cairn. He stopped, squatted, and retrieved his binoculars. Through the lenses, he spied Brian kneeling before a dark figure in the shadows. It had to be Alex. He must be alive. But why was Brian keeping his distance? He guessed Alex had a weapon.

From this direction, no cover existed between Jenner and the cairn. He needed to get to Alex unseen, then take him from the rear. Jenner had to backtrack and find another approach.

But he had to hurry.

CHAPTER FIFTY-ONE

Every time Alex's eyes turned away to peer into the darkness, Brian inched closer to the cairn. When his friend's eyes darted back, Brian froze. He saw the scared-dog look on Alex's face and heard his labored breathing. Below Alex's left arm, drops of blood stained the snow.

"You're bleeding." Brian leaned forward as if to stand.

Alex thrust out the knife. "Stay back."

"But —"

"Stay where you are."

"You're hurt."

"It's nothing."

"Let me help you."

Alex twisted his knife closer to Brian's chest and studied his eyes. Neither man spoke. Finally, Alex raised his free arm and pressed the back of his hand against his mouth, then let it fall. "Do you have any water?"

Brian reached inside his coat, withdrew a water bottle from a mesh pocket, and tossed it to Alex, who caught it with his free hand.

"Thanks."

Alex sipped the water, slid to his knees, and sat back on his legs. He wiped his mouth with his sleeve, then used the blade of the knife to point to a slight wound on his left hand.

"I don't know if you can see this. I cut myself. . . . I know it's crazy, but I had no water, so I cut my palm. Not much, just a tiny slice. But enough to sprinkle blood on each side of the cairn."

Brian shook his head. "You shouldn't have cut yourself. I was here this morning with my father, and I poured water on the three sides . . . for you."

Alex's eyes opened wide. "For me?"

"I told you. I got you covered."

Brian grinned. "For you, Fucktard. You didn't have to spill blood."

Alex's face fell. "It was fitting. My blood for theirs."

"Their deaths were not your fault."

"Maybe, but it was me who left Aarmaan in the village."

"I ordered you to. Blame me."

"You know what they did to his body," Alex said with disgust.

Brian flinched. No one had ever found Aarmaan's body. The people from that village wouldn't reveal where, or if, they buried him. Brian could only guess at what desecrations they inflicted upon him before they disposed of his remains.

"If you're to blame for what happened to him, then so am I," Brian said. "And so are the generals, the politicians, and the millions of Americans who sent us over there. We're all to blame. For all of it. Not just Aarmaan. It sucks, but that's the truth."

Alex took another sip of water and nodded. "I'm in the eye of a storm, and there's no easy way out. The only way forward is to go through the worst of it. It's not just Hector and Aarmaan. It's all the rest before that. In Iraq and Somalia. I see dead people wherever I look. I talk to them. In my dreams, I bury people, but they keep crawling out of the ground."

Brian thought of Kate waking him from a nightmare, holding him, and singing Coldplay's "Strawberry Swing" until he calmed down. "I get nightmares too. It's normal. Our brains juice up like junkies every time we go out on a mission. We hate violence and we love it. Hell, we're human. Given what you went through, I'd worry if you had no nightmares."

"But do they ever end?"

"They fade in time. Or so my father says. He says we need to help each other heal."

Brian could almost reach out and touch Alex. Could he grab the arm holding the knife before his friend used it?

Instead of obeying, Alex brought the blade's sharp edge over his left wrist. "I told you to stay back."

Brian held up his palms and leaned back to create more space. "Whoa."

"Why are you here?" Alex asked.

"I got your letter."

Alex shook his head. "I don't know what I was thinking."

"You wanted me to know so I could tell your mother, remember?"

"You spoke to her?"

"We drove with her from the airport. She's trying to help. I know she wants you to come home."

Alex bowed his head.

"Put the knife down, Hammer. Talk to me. Tell me what happened the night we came back from the raid."

Alex's chin lifted and his eyes watered.

"Hammer, in your letter, you wrote you let something happen. What was it?"

Silence.

Brian leaned forward. "Were you with Jenner?"

"No."

"Not at all that night?"

"I was, later. He wanted me to go to the MWR, but I wanted to be alone, so he left. But then, I don't know . . . I couldn't stay in my room anymore, so I went looking for him."

He wiped his mouth. "That's when I met this other soldier."

"An Afghan?"

Alex's face looked like someone had slapped it. "Yes. He . . . was a young guy. Spoke a little English. He asked me for a cigarette."

Alex paused as if he needed to clear his throat. Then the words gushed out of him.

"He said he was from Kandahar. Said he hated the army and wanted to go home. He asked me for a second cigarette even though he was still on his first. I told him I had none to spare. But I don't think I would have given him one if I did. There was something strange about him. He wouldn't let me be."

Alex choked up. When he spoke again, he parsed each word. "He kept tagging along asking for things, always talking, touching my shoulder, muttering in Pashto, showing off the rifle by his side like he wanted me to know it was there. Kind of threatening me with it. I don't know how long we walked like that, side by side, him talking, yelling at me, and me trying to lose him. When he raised the muzzle of his rifle to my face, I just lost it."

"What did you do?"

"I hit him and hit him and hit him. I kept on hitting him. Even when he was down. In my head, I saw Aarmaan below me and I wanted to kill him. If Jenner hadn't pulled me off, I would have."

"Jenner was there?"

"I don't know where he came from. He held me until I calmed down. Then he checked out the soldier to see if he was still alive. He was, barely. So, we took him as close as we could get to the hospital, without somebody seeing us, and left him for somebody to find."

He paused, then added. "Later, when I heard he was in a coma, I wanted to tell you what I did . . . But I didn't."

"So that's what you've been carrying around all this time," Brian said, wondering why Alex hadn't come to him.

Brian needed to get Alex's knife. He was about to lunge forward when he saw Jenner stealthily moving toward them from behind the cairn.

Alex rose to his knees and twisted his torso to look in each direction. "Where's Jenner? He's here, isn't he?"

He raised his voice to a feverish pitch. "Icarus, show yourself, goddamn it, or I'll cut myself bad. I swear."

Jenner didn't answer.

The silence weighed on Brian's chest. He froze in place, his eyes shifting back and forth from Alex to Jenner.

Alex's jaw clenched. "Icarus, you'd better show yourself. I'm counting to three. One . . . Two . . ."

Jenner strode from behind the cairn and circled in front of Alex, his arms extended to his sides with palms upward. His smile curled as if he were a smart-aleck teen caught smoking in school.

"Greetings, Brothers. It's a fine night for a stroll. The moon's out, the air's clean, we're all here, and beer is in the fridge when we get back."

"Stay away from me, Icarus."

"You have nothing to fear from me, Hammer Man. I'm a peaceful warrior. I'm here on Mount Olympus to pray to the gods for our safe journey home. Isn't that what we all want?"

Jenner took a step toward Alex.

"Get back," Alex said. "Or else."

Jenner halted.

Brian gestured to Jenner to stand down. "Take it easy."

Jenner sneered. "Don't tell me what to do. If you hadn't looked my way a second ago, I would have had him."

"Jenner —"

"I heard you two talking about the Afghan soldier."

Brian glanced at Alex, then spoke to him as well as to Jenner. "Calm down, both of you."

Jenner took a half-step towards Brian and halted. "Calm down? What are you talking about? Hammer, do you hear our fearless leader? We're in the middle of the wilderness, on top of a mountain, freezing our oysters off, and he's worried I'll do something crazy when it's you who's holding a knife in your hand."

Jenner turned back toward Alex. "It's crazy to do what you're doing, you know? If you want to die, there are five hundred ways to get killed in Afghanistan. You don't fly back home, climb a mountain, and get your friends involved. That's not what you do if you're a true warrior. Put the Yarborough down and let's get out of here. C'mon, Honcho, I'll get a brownie badge for saving your ass again."

Jenner inched closer.

Alex pressed the knife harder against his wrist. "Stay back!"

Jenner paused.

"Stand down," Brian said. Then louder, "Back off."

Instead of retreating, Jenner whirled around toward Brian with his 9mm pointed at Brian's chest. "I told you not to fucking tell me what to do."

Brian raised his arms, palms facing Jenner, who was in a soldier's fighting stance.

"Don't do it, Jenner," Alex said. He rose to one knee.

Jenner held his hand. "It's okay, Hammer. Stay right where you are and no one gets hurt. Right, Brian? Except for Hammer and me when you turn us over to the CID."

Holding the gun steady, Jenner moved in a semicircle toward Brian. "You had to come out here, didn't you? I told you I'd find him. But no. You've got to act like the hero. I could have brought him back; talked to him before you or the Army got to him. We would've been all right. Now, who knows what the Army will do to us because of that damn code you live by. That's the truth, isn't it?"

Brian said, "I don't know anymore."

"Well, that's something, at least. Your concession will make it easier for me when they lock me up."

"Hammer could plead self-defense."

Jenner pointed at Alex. "Look at him. Do you want him to go through a trial after what he's suffered? You don't get it, do you?

I came to Glacier to save Hammer from himself, and from you."

"From me?" Brian asked.

"You and that list of Army regs you've got buzzing like bees inside your brain. This isn't about following the rules; it's about doing the right thing."

"I'm here to do that."

"Like hell."

"Then shoot if you don't believe me."

Jenner stared at Alex, then at Brian, as if he were figuring out what to do.

"Stand up, Brian," he said.

Brian rose to his feet and stretched out his hand like a beggar. "Give me the gun."

"Put your hand down."

"Jenner . . . "

"I said, put your hand down or I —."

Alex cried out. "Jenner, drop the weapon."

Jenner smirked. "Take it easy, Hammer."

"Don't do this. Put it down. Please."

Jenner looked over his shoulder and gave Alex a half-smile. "OK, whatever you say. Watch me."

He lowered the 9mm carefully until it pointed at the ground, then released his left hand from the grip and shifted the gun to one-hand control. When done, he moved within a few feet of Brian and stood face-to-face with him.

Then Jenner winked and smiled.

Taken aback, Brian waited to see what Jenner would do next.

Slowly, Jenner performed a series of tactical hand signals only Brian and he could see.

Brian answered him with the same.

Understood? Jenner signaled.

Understood, Brian motioned.

With that, Jenner dashed to the side and fired two quick shots into the ground to distract Alex.

At the sound of the first report, Brian sprang forward and grasped Alex's right hand with his left, pushing Alex's hand and arm back and smashing the knuckles against the hard stone. The knife fell, and Alex let out a cry of pain as Jenner tackled him and pinned him to the ground.

Brian tossed the knife as far as he could. With Jenner, he lifted Alex from the ground. Alex sobbed and slumped against them. In response, they held him in their arms.

"It's OK," Brian said. "Let it all out."

For several minutes, the three men stood together without a word, their heads bowed, their arms intertwined around each other's shoulders.

Finally, Alex lifted his head and mumbled, "I don't want to die."

Brian looked at him and nodded. "We know that. Right, Jenner?"

Jenner grinned. "Knew it all the time, Hammer. You were just doing your Odysseus thing."

Alex shook his head. "God, I miss them."

"Hector and Aarmaan are still with us," Brian said. "Always will be."

Brian gazed at his surviving team members. The strength of their arms comforted him. He glanced over their shoulders at the distant mountains. Standing on Triple Divide's summit with these men, he marveled at how far they had come from the Afghan village. And from the war. This journey may be their last together, but he knew the fiery furnace of war had forged their bond. What they were to each other connected them, wherever they went, and whatever they did.

CHAPTER FIFTY-TWO

The moon surrendered to a wakening sun as the three men picked up their pace on their way to the campsite. They hiked in single file, Brian in the lead and Jenner bringing up the rear. Alex marched in the middle, his head down, his arms wrapped around his chest to ward off the bitter cold. Sheets of frost clung to the ground. Virgin streams of melted snow crossed the trail and disappeared over the edge. In the valley, a bull elk bellowed. A startled catbird flew out of a mountain ash stretching its berry-heavy limbs skyward. The bird soared overhead, not a cloud masking the sky.

"I'm turning off my headlamp," Jenner yelled forward. "You might do the same, Team Sergeant."

"Thanks," Brian said, shutting off his lamp.

"No problem, Mate."

"It's not much farther."

They marched on.

Brian raised his arm when he spotted his father side-shuffling down the slope with a canteen and a space blanket.

"Thank God, you found him," Bill said to his son, then rushed to Alex and clutched his arm. He unfolded the heat-reflective sheet. "Here, take this. It will warm you."

Without a word, Alex swathed himself with the silvery blanket, then greedily drank from the old man's canteen.

Bill greeted Jenner with a wave.

"Do you have coffee on, Mr. McEnroe?" Jenner asked.

Bill shook his head. "No, but I'll brew a pot as soon as we reach our campsite."

"Then let's get to it," Jenner said. He gave Alex a playful shove.

The four men marched on. Five minutes later, they arrived at camp and busied themselves with tasks. Alex helped Bill make the coffee and ready breakfast. Jenner gathered wood and lit a fire.

Meanwhile, Brian retrieved the satellite phone from the tent and walked to a sheltered spot to make his call.

Teresa answered almost immediately. She sounded feverish. "Did you find him? Tell me. Is he —"

"He's safe."

Teresa screamed. "*¡Gracias al Dios!* Let me speak with him."

"First, I need you to listen. This phone's battery is dying. In case it dies while you're talking with Alex, I want you to do two things for me. First, call Gretchen and let her know we're all safe. Next, contact the rangers and tell them to end their search; that we're taking Alex out of the park via the Cut Bank trailhead."

"But I thought —"

"Just do it, Mrs. Villanova. We're running out of time. I'll go get your son."

Brian rushed to the improvised kitchen area where his father and Alex chatted like old friends. As Brian neared, his father pointed to a jar of raw cashew butter and gave Alex instructions. "After I finish cooking these grits in the boiling water, slowly stir in about two tablespoons of that stuff into the pot until you get the right creaminess. Then add some sunflower seeds for crunchiness."

Alex scoffed. "Where I come from, they'd shoot you for messing with their grits."

Bill chuckled. "Then don't tell anybody. Promise?"

"On my honor," Alex said, then turned when he heard Brian approach.

Brian handed the phone to him. "Hammer, it's your mom. Talk fast. The battery is dying."

Alex grabbed the device, handed his spoon to Brian, and hurried away as he lifted the device to his ear.

"Momma?"

Teresa cried out. "Are you hurt?"

"I'm OK."

"Are you sure?"

"Yes. I'm sorry for everything."

"Don't be sorry. No apologies. Just come home."

Alex tried to answer but the words stuck in his throat.

"I can't lose you, *mi hijo*."

"I saw the Big Show, Momma. Two nights ago. There must have been a billion stars in the sky. It was beautiful."

"Like you, Alejandro."

As Alex was about to answer, the battery died.

He pressed the "power" button off and carried the phone back to Brian. "It lost its power."

"That's OK," Brian said, trading a cup of coffee for the phone. "We'll stop at the ranger station at Cut Bank if we need to call someone."

Bill waved Alex over. "Hey, young man, finish your KP duties. Grits don't cook themselves."

As Alex joined Bill, Brian moseyed over to a stand of Western Larch trees glowing a brilliant Autumn yellow. Jenner was collecting firewood under its canopy. Brian walked up to him from behind and gripped his right shoulder.

"I'd like to talk with you," he said.

"Why?"

"To clear the air."

Jenner dropped his bundle of firewood, and faced him. "Shoot."

"I told you the truth on Triple Divide."

"About what?"

"About what I was going to do about Alex. I said 'I don't know.'"

"I heard you," Jenner said.

"What do you want me to say?"

Jenner stepped closer. "It's not up to me to tell you what to say. You figure that out for yourself."

Jenner was right. The dilemma was Brian's to solve. If he followed the law, his decision was clear. He had to report his friends to Command. If Alex had been on a battlefield and threatened with bodily harm, his actions would be justifiable. But Alex hadn't been on a battlefield. And neither he nor Jenner reported the incident nor carried the man to the infirmary.

"You're right, Icarus. It's up to me. But your actions make it harder."

"Listen, Falcon. You say we must live by the military code. But what code is perfect? Fallible human beings write the regulations. They pull down their pants before they shit, just like we do. What set of regulations can cover everything that occurs in war?"

"That's why we have commanders and judges."

"Sure, to interpret the law. But I'd wager they never faced what Alex did that night. Is it fair they determine his fate when he makes a tough decision in the blink of an eye?"

"I have a duty to tell the truth."

Jenner flung his arms up in the air and walked away, only to turn back. "Listen to yourself. You talk about your duty? You also have a duty to protect those you serve with."

"I know. And what about you? You kept Alex from killing that soldier but then left the man injured in the street."

"In a busy street near the hospital."

"In the street. What were you thinking?"

Jenner slid his hand over his eyes and head until it reached the back of his neck. "Maybe I was wrong. In your eyes, I can see that. I'm not proud of what I did. But my overriding concern was my comrade, not the scumbag who almost shot him. I made an honorable choice. Now, it's your turn."

Brian gazed down the valley, expecting to see a park police helicopter flying their way. "I asked Alex's mother to call the park rangers. They'll probably meet us at the trailhead."

Jenner made a face. "I guess your time is up to decide."

Jenner was right. Whatever Brian decided, he'd inflict harm. To Alex, Jenner, to himself, the oath he took; the trust others placed in him. What was the greater good in this situation?

"No simple answers, are there?" Jenner asked.

Brian's brow furrowed, and he met his friend's stare with his own. "Tell me. When you held the 9mm on me before you created that diversion, were you tempted to fire the gun?"

Jenner looked at him with unblinking eyes. "We'll never know."

"That's not an answer."

"It's the only one you'll get." He paused, then asked,"You made your decision, didn't you?"

Brian didn't respond, and Jenner grinned.

"You're not going to report him."

Jenner's declaration struck Brian like a slap in the face. His friend had read him so easily.

"Report him?" Brian said. "For what?"

"For what he told you on Triple Divide."

"He didn't tell me anything."

Suddenly, Alex came up behind them. "That's a lie, Falcon."

Startled, Jenner and Brian turned around. Alex had a pained look on his face. Unbeknownst to them, he had eavesdropped on their discussion.

"Listen. I appreciate what you're both trying to do, but forget it. I'm going to tell the CID what I did. It's what Aarmaan would have done. Maybe I acted in self-defense. That's something, but I let my rage take over. I almost killed the soldier; left him bleeding in the street. I need to live with my choices."

Jenner tried to argue, but Alex raised his hand to signal him to stop. "I'll leave it up to the Army to decide what they want to do with me, but I don't want to fight their wars anymore. And I don't want you two to fight my wars for me. You understand?"

Brian said, "But I —"

"No, I finish this journey on my own. I'll tell the CID that neither of you knew anything about the Afghan soldier. I never reported the incident to you, Brian. And Jenner, you and I parted ways before I ever met the man, and we didn't meet again until I had left him unconscious on the street. Are we all agreed?"

They didn't answer him.

"Do this for me. Lie this once. For our friendship."

"I don't get it," Brian said. "Don't lie to save you, but lie so you take all the blame?"

"That's right. If I let you save me, I'll never find peace."

"You sure about this?" Jenner asked.

Alex put one hand on each man's shoulder and tightened his grip. "I am."

Jenner peered at Brian. "Then I'm in. What about you, Team Leader? Hammer wants to do the right thing and shoulder the load. Least harm, I say. I'm OK with that. Are you?"

Brian nodded.

Alex playfully pushed Brian and Jenner. "Enough, you fucktards. We have things to do. Finish here, then come eat breakfast. We have a posse to meet."

Alex wheeled around and strode back to camp. The other two watched him go.

Jenner spat on the ground. "Didn't expect that."

Brian shook his head. "Neither did I. Do you think he'll be all right?"

"Maybe."

"He's tough."

"A goddamn warrior."

Brian turned and stared at the dead branches at his feet. "Fuck the firewood."

Jenner kicked his pile, scattering it in all directions.

Brian's eyes caught Jenner's. "I still want to know. And no bullshit this time. When you pointed your gun at me, did you think about pulling the trigger?"

"You don't want to know."

"I do."

Jenner threw his left arm around Brian's shoulder and pulled him close. He squeezed his shoulder, then nudged him to walk along with him.

"Never in a million years."

CHAPTER FIFTY-THREE
September 12, 2021

Brian gazed at his watch: Fifteen minutes to noon. He was strolling toward Hector's gravesite when he heard the bugle play and saw the gathering clustered next to a blazing red-leafed dogwood.

The sounds and sights drew him closer.

Brian watched as a young soldier in dress blues folded the American flag from the casket thirteen times and gave it to the stalwart officer in charge, who presented the flag to a dark-haired woman sitting in the first row of mourners.

The woman struggled to smile as she accepted it.

The captain spoke in a deep, constrained voice, "On behalf of the President of the United States and the people of a grateful nation, may I present this flag as a token of appreciation for the honorable and faithful service your loved one rendered this nation."

The woman's jaw quivered as she turned to face three children — two girls and a boy, all younger than ten — who leaned over to look at the flag, then glanced upward at the woman's sweet face, struggling valiantly to smile.

Brian suspected the soldier entombed here today was one of the thirteen Americans who died at the Abbey Gate in Kabul.

He knew too well what came next: An Arlington Lady approaches the widow and hands her a card extending the condolences of the Army Chief of Staff; the chaplain whispers something to the widow and children; a cemetery representative announces the service is over; then family and friends go home.

Suddenly, Brian felt like an intruder.

He backed away, leaving before the service concluded.

For Brian, military funerals stirred up mixed feelings: He appreciated the honor given, and his heart stirred every time he heard the three-volley salute and the bugler playing Taps. Yet every grave marker reminded him that many Americans found it far easier to honor dead soldiers than the ones who returned alive.

As he resumed his journey, he noticed the sparse lawn in this section of the cemetery reserved for Afghanistan and Iraqi war veterans. Now that the war had ended, burials would slacken, roots would take hold, and green would cover everything. Then they'd build a new section for a new war. What did Socrates say? Only the dead have seen the end of war.

Brian thought of Alex and Jenner, who had promised to meet him at Hector's gravesite at noon, nearly two years after the three men and his father had trekked out of Glacier.

The fallout had resembled a circus. In Kalispell, the men faced a horde of reporters, law enforcement officers, and celebrity hunters. Park Rangers threatened to bring charges against all of them but deferred to CID agents, who questioned the three soldiers for days about the assault on the Afghan soldier. Alex told his story, and he and Jenner stuck to their promises. No eyewitnesses ever came forward, and the Afghan soldier had no memory of the incident, so the Army reduced the charges against Alex and later dismissed them. Over time, an impeachment trial, a war in Syria, and a virus outbreak in China took the public's mind off Afghanistan. Army officials sent Alex to an inpatient PTSD program in Denver and Jenner and Brian back to the Hindu Kush.

But now, Brian thought, we keep our promise to Hector.

He walked until he found Hector's granite gravestone. Fresh cuttings of Lily of the Valley gave off a faint, sweet scent. The white, bell-shaped flowers also adorned the graves on either side.

Brian glanced to his left and right, then behind him, before looking at his watch. Three minutes to noon. Alex and Jenner were nowhere in sight.

He stared at the name chiseled in hard stone: Hector Flores.

Without intending to, he spoke to the stone and the man who lay beneath it.

"It may just be you and me, bro. The dudes said they'd be here, but they might not make it. I know we all promised to meet up with you when the war ended, no matter what, but things happen. Jenner is supposed to be on leave, seeing his new girlfriend in Virginia Beach, but for all I know, he's hunting down Al-Shabab jihadists in Mogadishu and sending them to Allah as we speak. And Hammer just started a new job my father got him, working with vets for Outward Bound in Colorado. So maybe he stayed home. I don't know. He's doing okay. He had it rough for a while: twenty-eight days in a PTSD unit, trouble getting his benefits, and he lost his apartment. But he's better. The job's a big deal, I think."

He glanced at his watch.

"I left the Army six months ago, and Kate and I live together in a small apartment in Corona, Queens. You'd love it there. Hondurans live next door. I haven't told them I'm Irish, so they haven't moved out yet."

He chuckled and looked to the side.

"I'm teaching science in a Catholic high school and studying for a master's degree in environmental engineering at City College. Me, an engineer? Can you believe it?"

His eyes watered, and he sighed.

"Marianna emailed me a picture of her and the kids. She lives with her family in Honduras, but I guess you know that. She misses you, you fucktard, but I guess you know that, too. None of us gets a pass on grief, not if we're human. I guess it's one of the things that make us human."

Brian took the leather pouch out of his pocket, removed a small rounded stone, then placed it on top of the gravestone. He, Alex, and Jenner had each picked up a stone before leaving the summit of Triple Divide Peak.

"I miss our team and the bond we had. My past is an undertow constantly pulling me back into deeper waters. Sometimes I want to just lie back and float away. It's so damn hard, but I must move forward, right? I need to live my life."

Brian looked around. It was past noon and no one was in sight.

He turned back to the gravestone and knelt. With his index finger, he traced Hector's name chiseled into the surface. "I guess it's only you and me this time. Hope it's okay. I miss you, my friend. We all do. You're loved by Marianna, the kids, all of us. You know that, don't you?"

Brian bowed his head and buried his face in his hand. He didn't know what else to say. This is so painful, he thought. After the war ends. Saying goodbye. So final, like a burial.

"But death doesn't bury love," Brian muttered. He closed his eyes. In his mind, Hector was kneeling beside him, his arm around him, goofing off, as usual, making fun of everything sacred, smiling that smile, alive.

Don't be so serious, man, Hector was telling him.

A voice sounded in the distance.

Brian spotted two tall men running toward him with a loping gait. Unmistakable. One of them raised his arm in greeting.

Brian pulled himself up and shielded his eyes from the overhead sun. He took a step forward, smiled, and waved to his brothers-in-arms.

ACKNOWLEDGMENTS

Writing a novel involves—like our lives—a journey with daunting obstacles, moments of triumph, and a final chapter that, at times, feels elusive. And like any pilgrimage, travelers must often rely on others along the way.

The genesis of this book began in a VA hospital in New Jersey where I spent a year working with war veterans, learning the ways trauma affected them, and vowing one day to write about their emotional journey home. Without the insights these men and women gave me, this novel would not exist.

I would also like to thank my cousin, Brian McLaughlin, a distinguished philosophy professor at Rutgers University. We spent hours discussing Homer's *The Odyssey*, the original saga of returning war heroes, and how its themes of homecoming and perseverance might deepen *Triple Divide*'s depiction of modern warriors. He also opened my mind to the concept of *moral dilemma*, the situation in which one must choose between two or more equally unsatisfactory choices. Such choices are at the heart of this novel.

Another big thank you to John Conlee and Sally Stiles at Pale Horse Books for transforming my rough-hewn writing into a polished book with a stunning cover design. Gratitude goes to them and fellow writers, Kathleen Jabs and Len Shartzer, graduates of the U.S. Naval and Military Academies respectively, who shared their military life experiences, and to Petra Schwiertz for her German translations.

Lastly, I am grateful to my wife, Jean, who continues to be my most loyal reader and champion. She makes my journey so much easier.